Naughty No More

Naughty No More

Brenda Hampton

www.urbanbooks.net

Urban Books, LLC
78 East Industry Court
Deer Park, NY 11729

Naughty No More Copyright © 2010
Brenda Hampton

ISBN 13: 978-1-60162-370-6
ISBN 10: 1-60162-370-4

First Mass Market Printing November 2012
First Trade Paperback Printing April 2010
Printed in the United States of America

10 9 8 7 6 5 4 3 2 1

This is a work of fiction. Any references or similarities to actual events, real people, living or dead, or to real locales are intended to give the novel a sense of reality. Any similarity in other names, characters, places, and incidents is entirely coincidental.

Distributed by Kensington Publishing Corp.
Submit Wholesale Orders to:
Kensington Publishing Corp.
C/O Penguin Group (USA) Inc.
Attention: Order Processing
405 Murray Hill Parkway
East Rutherford, NJ 07073-2316
Phone: 1-800-526-0275
Fax: 1-800-227-9604

Naughty No More

Chapter 1

Nokea

Who would've thought that my husband Jaylin and I would be celebrating our three year anniversary? After many years of trials and tribulations, a failed marriage to my now ex, Collins, and Jaylin being able to put Scorpio, a woman he was engaged to behind him, here we were. We had our children, Jaylene who was two years old, and Jaylin Jr., a.k.a. LJ, who was now four. Life couldn't be any better for us. Jaylin's inheritance at the age of sixteen, from his grandfather's estate, and his numerous years as an investment broker, brought him to millionaire status. Several years ago he retired. Once we got married, he required that I retire too.

Our mansion in Florida was by the beach, offering us nothing but peace and quietness. I in no way missed living in our hometown, St. Louis, but I often missed being with my parents, and my best friend, Pat, who still lives there. Our fifty or sixty-something-year-old nanny, Nanny B, takes good care of all of us and she wouldn't have it any other way. It took a lot of work for us to get to this point. If anyone thinks that relationships are easy, they are fooling themselves. I have known Jaylin since elementary school. We didn't become an item until I was in my twenties. Still, his womanizing ways caused us many setbacks. When he finally asked me to marry him, it wasn't until I was almost thirty-three. He was thirty-four and time was starting to run out on us. I hadn't planned on waiting this long for him to get his act together, but through dealing with him for so many years, I knew there was a step-by-step process.

Many people had to be cut from our lives, but the one person that I hated to see distance himself was Jaylin's best friend Shane. Reason being, Shane and Scorpio had started dating, causing Jaylin much headache and jealousy. He hadn't admitted his anguish to me, but I knew my husband and knew him well. When Shane declined Jaylin's offer to leave St. Louis and start his architectural business here, their friendship went downhill. I figured Jaylin had made the offer to get Shane away from Scorpio. As far as I know, that hasn't happened, especially since

Scorpio was *supposed* to be pregnant. She and Jaylin had only dated for a few years, but the way she had a hold on him, you would have thought they'd known each other for a lifetime. She was the kind of woman who often toyed with a man's feelings. Her jaw-dropping body and movie star attributes made many men eat out of the palms of her hands. More than anyone, I'm so glad that Jaylin got away from her tight grip. To this day, it still bothers me that she has a beauty shop named Jay's, and that Jaylin still considers her seven-year-old daughter, Mackenzie, his child. He adopted her several years back, and I guess there's not much I can do about that. What I can do is make sure my man is the happiest man in the world. He's had his trust issues with me too. Once upon a time, I had been engaged to his cousin, Stephon, but he was set up and killed by someone. Stephon was Jaylin's right hand man until Stephon got on drugs and started pursuing me and Scorpio. Needless to say, things got ugly. Even in Stephon's death, Jaylin has never forgiven him. It was only a few years later that I took it upon myself to kiss Shane. I was upset that Jaylin had gone to St. Louis for a visit where he wound up having an encounter with Scorpio. I consulted with Shane about my concerns. Even though he convinced me that nothing had happened between the two, I still *offered* Shane my thanks.

At the time, I wanted to offer him more than that. I'll never forget the way he looked that day with his shirt off. Jaylin's body was cut, but Shane's was cut to perfection. His caramel skin always had a smooth look to it, but what sent me into a trance that day were his light brown eyes. Scorpio was lucky to have Shane, but not as lucky as I was to have a man who loved me as much as Jaylin. He had swagga, and even a man like Shemar Moore didn't have anything on him. His bedroom gray eyes had broken many hearts and his nine plus inches of goodness had injured many backs. He was great . . . excellent in the bedroom, and even though I hated it, there were plenty of women who could testify.

A while back, I told Jaylin about the kiss between me and Shane. For whatever reason, he wasn't that upset. He knows how much I love him and him only. There is no other man in the world that I want, need or desire. Jaylin is my destiny, and no matter what, we will be together for the rest of our lives.

Today, on our anniversary, he surprised me. Instead of using our neighbor's yacht to sail the ocean, Jaylin purchased a yacht for our family. Of course, he named it after our son, LJ. Once I saw how beautiful the huge forty foot vessel was, I almost cried.

The majority of it was white with navy blue trimmings around the outside. LJ's initials were scripted on the front in big bold letters. Navy blue and white adorned the interior too. The floors were covered with soft white carpet. The walls were draped with silky navy blue fabric and cherry oak panels covered portions of the walls as well. In the saloon there were two navy swivel leather chairs and a leather sectional in front of them. There was a cherry oak bar for our drinking pleasures. Once Jaylin took me up the spiral staircase to the master stateroom, I couldn't believe my eyes. Multi-colored fiber-optic lighting lit up the queen-sized bed and made the room feel and look like the most exquisite place I'd ever seen. As Jaylin wrapped his arms around me from behind, all I could do was think about how lucky I was.

"Do you like it?" he asked while nibbling my earlobe.

"I . . . I don't know what to say, other than, yes, I love it! How did you have time to plan all of this and . . . and I know this must have cost you a fortune?"

"It took almost eight months to build and if I tell you how much I paid for this thing, you'd kill me. The company I purchased it from promised they'd have it ready for today and it's been docked for almost a week. A few days ago, I saw it for the first time, and baby, I almost cried my damn self. We are so fortunate and I am enthused about spending our anniversary weekend here."

I turned to face Jaylin, placing my arms on his broad shoulders. "Me too. I love you so much. I'm afraid my little present for you doesn't even compare to this. I'm almost ashamed to give it to you."

"You know I'm a simple man, Nokea. All you gotta do for me is get naked and show off your sexy caramel skin. That's how I get excited. Whatever you have for me can't possibly compare to you walking around the entire weekend without any clothes on. No negligee, no thongs, nightgowns, swimming suit . . . nothing."

"Nothing?" I asked, rubbing my nose against his. "What about when I go outside and stand on the deck? You don't want me naked out there, do you?"

"Trust me. For the next few days, you won't even see the outside. I'm going to satisfy your every need in here. Whatever is on the outside won't even matter."

From experience, I knew Jaylin's statement to be all so true. I gave him a long, wet kiss. Before things got heated, he continued to show me around.

After the rest of the yacht was shown to me, I decided not to show Jaylin the silver electronic picture book I'd gotten him for our anniversary. The inside screen displayed some of my favorite pictures of us but I'd only paid two-hundred bucks for it. I knew Jaylin wouldn't trip, but compared to the yacht, I felt as if my gift was rather cheap.

As our hype started to settle, Captain Jack, whom Jaylin had hired to navigate our vessel, took off. Being on the ocean always provided a sense of peace, while dressed in our silk blue matching robes, we held up our glasses to give a toast.

"Here's to fifty more years," I said, while sitting at the bar. Jaylin stood tall behind it, clinking his glass with mine.

"Fifty? Fifty years is a long time to be with somebody, Nokea, and I . . . I can't drink to that kind of commitment. Besides, you looking like Nia Long today, but ain't no telling what you'll look like in fifty years," he joked.

With my glass in my hand, I walked away from the bar and took a seat in one of the swivel chairs. "Oh, well," I shrugged. "Then, I'll just have to find someone else to spend my life with."

Jaylin came from behind the bar and kneeled down in front of me. He removed my glass from my hand and set both of our glasses on the circular table between the chairs. As his hands roamed up and down my legs, he looked deeply into my eyes. "Fifty, sixty, seventy . . . whatever. We'll be together forever, Mrs. Rogers. You can count on that and when we toast again, make sure it's for a lifetime, all right?"

"Got it," I smiled. "Now, Mr. Lifetime, other than sex, what are we going to do to keep ourselves busy for the next few hours?"

Jaylin showed his straight pearly whites and snapped his finger. "Somehow, I knew you'd ask that question. Trust me, your husband already got this shit planned out."

He went over to the bar, picked up two large bottles of Remy and reached for two shot glasses. He placed them on the table, and invited me to sit on the floor with him. While looking at each other from across the table, Jaylin poured Remy in both glasses.

"What are you doing?" I laughed.

"We're about to play strip poker. If not that, truth or dare. Loser or liar must drink up!"

"Are you serious?" I laughed.

"Very. It'll be fun. Besides, you are always at your best when you're sloppy drunk."

"I've never been sloppy drunk. You must be thinking of someone else."

"Nokea, on your birthday last year, you were sloppy drunk. Remember? You passed out on the beach and I had to carry you . . . ."

"Yeah, yeah, I remember. I also remember what you did to me that night and if you think you're going to do *that* to me again, you might as well forget it."

"Please," he begged. "I . . . we had so much fun that night. Besides, I like taking advantage of you. Sometimes you be holding back, but when you get that oil in your system, baby, you get looser than a mutha."

My mouth hung open. "Loose? That's a terrible to say about your wife. You should be ashamed of yourself. For the record, the liar will lose and that will be you. I'm feeling truth or dare and I get to ask the first question, right?"

"Shoot," he said, and then shot the full glass of Remy to the back of his throat. He coughed, then smiled. "Just trying to prepare myself."

I chuckled and reached across the table to rake my fingers through Jaylin's thick, naturally curly hair. "Do you miss Shane? It's been a long time since you last spoke to him, and you seem kind of, at times, in another world."

"I talk to him every now and then, Nokea. I would be lying if I said I didn't miss our friendship, but for the time being, things must stay as they are."

"You mentioned that things were just okay with him and Scorpio. By now, I thought you and Shane would put the past behind and work on your friendship."

Jaylin gulped down another glass of Remy. Obviously, because of Shane and Scorpio's relationship, Jaylin had put his friendship with Shane on the back burner. I could tell it bothered him, but for months, he hadn't said much about it.

"Why are we talking about this right now?" Jaylin asked, rubbing the goatee that suited his chin well. "I thought we're supposed to be playing truth or dare?"

I traced my finger along the side of his smooth, light skinned face. "I know, baby, but I worry about you. I want you to be happy and you seem bothered by Shane declining your offer to come here and live."

"I was bothered, but I'm over it. The only thing I'm bothered by is you leaving next weekend to go to St. Louis. Even though it's only for the weekend, you know I'm going to miss you, right?"

"Then go with me. You don't have to go to Pat's baby shower with me, but you can still go to St. Louis. Maybe even stop by Shane's place and kick it with him. I know he'd be happy to see you."

"Naw, I'm cool. You need this time to yourself and I want you to have a good time."

"Okay," I said, taking a sip from the glass. Jaylin took another one as well. "Your eyes are getting really, really glassy looking. You might want to slow it down a bit, Jaylin."

"You know I'll have to consume a lot of alcohol before I get drunk. A few shots of Remy ain't gon' do nothing to me."

"If you say so. But, uh, let's continue our game. Since you already know everything about me, I'll take a dare."

"Yes, I do know everything about you. So, I dare you to drink this whole bottle of Remy without stopping."

"If I drink that whole bottle of Remy, I will be sick as a junk-yard dog. You don't want me to be that sick, do you?"

"Then drink half."

"Some," I smiled. "And whatever I drink, you must do the same."

"Bet," he said.

I opened the other bottle of Remy, taking a few sips from it. Jaylin carefully watched me, but when he walked over to the bar to get some ice, I filled the wineglasses with Remy and placed them behind the chair so he wouldn't see them.

"Damn," he said, looking at the half empty bottle upon his return. "You doin' it like that, huh?"

I smiled and nodded. "I sure am. Now, it's your turn."

No questions asked, he turned up the bottle, guzzling down the alcohol. "Okay, stop," I laughed, trying to pull the bottle away from his mouth. I showed him the wineglasses I'd filled. "I'm sorry, baby, I cheated."

Jaylin slammed the almost empty bottle on the table and looked a bit dazed. "Why you cheat like that?" he softly said. His gray eyes were watered down and there was no smile on his face.

"Are you okay?" I asked. "You look . . . ."

"Look like I'm fucked up, don't I?"

"Very."

Jaylin sucked in a heap of air, wobbling a bit as he stood up. With a universal remote, he dimmed the lights and turned on some music. Seeming awfully woozy, he fell back in the chair, staring at me as if he wanted to eat me alive. I'd seen that look many times before and I definitely knew what it meant. It was show time and I had no problem standing up to show my handsome husband everything I had.

I kept my eyes connected with his and removed my robe. Naked, I pulled him up from the chair and held his muscular frame close to my petite body. He worked his way out of his robe too and as the tunes of Prince kicked in with "Purple Rain" we embraced each other.

"Your body . . . damn your body feels good," he slurred. "I . . . I remember that time I rented a boat for your birthday and you . . . you couldn't hang with my ass . . . ."

I moved my head away from Jaylin's buffed chest and looked up at him. "Are you talking about when I was thirty and still a virgin?" I asked.

With his eyes closed, he smiled and nodded.

"What in the world would make you think of that?" I asked. "That night, I was so hurt and not because your dick . . . penis was too big for me either. If your memory serves you correctly, you left that night to be with Scorpio."

"I ain't do no shit like that, quit lying!" he challenged, opening his eyes.

"Yes you did! And, I drove to your house and found the two of you in the shower, remember?"

Jaylin smirked, knowing darn well he remembered. "Damn, you did, didn't you? I was tripping, wasn't I? You should have kicked my butt and left my ass alone. Instead, you gave me another chance, didn't you? A few weeks later, I tapped that ass and we made our son, didn't we?"

"Yes, we did."

We stood in silence and I could feel Jaylin's body getting heavy.

"Baby, I think you might want to sit down for a minute."

"I'm guuud," he said, and then backed up to the leather sectional. He dropped his head back and tightened his eyes. I could tell he was doing his best to shake off the liquor. He opened his eyes, and licked his lips as his eyes dropped between my legs. "Come here girl, wit yo' sexy li'l self. I got myself a bad-ass wife. I got to be the luckiest man in the world."

"Wit yo' what?" I said, appreciating his compliments. I headed his way and straddled his lap. Jaylin touched my inner thighs, and when he slid his finger deep in my tunnel, he snickered.

"Wit yo' slippery and wet, sexy, horny-ass self."

"Very horny self. Now, sober up and take care of this slippery wet mess, would you?"

Jaylin sucked his finger, tasting my sweetness on his finger. I slid off his lap and lay back on the couch to get into position. He sat up, rubbing his temples with his eyes closed.

"Baaaby," he slurred. "I'm fucked up. Would you, uh, go get me some ice cold water, please?"

I hurried off the couch to get his water. Within a few minutes, I came back and handed the water to him. He was lying back with his eyes closed.

"Jaylin, wake up," I said. "Here, drink some water."

He threw his limp hand back at me while massaging his goods. "I'm tired, baby. Real tired. Come on, though, so I can make use of my nine, plus some."

"We have all night for you to make use of that. Just drink some water and let's go lay down, okay?"

"Nooo," he ordered. "Lay back down on the couch. I . . . I wanna taste that pussy."

Those words always excited me, but it was obvious that Jaylin had too much to drink. I tried to get him to drink some water, but he pulled me down on the couch. He parted my legs, and with his curled tongue, he took slow licks up and down my already juiced slit. I pressed his head in closer, inviting him to sink his tongue further inside of me. As he did, he widened my coochie lips, exposing my clit that he knew how to stimulate so well. He licked along the furrows of my walls, causing my breathing to become intense. I sucked in a heap of fresh air, releasing it to calm the electrifying feeling that was stirring between my legs. I was so ready to start raining cum, but the excitement Jaylin was bringing came to a screeching halt. I sat up on my elbows, looking down at him.

"Jaylin?" I questioned. There was no answer, so I called his name again.

"Hmmm," he moaned.

He slowly sat up and leaned to the other side of the couch. Wanting so badly to continue, I lay on top of him. I kissed his lips, sucking them with mine. I licked down his chest, giving special attention to his sexy abs by pecking them. His stomach heaved in and out, and when I picked up his hardness to put it into my mouth, it had no reaction.

I sighed, making my way back up to him. "Honey, are you okay?" I whispered. He slightly cracked his eyes and nodded. His eyes faded again and true disappointment was written on my face. "You know I'm going to make you pay for bailing out on me like this, don't you?" He slowly nodded again and I continued. "I am horny as hell. How dare you do me like this on our anniversary. You do know it's your anniversary, don't you?"

At that point, he was out. He didn't provide any gestures and started to snore. What else could I do but go down low again. That didn't do me much good at all because *it* was as limp as he was. "Darn-it!" I yelled and tried to wake him again. I lightly shook his shoulder. "I got your present, baby, look." He didn't budge. I huffed, realizing that this night was over. I cut my eyes at the almost empty bottle of Remy and frowned.

Chapter 2

Nokea

I was headed to my best friend's baby shower in St. Louis. After many years of trying to have a baby and using fertility drugs, Pat and Chad were expecting. Also, I hadn't seen my parents in four months, so I had plans to spend a few days with them.

I wanted to take the kids with me but Jaylin and Nanny B encouraged me to take some time for myself. I hadn't had a vacation in almost three years. Even though living close to the beach in Florida always gave us that vacation feeling, I knew I'd enjoy being in another city.

As I packed my suitcase, Jaylin lay shirtless on our California king bed with his hands behind his head. He kept watching me go in and out of my walk-in closet, occasionally looking up at the sky view ceiling. I couldn't help but question his frowned up face.

"Are you sure you're okay with me leaving?" I asked.

"I'm fine. I just can't believe I'm letting you leave me for a few days. Besides that, how much more do you think you can stuff inside of that suitcase? You've got damn near a month's worth of clothing in there. The deal was only for the weekend."

"I like variety, Jaylin. I have less than six outfits in there and that's it. As for you *letting* me go to St. Louis, thanks a lot Daddy. It was so nice of you to *let* me out of the *palace*."

"You're welcome. And, before you go, I hope you have time to thank me like I deserve to be thanked."

Already dressed to go to the airport, I eased on the bed, crawling up to Jaylin. "On our yacht last weekend, I thanked you enough, didn't I? Any more gratitude on my part will have to wait until I get back. My plane leaves in two hours, so it would be nice if my husband would get out of bed and get dressed so we can go."

Jaylin kissed my forehead and pulled the covers back. He looked down at his hardness. "I gotta be out of my mind letting you leave me like this. What in the hell am I going to do for three whole days without you?"

"You can always watch those video tapes we made and I'm sure you're still hanging on to those pictures I gave you a few years back."

"We made one tape, Nokea," he said, walking into his walk-in closet. I thought he was looking for something to put on, but he came back with the tape in his hand. "See, one tape and it's an old one."

Jaylin stepped over to the entertainment center built into the wall. He slid the tape into the VCR/DVD combo unit and waited for the seventy-two inch plasma TV to show a picture. Soon, the tape that we made showed. While staring at the TV, he slowly inched his way back and sat on the bed. In disbelief, I tapped my watch and cleared my throat.

"Excuse me, but I really, really need to be—"

"Shhh," Jaylin said, placing his index finger on his lips. He turned up the volume, and once I saw the position he had me in, embarrassed, I turned my head. My moans were loud and Jaylin was ecstatic.

"Baby, what's up?" he asked. "You don't moan like you use to. And, look at your expression. You sucking the shit—"

"Jaylin!" I yelled and grabbed the remote. "If you don't mind, I need to get going."

"I was just talking about the way you sucked your bottom lip. Why you don't suck your bottom lip anymore?"

I playfully rolled my eyes and walked over to the TV to turn it off. "For the record, when we're making love, I still moan and bite my bottom lip, so there."

"But, not like you use to do. Damn, I got some work to do, don't I?"

I walked up to Jaylin, pulling him up from the bed. I put his arms around my waist and hiked up on the tips of my toes to kiss him. "Listen, there is no woman on this planet who is more sexually satisfied with her man than I am with you. That tape was a long time ago. It doesn't compare to what I say, do or feel whenever you're inside of me. Now, if you would please, please go get dressed, I'd like to go. If you'd like to stay here and reminisce about the past, I'd be happy to ask our driver Ebay or Nanny B to take me to the airport."

Jaylin stood tall over me and looked down. He sucked in his bottom lip and bit into it. "I don't want no shit out of you, Nokea. That punk-ass ex-husband of yours, Collins' house, is off limits and I want a phone call from you as often as possible."

I pulled my head back and couldn't believe he'd gone there. I hadn't thought about Collins and I knew, more now than ever, that our marriage had always been a mistake. "It sounds as if you don't trust me," I said.

"I trust your pretty ass as far as I can see you. If I can't see you, I don't know what the hell you're doing."

I removed Jaylin's arms from around me and he smiled. He walked off to the closet to get dressed. I left the room to say good-bye to my babies.

Finally, thirty minutes later, Jaylin and I were on our way to the airport. I waved at Nanny B, Jaylene and LJ, as Jaylin drove off in our black Hummer. He seemed rather quiet. I could tell something was on his mind.

Trying to put him at ease about my trip, I reached over, touching his hand. "Look, I know you're going to miss me, but don't look so sad."

"I don't know what's up with me, Nokea. I want you to go and have yourself a good time, but I'm already feel . . . feeling empty."

"I feel the same way when you're gone, but that's because we complete each other so much. When either one of us is away, it feels as if something is missing."

Jaylin nodded.

"So, other than the baby shower, what other plans do you have?"

"Other than going to see my parents, not much. This morning, when I spoke to my mother, she said that an ice and snow storm is on the way. You know how much I hate to drive in that mess, so I will probably spend most of my time at Pat's house."

"Well, be careful. And, watch out for Pat's husband Chad. I remember when that mutha-fucka tried to hit on you. I'm skeptical about you spending the night at their house. You might want to think about staying at a hotel."

"Jaylin, at the time, Chad and Pat were going through something. He's changed and I'm sure he's just as excited about the baby as Pat is. They've waited a long time for this baby and I'm excited for them."

"That's all fine and dandy, but if he *rubs* you the wrong way, promise me that you'll go to a hotel and call me."

"I promise," I said. "In the meantime, whatcha going to do for the next few days?"

Jaylin let out a deep breath. "Shit, I don't know. But, tonight, I got myself a date with the VCR. I need to figure out what I was doing back then, that I'm not doing now, to excite you like that."

"Did you hear anything I said earlier?"

"Yeah, I heard you. But, I saw you on that tape too. Baby, you were overly thrilled about my dick being inside of you. Tears were in your eyes."

I threw my hand back and blushed. "Oh, please. During our love making sessions, tears have never been in my eyes. Even though your stuff is superb, it's never made me cry."

"Bullshit Nokea! Please don't make me recall those times, okay?"

I folded my arms and thought about some of my emotional times with Jaylin. There had been a few times I'd cried as we made love, but there was just something special about the man I loved being inside of me. I told Jaylin he was right. When I turned my head to look out the window, he laughed and put his foot on the accelerator so we could hurry to the airport. When we got there, Jaylin helped with my bags and checked them in. There was an hour delay. For security purposes, if I went through the gates, Jaylin couldn't wait with me. Instead, we waited in another waiting area together. We sat side by side, tightly holding hands.

"Do you have enough money on you?" he asked.

"I have very little money on me, but I have plenty of credit cards."

"You still need to have a little cash on you. Some places don't accept credit cards." Jaylin stood up. "I'll be back. I'm going to the ATM machine over there and to get a soda. Would you like anything?"

"No, I'm fine."

As Jaylin made his way to the ATM machine, I checked him out from head to toe. He was so clean cut. No matter where he went, he always dressed at his best. His dark gray pants slightly hung over his square-toed leather shoes, and his sheer gray button down shirt, trimmed with a white collar, exposed his jaw dropping muscular frame. His sparkling Rolex and diamond bracelet that draped from his wrist enhanced his attire and gave off the smell of a brotha with mega money. The tinted glasses that covered his eyes instantly drew several, if not all women to him. Of course, he had no problem with all eyes on him and the attention didn't seem to faze him one bit. I knew who he belonged to. As I sat back and watched three females approach him, I watched his reaction. He smiled and when he pointed to me, the women turned. I turned my head too, looking in another direction.

Jaylin came back over to his seat, reaching out to give me some money.

"Here. That's five hundred dollars. It's all the machine would allow me to get. Put it in your purse so you don't lose it."

I looked at the money. "Jaylin, I told you I had credit cards. I don't like to carry this much money on me when I'm traveling."

"Just take it, all right?"

To not attract attention, I put the money in my purse. "What did those women want with you? Did you know them?"

He smirked while rubbing his goatee and sucking in his sexy bottom lip. "No, I didn't know them, and I'm sure you already know what they wanted."

"Well, too bad you're married, huh? If you weren't, I'm sure you'd be on your way to a hotel room right now, especially with the chick with the big ole booty."

"Big booty? I didn't even notice."

"Stop lying. There was no way to overlook her butt. I'm sure you saw it."

Jaylin shrugged. "Like I said, I must have overlooked it."

I didn't believe Jaylin for one minute. I don't know why his being approached by women still upset me. He was my husband, and if anything, I should be proud to have a man that so many women wanted. *Yeah, right,* I thought. I was pissed and my tone implied it.

"I'll be back," I said. "I need to go to the rest-room."

"Do you need some help?" Jaylin smiled.

"No. I'm sure I can handle it."

I walked off to the bathroom. Before going into a stall, I looked in the mirror and moved my short bangs away from my forehead. With the tip of my finger, I straightened my perfectly arched eyebrows and tightened the belt around my cream knee high sweater dress. It buttoned down the front and the brown buttons matched my Nine West brown boots and hand bag. Satisfied with my appearance, I turned to the side and was pleased at how well the dress clung to the curve in my butt. I smiled and made my way to the stall.

Once inside, I took a leak and flushed the toilet using the heel of my boot. As I pulled up my panties, I heard Jaylin call my name.

"What?" I said.

"What's taking you so long?"

"I haven't been gone that long, but . . . are you in the ladies restroom?"

Jaylin pushed on the door, but it was locked. I hurried to unlock it.

"What are you doing?" I whispered. "Is there anybody else in here?"

"Who cares?" he said, stepping into the stall with me.

"I care," I whispered again. I tried to open the door, but he held it shut. He looked deeply into my eyes, like he always does when he has something serious to say.

"Just so you know, I have no desire for any woman but you. Beyonce, Janet, Nia and Halle have been put on the back burner for you, baby. You have nothing to worry about when it comes to us."

"Are you sure about that? Because, Denzel is still my number one. There's no way for me to put him that far back on the burner."

"Well, unfortunately, Denzel will never love you like I do. And," Jaylin moved closer to me and held my belt in his hand. "No man will ever make love to you like I'm about to do."

"Uh, anywhere else, but not in this stall. It is not clean enough for me, and the last time I checked, this was considered a public restroom."

"Then, be quiet," he whispered. "I will hold you up in my arms and no parts of your body will touch the stall or the floor. Besides, I told you I'd make our anniversary night up to you, didn't I?"

"Oh, you've already done that. I . . . I just can't get into it in a place like this. How do you expect—"

Jaylin kissed me and undid his pants. They dropped to his ankles and he positioned me around his waist. I rested my arms on his shoulders, and instead of removing my dress, he unbuttoned the bottom three buttons. He held me with one arm, using his other hand to stretch the crotch of my panties to the side. Within seconds, he inched his way in, causing my pussy to moisten right away. I took several deep breaths. As he guided his goodness in and out of me, I held his neck tightly, whispering in his ear.

"I love the way you turn me on. You make me want to say to hell with St. Louis. I . . . I don't want to go."

"You excite my ass too. I'm about to give this pussy something to think about while you're in St. Louis."

Jaylin did just that. All it took was a few more strokes of his hardness, slightly touching against my clit and I cut loose. He felt my legs tremble and he backed me against the door. He gave it to me good, expanding my insides with every thrust. We felt the explosion about to go down, and placed our hands over each other's mouths. He tightened his eyes and I let out a loud, yet satisfying moan. To silence me even more, he moved his mouth away from my hand and took his hand off my mouth. His lips met with mine and he silenced me with a juicy and memorable kiss.

"You're going to miss your plane," he smiled.

"So. I want to go home. Besides, what good is a vacation without you?"

"No good, but you can't play Pat like that. Your mother is expecting you. I will be waiting patiently for your return."

Jaylin lowered my legs and pulled up his pants. He cleaned me up with toilet paper and straightened my panties and dress.

"My silk panties are soaking wet. They are really uncomfortable and must come off," I said.

Jaylin lowered my panties and I stepped out of them. He grinned and put them in his pocket.

"These are going home with me. Air that coochie out, and as soon as you get your luggage, put on another pair. I don't want my wife walking around without any panties on, unless you're with me."

I laughed. Before exiting the stall, I looked to see if the coast was clear. There were two ladies washing their hands by the sinks, another lady stood by the trashcan and one lady was on her way in. The ladies at the sink eyeballed me. My face was covered with embarrassment. Jaylin had no shame in his game and pulled the bathroom door open to exit. He stepped up to the sink and washed his hands.

"The men's restroom was flooded," he said to the ladies. "I apologize for the intrusion, but I had to go."

The ladies assured Jaylin that it was okay. After I washed up, we walked out holding hands.

Finally, my plane was getting ready to load passengers. Jaylin walked me to the security checkpoint and stood with his hands in his pockets. He winked at me and mouthed that he loved me. I mouthed the same and blew him a good-bye kiss.

As he walked away, I took a seat and stepped back into my boots that I removed at the security checkpoint. When I looked up, I saw an extremely attractive woman tap Jaylin's shoulder. Her light skin and long hair reminded me of Scorpio and so did her figure. Whatever she said to Jaylin, he bent down and picked up something from the ground. It was obvious he'd dropped something. When I saw him look up for me, I eased behind a man who stood in front of me. The female kicked up a quick conversation. Whatever she said put a smile on his face. He blushed. I saw her go into her purse pull out a card and hand it to him. He accepted the card and removed his tinted glasses to get a closer look at it. He nodded and put the card in his pocket. The big test came when she smiled and walked away. If she was a woman trying to sell something to Jaylin, I'm sure he would have walked away without giving her a second look. Instead, he took a few steps, turned and thoroughly checked out her backside. He then pulled out the card again, studied it and put it back into his pocket. Of course, I wanted to see what that was all about, but I didn't want to miss my plane. I hurried to it. As soon as I took a seat, I quickly called Jaylin's cell phone. He answered.

"Yeah, baby," he said.

I wasted no time asking him what was up. "What was on the card?"

"What card?"

"The card in your pocket."

He paused. "A, uh, a travel agent gave it to me. She said if I needed a travel agent in the future, to contact her and she could get me some decent rates."

"Oh. I didn't mean to sweat you, but I just happened to see the interaction."

"Well, that's all it was. Right before you called, I tossed the card in the trash."

I felt unsure about his response. "Okay, well, uh, I'll call you when I get to St. Louis. Be careful. I'll see you soon."

Jaylin hung up. When I looked up, heading my way was the woman who'd given the card to Jaylin. For whatever reason, God surely had a way of confirming things that I wanted to know. The woman sat directly across from me. Once the plane took off, I drummed up a conversation with her.

"So, are you on your way to St. Louis too or do you have another plane to catch?" I asked.

"No, this is it. I'm on my way to St. Louis to visit my brother and his wife. I'll be there for two weeks. I'm looking forward to it."

"Do you live in Florida?"

"I've lived here all my life. What about you?"

"I'm from St. Louis, but I moved to Florida several years ago. I love it too and it couldn't have been a better move for my family. Do you have a family? I saw that handsome man you were talking to at the airport. Was he your husband?"

She chuckled. "Oh, I wish. He just popped up out of nowhere. When I saw that he'd dropped his parking ticket, I saw an opportunity to confront him. A man that gorgeous doesn't come around too often. Since I've been single for quite some time, I gave him my phone number. He said he'd call and I hope he does."

That was not what Jaylin said. My insides were boiling because he'd lied. "I . . . I checked him out too, but I noticed a ring on his finger. That said he was taken, so I backed off."

"Honestly, I didn't get a chance to look at his fingers. I was so wrapped up into his eyes. It was like . . . like I was in a trance or something. If he's married, though, all I can say is, I hope not happily," she laughed.

I swallowed. "I'm sorry, we've been chatting and I didn't get your name. My name is Nokea."

"Mine is Mariah. Everyone calls me Mia for short."

"Mia, I work for a major marketing firm in Florida," I lied. "What do you do?"

"I'm a school counselor. I'm also a part-time waitress at a restaurant. With this economy, everyone needs two jobs in order to make ends meet."

At that moment, I was speechless. *Why did Jaylin lie to me?* I thought. All he had to do was be honest. I guess that was asking for too much. I couldn't wait to get settled in at Pat's house so I could call him.

Pat was so happy to see me. She knew that I was coming, but had no idea that her mother and I had planned a surprise baby shower. I told her I was in town to visit my parents and that's all she knew. For hours, we sat around and talked about her marriage, her baby, and how much we'd missed each other. The time had flown by. Since I wasn't making my way to my parents' house until tomorrow, I told Pat I was going to take a shower and call it a night.

"Are you sure?" she said, waddling around the kitchen with her big belly.

"Yes, I'm tired. Last night, I didn't get much sleep and I hoped to rest on the plane. That didn't happen either so I'm turning in early."

Pat walked me to the guestroom and offered to bring me some extra pillows.

"No, two is enough. I already know where your towels are and your relaxing Jacuzzi tub is calling me. I'll see you in the morning, okay?"

Pat gave me a hug and left me in peace. I closed the door and looked at the phone on the nightstand. I hadn't called Jaylin, like I told him I would, so I sat on the bed and dialed out on the cordless phone. On the first ring, Nanny B answered.

"Hello," I said.

"Hi, Nokea. Have you already made it to St. Louis?"

"Yes and I had a smooth flight too. Is Jaylin around?"

"He's out back with the kids. Hold on, I'll get him for you."

"Nanny B," I said. "Would you do me a huge favor?"

"Sure."

"Earlier, Jaylin had on some dark gray pants. Most likely, they're hanging in his closet. At the airport, we met a travel agent and I wanted to call her about some rates for a future trip. Would you get the card out of his pocket for me?"

"No problem," Nanny B said. We talked about the kids, until she stated that she was in the closet and didn't see a card in Jaylin's pockets.

"Are you looking into the pockets of his dark gray pants? I know he has several pair of gray pants. I think there is only one pair with cuffs at the bottom."

"I'm still looking, but I don't see . . . wait a minute, here it is."

"Is it the card?"

"Yes, but the card is not from a travel agent. A counselor's name—"

"Is her name Mia . . . I mean, Mariah?"

"Yes. It's Mariah Davis."

"Thank you, Nanny B. That's the card I'm looking for. Would you put it in my drawer for me and please ask Jaylin to come to the phone."

"Okay, sweetie, hold on. Have a good time and I'll see you soon."

I heard Nanny B call for Jaylin, and soon after, he got on the phone.

"What took you so long to call?" he immediately griped. "I've been worried sick about you. You promised me that you would call as soon as you got there."

I ignored his comment and was so ready to tear into him. "Are you happy?"

"What?"

"I asked if you were happy."

"Very."

"Then, why did you lie to me earlier?"

"Lie to you about what?" He snapped.

"About the travel agent, Jaylin. Before you get caught up, again, I must warn you that Mariah and I shared good conversation during our flight to St. Louis."

"So, she gave me her damn number. What's the big deal?"

"And you threw it away, right?"

"I told you I did, didn't I?"

"I don't know what has gotten into you, but lying to me is unacceptable."

"Nokea!" he yelled. "Have you listened to anything I've said? The card is in the trashcan at the airport. Now, if you want—"

"Don't yell at me, Jaylin! The f-ing card was in your pocket, where you left it! I already asked Nanny B to check your pocket. How in the heck can the card be in the trashcan at the airport, if it's still in your pocket! Besides that, Mariah is not a travel agent. She's a counselor and her card, that you clearly looked at, specified that. Now, I'm asking you again . . . why did you lie to me?" He didn't say a word. "If you don't talk to me, I'm hanging up. You will not get another phone call from me. I'll see you when I get back."

"I lied because . . . I don't know. I guess I just didn't want to tell you the truth about another woman approaching me. I see how uncomfortable it makes you and I was trying to spare your feelings."

"Well, lying to me does not spare my feelings in any way. I don't know what to say about you. If your concern was all about me, then her card would have gone into the trash like you told me it did."

"Look, you're right Nokea. I'm not going to argue with you, baby, but I had no intentions to call her."

"That's what your mouth says. Your true actions tell me something different. Either way, I'm safely here. I'll call you tomorrow. I'm going to give you Pat's new phone number, but please do not call here constantly checking up on me. If you just happen to experience a *funny* feeling inside, remember, you brought those feelings upon yourself."

"If you gon' put it like that, don't bother with giving me Pat's number. You know what you got at home waiting for you. If you feel as if another man can give you something better, then go for it."

"This has nothing to do with another man. Take responsibility for your own mess and don't go blaming—"

"Damn, Nokea! I said I was sorry. Now, I got a banging-ass headache. You act as if I fucked the bitch right there in the airport or something!"

"I'm sure if you hadn't screwed me, she might have been on your agenda. In the meantime, you need to watch your tone. Maybe you've forgotten who you're speaking to."

"I know damn well who I'm talking to. If you wouldn't be acting so stu—"

I hung up on Jaylin. Obviously, he just wasn't getting it. As always, he acted as if I had no right to question him. He was sadly mistaken if he thought I wasn't going to trip off his lying. I knew the thoughts of him would ruin my vacation, and so far, that's just what they were doing.

Chapter 3

Shane

On Sunday, I was hard at work in my home office, sketching some new designs for The Mayor's Group. Since Scorpio seemed so devastated from losing the baby, I started to spend a lot of time with her and her family. I was wounded by our loss too, but there was a small part of me that believed there never was a baby. For me, some things didn't add up. When she came to me crying, and broke the news, I kind of expected it.

Either way, we were still a couple. Over the weekend we'd been ice skating, to the movies, and last night, Scorpio and I went to the Jazz Corner. I was so, so tired, but I didn't want to get too far behind on my work. Scorpio was still asleep, but she told me to wake her at noon. I didn't, but around 2:00 P.M. that day, she woke up. She came into my office, rushing to put on her clothes.

"Baby, why didn't you wake me?" she asked. "I was supposed to open up Jay's for one of my stylists, Bernie."

"I did wake you, but you wouldn't get up. Besides, have you looked outside? There's no way you're going to make it to Jay's with all that snow and ice out there."

She pulled the curtains aside to look out the bay window. "When did all of this happen?"

"It started early this morning. According to the weather channel, it's going to get worse."

"Shane, I have to get home. If Bernie hasn't called my cell, then I know she's cancelled her appointments. Still, I need to get home."

"Go call Bernie to make sure everything is cool. If so, I'll take you home because I'm not about to let you drive in that mess all by yourself."

Scorpio pulled out her cell phone and left the room. As soon as she left, my phone rang. I looked at the caller ID and didn't recognize the number. Not wanting to be bothered, I let the call go to voice mail. A few minutes later, the phone rang again. This time, Jaylin's phone number came up. I hesitated, but then answered.

"Hello," I said.

"Shane, it's Jay. What's up?"

"Nothing much," I said, keeping my response short. I hadn't heard from him in a while. The last time we spoke, he seemed kind of bitter because I decided not to make a move to Florida.

"I'm, uh, sorry to bother you, but I need a huge favor. I was wondering if you could help me."

"It depends on what it is."

"Nokea attended her friend's baby shower this weekend, and now she's stranded at the airport. Because of the weather, they have no idea when her plane will depart. Nokea said it could be a couple of days and she's ready to come home. Would you mind picking her up for me and bringing her home? I would really appreciate it."

St. Louis to Florida was a nineteen-hour drive. With the weather being so bad, I knew it would be longer than that. Damn. "That's a long drive, Jay. Are you sure she won't get home faster by waiting on a plane?"

"The way things are looking, I don't think so. I know the streets are pretty bad, but if you take your time things should be cool. Besides, being at the airport all day is driving her butt crazy. I know she's ready to get the hell out of there."

I thought about when Jaylin and Nokea drove to St. Louis to see me in the hospital. I had to be there for him, just like he was there for me. "I'm sure getting her safely to you is of key importance and it sounds like you might be missing your wife."

"Possibly," he said. "Not only that, but it'll give us a chance to talk face to face. I know I haven't called you that much, but I've been trying to work out some things."

"If you remember, I suggested that you take all the time you needed. Wha . . . what entrance is Nokea at?"

"Take down her cell phone number and call her. She'll tell you exactly where she's at. Your generosity will be well rewarded."

"You don't have to pay me, Jaylin. I'll call Nokea and I guess we'll see you soon."

Jaylin gave me Nokea's number and I wrote it down. After we hung up, I called Nokea. She was happy to hear my voice.

"Shane, I'm so, so sorry to bother you. All of the hotels are booked and I'm ready to go home. Another day or two here would drive me crazy."

"Well, meet me by the baggage claim area. I have to take Scorpio home, and depending on how bad the streets are, it might be longer than that. Just be patient. I'll get there as soon as I can."

"Thanks again, Shane," she said.

Scorpio came inside of my office with her arms folded.

"What was that all about?" she asked.

"Nokea is stranded at the airport. She needs a ride home."

"And you're going to drive her all the way there? Shane, the streets are a mess."

"I'll drive very, very slowly," I said.

"How long do you intend to stay in Florida?"

"Maybe for one day, and that's only so I can get some rest before hitting the road again."

"You know how I feel about this. Why do you and Jaylin always feel the need to cater to Nokea?"

I gave Scorpio a simple look. Obviously, there had always been bad blood between Scorpio and Nokea, but hadn't we all moved on? I knew Scorpio hadn't known about Nokea's and my tiny kiss that day. It was odd that Scorpio felt as if I were catering to Nokea.

"Now, where did that come from?" I asked. This has nothing to do with catering to Nokea. I'm just trying to help, and by seeing Jaylin face to face, this will be a perfect opportunity for me to get some things off my chest."

She threw her hands back. "Look, forget about what I said. Adding my two cents ain't going to do me no good. Let's just go."

I changed into my crisp button down over-sized tan shirt and starched Sean Jean jeans. After I put on my clothes, I reached for my brown leather jacket and lay it across my arm. I slid into my Timberlands, and made sure my day-old twisties still had a shine. Scorpio and I left, but she gave me the silent treatment. Thick ice was on the ground, so we slowly made our way to my car. Scorpio got inside, turning on the car to warm it. I scraped the snow and ice from the windows. Afterward we left.

By the time we reached Scorpio's place in Lake St. Louis, it was nearly an hour and a half later. The roads were slick. I couldn't believe that I'd offered to drive Nokea all the way home. I wanted to change my mind, but I knew Nokea and Jaylin were counting on me.

Scorpio placed her hand on the doorknob, then leaned over to kiss me.

"Thanks for the safe ride home. Please be careful, okay?"

"You know I will. I'll call you, and if you need me," I lifted my shirt to show her my phone clipped to my jeans. "I'm just a phone call away."

She leaned in again, giving me another kiss. "I love you," she said.

"I love you too."

Scorpio slowly made her way to the door. Before I pulled off, I waited until she was inside. I then left, making my way to the airport.

***

Nokea was nowhere in sight. With so many people standing around, it was hard to find her. When I called her cell phone, she said she was in the restroom and was on her way to the baggage claim area. A few minutes later, she came from behind, placing her hand on my back.

"Hi, Shane," she said, opening her arms for a hug. I gave her a tight squeeze and kissed her cheek.

"What's up, Lady? I bet you can't wait to get out of here."

"Oh, you just don't know. This place is packed with irate people and I can't blame them. This is ridiculous. Do you know how many people are lying on the floors around here?"

"Yeah, I saw several of them over there. After I go take a leak, and get me a quick bite to eat at an eatery around here, we can go, all right?"

Nokea nodded.

"Have you eaten anything?" I asked.

"Yes. I already had a salad and I'm not hungry."

Nokea waited by the restroom for me, then we found an eatery where I ordered a sandwich. The lady behind the counter handed me my bag. "There you go, handsome. Is there *anything* else I can get for you?"

I looked up at her and she smiled.

"That'll be it. Thanks, though."

Nokea shook her head. "I don't know if it's worse being with Jaylin or with you."

"Damn, what's that supposed to mean?"

"The stares, Shane. Don't you notice all the stares and pay attention to the advances?"

"Yes, I noticed the two security guards nudge each other when you walked past, and those tight jeans you have on got those three men behind us checking out your rump shaker."

Nokea turned her head and one of the men waved at her. She waved back and turned around. "I wasn't talking about me. I was talking about you."

I laughed and strolled her luggage. She walked in front of me. It was so hard for me not to admire her petite and well shaped body. The blue jeans hugged her hips, and the way she walked with confidence in her black high heeled short boots brought much attention her way. When we made it to the door, another security guard's eyes were glued to her. He reached out, giving me a slamming handshake. Nokea ignored him and turned to question me.

"Are you parked close by?" she asked.

"I'm right there," I said, pointing to my car with a ticket on the windshield. "My fifteen minutes turned into thirty minutes."

"I'll pay for it," Nokea said. She headed toward the car and the security guard let go of my hand.

"Damn, man, you hooked up the right way. Is she from the Lou?"

"Born and raised. The Lou be representing some bad-ass women, but unfortunately, that one is taken. Maybe you need to get out more often."

"Maybe so," he said, looking at Nokea as if he could eat her alive. It was a good thing that I wasn't Jaylin. Even though I wasn't, I found the man's stares to be a bit overboard. Nokea waited patiently by my car so I headed her way.

Once she helped me put her luggage in my trunk, we got in the car. She looked cold. Even though she had on a short jean jacket, I asked where her coat was.

"I put it inside of my luggage. I didn't expect for it to be this cold out here."

"Do you want me to get it for you?"

"No, once you crank up the heat, I should be fine."

I started the car and carefully drove out of the parking lot. I turned on the heated seats and Nokea rubbed her hands against the vents to warm them.

"Ahhh," she said. "That feels so, so good. You don't mind if I drop this seat back and take a quick nap, do you? Pat and I stayed up all night and I haven't gotten much rest this weekend."

"Just so the drive would go by quickly, I was hoping that you'd keep me company. But, if you're tired, you're tired. Just make sure you put on your seatbelt."

Nokea reached for the seatbelt and dropped the seat back. She placed her arm across her forehead, apologizing for needing a quick nap.

At least an hour had gone by, before Nokea's sleep was interrupted by her ringing cell phone. She popped up and reached into her purse. When she looked at the number, she mumbled Jaylin's name and dropped the phone back into her purse.

"So, you're not going to answer that?" I asked.

"No," she said. She lifted the seat and sat up straight.

"What's going on Nokea?"

"Lately, Jaylin . . . he's been kind of to himself. He lied to me about keeping a woman's phone number. Since I've been here, today was the first time I'd spoken to him, and that's because I was stranded at the airport. I'm so upset with him. I can't wait to tell him how much his lies hurt our marriage."

"Just because he took a woman's phone number doesn't mean he planned to use it."

"I knew you'd defend him, Shane, but whether he intended to use it or not, he shouldn't have taken it."

"In Jaylin's defense, Nokea, sometimes you don't want to hurt people's feelings. If Jaylin had not accepted the number, that woman might have gotten her feelings hurt."

She pointed to her chest. "What about the feelings of a wife who might have seen the entire exchange? Or the wife who finds the number in her man's pocket? Shouldn't my feelings be the priority?"

"Of course."

"That's all I'm saying. My feelings were deeply bruised and when I tried to talk to him about it, he got defensive and started cursing. Through my eyes, that made him guilty of something. I can't wait to see him to tell him how I really feel."

"Trust me, ignoring his phone calls ain't going to help. If you've been ignoring them all weekend, I'm sure you have an angry and upset man waiting for you at home."

She threw her hand back and tooted her lips. "Who cares? He shouldn't have lied and that's all there is to it. Anyway, how are things going with you and Scorpio?"

"Just okay. She lost the baby, but we're managing."

"She was pregnant?"

"Yeah. Almost four months, but something went wrong. What? I really can't say."

"I'm sorry to hear that. Did Jaylin know?"

"Yes, he knew. He didn't say anything to you about it?"

"Not one word."

Nokea looked out the window, as if she was thinking about something. Her phone rang again and she ignored it. When she didn't answer, mine rang. I removed it from my jeans and looked at the number. It was Jaylin.

I looked over at her. "You know I gotta get this, don't you?" I said.

"That's your phone and you should. If he asks for me, I'm busy."

I shook my head and answered my phone.

"What up?" I said.

"Is that crazy-ass woman in the car with you?" he asked.

"Uh-huh?"

"Did you hear her cell phone ring?"

"Yep."

"Did she know it was me calling her?"

"I believe so."

"Tell . . . tell her to answer her fucking phone. As a matter of fact, give her your phone."

I held my phone out to Nokea and she turned away.

"She won't take it."

"Stupid ass shit," he yelled. "Tell her she's got a good ass kicking coming when she get home and I ain't playing either."

I repeated Jaylin's words to Nokea.

"You tell him that I look forward to it and the only butt that's going to get kicked is his."

"You heard her, didn't you?" I said.

"Yeah, I heard her smart-ass. She showing that ass 'cause you're in the car and she's many miles away. When she get on my turf, we'll see how quickly her tune changes. Now, tell her that."

"Man, seriously, I'm trying to drive. The roads are slick and y'all got me in the middle of this."

"Yeah, you get off the phone and make sure you get her here safely. I know she's been in the car venting. Did she tell you what for?"

"Yes."

"Ain't that some stupid shit? I was minding my own damn business and this woman approached me. Nokea act like she saw me pull down my pants and fuck the woman. All I did was take her number and put it in my pocket. When Nokea asked me about it, I lied to protect her feelings. She always getting emotional and shit and I didn't feel like hearing it."

"I feel you," I said. "I know exactly what you're talking about."

"All right," he said with frustration. "I'll see ya soon."

I hung up and Nokea glared over at me. "So, I guess you're feeling his side of the story, huh?"

"Well, it does make sense Nokea. Don't you think you might be blowing things out of proportion? You know Jaylin wasn't going to call that woman."

"Shane, please don't make me disrespect you. I know men and women view things differently, but you all couldn't be that darn stupid. I don't care what anybody says, Jaylin took that woman's number for a reason. By all means, he loves me to death, but Jaylin will always be Jaylin. No offense to Jaylin, but my girlfriend Pat said it best. If you keep a ho under lock and key, they'll do just fine. But if you put a ho into a *busy* environment, a ho will turn himself loose. I'm starting to see what she meant."

"Damn, that's deep. Are you perceiving your husband as a ho? If so, I wouldn't repeat that to Jaylin. He might be offended."

"I don't know what I'm saying Shane, but I'm mad. Personally, right now, I don't care if he's offended or not. I call it as I see fit."

I shut my mouth and dreaded pulling up to their house. Obviously, some shit was bound to go down. Since Jaylin and I weren't exactly on *good* terms, I wasn't sure what to expect.

For the next few hours, Nokea and I made good conversation. I felt a few extra bumps in the road, so I got off the highway, heading for the nearest gas station. The side road was dark as hell, and it appeared that we were in a rather hick little town. Not seeing a gas station in sight, I quickly pulled over to see what was up. When I got out, I saw my rear left tire was flat. I checked the trunk for a spare. Even though it was there, it had no air in it. Freezing cold, I slammed down the trunk and got back into the car.

"What's the matter?" Nokea asked.

"I got a flat tire. I'll call roadside assistance. It shouldn't take long for them to get here."

I dialed out on my phone, and the dispatcher said someone would be there in about thirty minutes. To keep us warm, I kept the car running and told Nokea someone was coming soon.

Nokea and I continued to talk and another hour must have passed. I called roadside assistance again, and they assured me that someone was on the way.

"Well, my car has been running for over an hour. I'm running out of gas and if you can give me a definite time, I'd be grateful."

"Sir, there's no way for me to give you a definite time. All I can tell you is that someone will be there soon."

I wanted to curse somebody out, but remained calm. Nokea looked worried and I didn't want to make matters any worse.

"Are you okay?" I asked.

"As long as we don't run out of gas, I guess I'm fine."

We waited for another fifteen minutes. Shortly after, a police car pulled up behind me. He aimed a bright white light inside of my car.

"I'll be right back," I said, getting out of the car.

I walked up to the police car and the police officer looked scared. "Put your hands up where I can see them," he ordered.

I held up my hands and leaned down to talk to him.

"Excuse me officer, but, uh, I got a flat tire. I've been waiting for roadside assistance for hours. I wonder if you could tell me where the nearest gas station is."

He spoke in a southern tone. "Well, let's see . . . it's about ten, maybe twenty miles down the road.

I doubt that you'll get any roadside assistance 'round here. If they haven't gotten here by now, young fella, they ain't a coming."

Cold as hell, I took a deep breath, showing frustration. "Look," the officer said. "Why don't you and the misses get in the car with me? I'll take you to a gas station and you can have that there tire fixed."

It sounded like a good plan to me. "Thanks officer. I hope you don't mind."

"Not at all," he assured me.

I went back to the car and told Nokea the deal. She got out of the car, and instead of taking the flat tire off my car, I opened the trunk and removed the spare. I figured it would save me much time if I put air in the spare tire and bought a new one from a tire shop on the way.

"Make sure you lock your doors," the police officer yelled out the window. "There's been a lot of theft in this area."

I checked my doors and asked Nokea if she wanted to take her luggage. She said there wasn't nothing but clothes inside and she wasn't worried about them. Seeing how cold she was, I took off my leather jacket, wrapping it around her.

"Come on. Let's go," I said.

We made our way to the police car. The officer unlocked the doors for us to get in. Nokea sat in the front and I sat in the back.

The officer didn't lie. The gas station was more than twenty miles down the road. When we got there, it was closed.

"Damn," I said, as I looked inside and saw racks of new tires. I also saw an air pump, so I asked the officer if he would wait until I put some air in my tire. He said yes. Just to be on the safe side, I made Nokea get out of the car with me. She walked with me over to the pump and I put the air pump on the stem.

"This place looks like a ghost town, doesn't it?" Nokea said, observing her surroundings.

I nodded. Even though the entire town gave me the creeps, I didn't want to alarm Nokea. I pushed the button to the air machine, and just my luck, the damn thing was broken. I slammed my fist against the machine a few times. When the front of it fell off, I looked up at Nokea.

"Let's go," I said, thinking about how much time we'd wasted. Even though the icy streets weren't as bad as I thought they would be, we were still at least four hours behind schedule. We walked back to the police car. Once inside, the officer looked in the rearview mirror at me.

"Where to now?" he asked.

"Would you mind taking me back to my car? By now, maybe roadside assistance showed up."

"I doubt it, but let's go see," he said turning the police car around.

Disgusted, I dropped my head on the back seat, closing my eyes. I prayed for a quick solution to my problem, but when we got back to my car, it was obvious that no one had shown up.

"That gas station we just left opens up pretty early, young fella. You and the misses can stay the night at a motel, and get yourselves a new tire in the morning. By then, the roads should be clearer. There's no more snow or ice in the forecast. I gotta get back to work, but I'd be happy to take you to the motel and pick you up in the morning."

I sighed and turned to Nokea for her suggestion. "Nokea, what do you think?"

"I think we really don't have much of a choice. I'm tired and I guess we'll have to wait until morning."

"I guess so," I said.

The officer drove off and took us back down the long and dark curvy road. On the way to the gas station, we'd passed a motel. I remembered thinking that the motel looked like the Bates Motel in the movie *Psycho*. Nokea turned to the officer.

"Isn't there another motel close by? This one looks pretty crappy, you know?"

"The inside doesn't look too bad. A few months ago, they remodeled the entire inside."

"Nokea, if you don't want to stay, we don't have to. We can chill in my car, until morning."

"And freeze to death," she said, opening the door. I thanked the officer. Before he drove off, he waited until we got our room. He said he'd be back in the morning. I gave him one hundred dollars for his trouble.

When I opened the door to the room, it was old fashioned. Surprisingly, it was neat and clean. There was a queen sized bed covered with white fresh sheets and a quilted plaid blanket. A dark wood entertainment center was in front of the bed, and a plaid green and blue chair was in the corner. A round dark wood table sat next to a chair by a tiny window, and a huge picture of painted orchids hung above the bed. The only problem was the damp and musty smell.

"Well, this is a surprise," Nokea said. She walked off to look in the bathroom and said it was just as tidy as the rest of the place.

"All I can say is make yourself at home for the night. You can have the bed and I'll sleep in the chair. Before we do anything else, please call Jaylin to let him know what's up."

"I'll call him in the morning. I'm too tired to argue with him again."

Earlier, when I had gotten my spare tire from the trunk, Scorpio had called. I sat on the bed to return her call from my cell phone.

"Hey baby," I said. "Sorry I missed your call, but I caught a flat tire and was in the middle of trying to change it."

"How'd you get a flat tire? Did you get it fixed?"

"I must have hit something on the road. I haven't gotten it fixed yet, but I will get it fixed in the morning. Nokea and I are staying the night at a motel."

"Really?" she sounded shocked. "I hope the two of you have separate rooms."

"Yeah, baby, we got separate rooms, and if we didn't, you know she's a married woman and I'm soon to be married."

Scorpio laughed. "You are so, so good. Soon to be married my butt. I had a feeling that something would happen. I've been worried about you. Be careful, okay? Get some rest and hurry back home."

"You know I will. Stay sweet and I'll call you in the morning."

Scorpio and I ended our call and Nokea stared at me again.

"I already know what you're thinking," I said.

"Why Shane? Why must men lie so much? Scorpio knows that you and I don't have anything going on, so was it necessary for you to tell her we had separate rooms?"

"In an effort to protect her feelings, yes. If I had told her we were spending the night in the same room, that would have caused major problems."

"No, if you had been honest with her, she would have known that you had nothing to hide. By the look on your face, I can see that this conversation isn't going anywhere so I'm going to leave well enough alone."

"Thank you. I will feel so much better if you would call your husband and tell him what's up. If you don't call him, I will."

"Shane, please stay out of my business. I said I will call him in the morning and I promise you that I will."

"All right," I said, making my way to the bathroom. "I'm taking a shower. Before you get in the bed, if you wouldn't mind tossing the covers or quilt in the chair, I'd appreciate it."

"You can have the quilt. The sheets will work for me and I'll be kind enough to give you a pillow."

"Thanks," I said, closing the door.

Tired, I took a rush shower and dried myself with a white towel. I wrapped the towel around my waist and opened the bathroom door. Nokea was laying on her side and had already fallen asleep. She still had on her jeans, but had removed her jacket and shirt. With her lace turquoise bra on, she was snoring her butt off.

I shook my head and made my way to the chair. It was comfortable and I had no problem snuggling up with the quilt and falling asleep.

I was awakened by a knock at the door. Nokea woke up too and we both looked at each other. I got up and when I looked through the peephole, the officer was standing outside.

"Who is it?" Nokea whispered.

"It's the officer who brought us here."

"Well, open the door. He might want to tell you something about your car."

Having the same thought, I opened the door and the officer smiled at me.

"Did you folks get all settled in?" he asked.

"Yes," I said, stepping aside as he made his way inside. I looked at my watch. "Did you need something? It's almost one o'clock in the morning and I'm sure the gas station ain't open yet."

"I was just checking up on you folks. Didn't know if you all had something to eat or not."

"We're not hungry," Nokea said. "We were sleeping and resting quite well."

"Gud, gud," he said chewing on what appeared to be tobacco. The officer looked at me still standing by the door with it opened. He placed his hand on his holster and slowly pulled out his gun. He aimed it at me. "I'm gon' need you to close the door and step away from it."

My forehead lined with wrinkles, showing confusion on my face. "What's this all about?" I asked.

He spoke sterner. "I said, close the door and slowly step away from it."

Nokea pulled the covers over her, looking frightened as ever. I closed the door and moved over to the bed with her.

"Get behind me, baby," I said, trying to throw the officer off. I wanted to rush him, but with the gun aimed in my direction, I knew my timing wasn't right.

"What do you want from us?" Nokea asked.

"If it's more money, my wallet is in my pants pocket on the dresser," I offered.

"Well, that there is a start," he said, and made his way over to my jeans. He picked them up, tossing them to me. "Take the money out and lay it on the nightstand. Missy, if you got any money in your pocket or purse, now is the time to come clean."

Nokea reached for her purse on the nightstand and pulled out some money. She set it on the nightstand, along with my money.

"You can take the money and leave," I said. "There ain't no reason for you to cause us any harm."

The officer laughed. "I haven't caused you any harm. Not yet anyway. I need for you to move away from Missy and she needs to get undressed."

Nokea panicked and held me tightly around my waist. My heart quickly dropped to my stomach. "I'm sorry but she can't do that. You will have to do whatever you came here to do, but I will not let you touch her."

The officer's wrinkled face scrunched up and he quickly placed the gun on the side of my temple. Nokea started to whimper and quickly shouted out, "I'll do it! Please don't shoot him!"

"You'd better listen to your wife. I'm giving the orders 'round here, boy, and I hope we have an understanding." He pressed the gun harder against my temple and pushed my head. "Do we have an understanding?"

My fist tightened and sweat had started to form on my forehead. I was so damn mad and couldn't respond. Nokea quickly spoke up. "Yes, he under-stands," she said, removing her bra. He focused on her perky breasts and backed away from me.

"Ohhhh, nice titties," he said, grinning and licking his lips. "Now, take off your bottoms."

I jumped up from the bed and the officer wast-ed no time cocking the gun. "Shane, stop," Nokea yelled, as I stared down the barrel of his gun.

"Sit yo' ass down, boy. As a matter of fact, go sit over there in the chair and don't move until I tell you to."

My chest heaved in and out. Nokea got off the bed, pulling me by my arm. "Shane, it's okay. Please cooperate. Don't make this harder than what it already is."

I kept my eyes on the officer and walked over to the chair feeling useless. For now, I planned to cooperate, but there was no way in hell I was go-ing to sit there and watch this man rape Nokea. I'd rather die first and I told her just that.

"Well, I don't want to die," she said. "And, I don't want you to either."

The officer interrupted us. "For the record, I don't screw colored women. And as luscious as her boobs and buttocks might look, I'll leave that up to you."

Once I sat in the chair, he turned the gun to Nokea. "Drop'em," he said, referring to her jeans.

Nokea cooperated and stepped out of her jeans and panties. For a moment, she stood naked and when he gestured for her to back up on the bed, she fearfully looked at me. She followed the officer's order and scooted back on the bed. Hurt was all inside of me and I held my face in my hands.

"Please don't hurt her," I pleaded. "You can do anything to me, but please don't put your hands on her. I can give you plenty more money and . . ."

"Shut the fuck up," he ordered and spat the tobacco from his mouth.

Nokea moved her head from side to side, implying that I be quiet. She could tell that my tone was irritating to the officer, but what else was I to do? Just then, her phone rang. When she looked at her purse, the officer told her to throw it to him. She did and he pulled her phone out of her purse.

"Would you like for me to answer and tell Jaw-lynn that you're tied up right now?"

Nokea didn't say a word. I knew she was thinking the same thing I was. Now, I bet she wished like hell she could answer her phone.

The officer dropped her phone and purse on the floor. He pulled some more tobacco from his pocket and put a fresh batch into his mouth. He chewed while studying Nokea's naked body.

"You are one pretty-ass Black woman. Hell," he said, looking over at me. "You got yourself a nice piece of ass over there." He rubbed himself down below. "I'm not gon' hurt her, though, I'm just gon' watch her."

Nokea surprised me by how strong she appeared to be. I was the one straight up losing it. I continued to think about the appropriate time to rush the officer, without me or Nokea getting hurt.

"The Rock," he said, turning to me. "Why don't you get up and get over there in bed with your wife. Remove the towel from your waist and show the woman a little appreciation for being so cooperative."

"Wha . . .what the fuck is wrong with you?" I yelled.

"You are a feisty nigger, aren't you? You'd better do like I tell you. I will have no problem blowing your fucking brains out if you don't listen to me."

"Shane," Nokea calmly said. "Just do what he says. Please. Come over here and sit on the bed with me."

I kept my eyes on the officer and walked over to the bed. The towel remained around my waist and I sat next to Nokea.

"You're a smart-ass," he said. "Missy, remove the towel from your husband's waist."

Nokea pulled on the towel, but I held it. "Why are you listening to him?"

She gave me a stern look. "Because I have too much to live for Shane. We'll be okay, trust me."

Nokea removed the towel and dropped it on the floor. The officer walked over to the chair and took a seat. He kept the gun on us and sat back.

"Well, well," he said. "Black couples look really good in porno movies and it's not too often that I get a chance to see colored folks perform in the flesh. I wish I had some fuckin' popcorn, but since I don't, my Vaseline will have to do."

I gritted my teeth. "Are you expecting me to sit here and make love to my wife in front of you?"

"No, smart-ass. I'm demanding that you start fucking your lovely wife. If you can't do that, I'll take her somewhere and get a real man to fuck her or do it myself!"

I couldn't believe this was happening. Nokea looked shocked too, but not saying a word, she courageously lay back on the bed. She swallowed, keeping her eyes on me. I got underneath the sheets and lay between her legs.

The officer laughed, slapping his hand against his leg. "You must think I'm awfully stupid. Take the fucking sheets off and hurry it the hell up so I can get back to work!"

Nokea slowly pulled the sheets off me, exposing a naked view of our bodies to the officer. She positioned me between her legs and I held myself up over her. For the first time tonight, her eyes watered as she continued to stare at me. My dick wasn't even hard and when I told the officer just that, he had another suggestion.

"If your husband's dick ain't hard, Missy, then you might need to put your mouth in action."

Nokea's eyes fluttered and she closed them. I leaned down over her and softly whispered in her ear. "Keep your eyes closed. Don't look at me and focus your mind elsewhere. I promise not to hurt you."

Nokea kept her eyes closed and I looked down at her pussy. I circled my thick head around her slit. When my dick hardened, I entered her. At first, she was dry as the desert and my strokes were painful for her. She held my hips, and as her insides started to moisten just a bit, she opened her watery eyes. Old boy was talking all kinds of shit, but I focused him out of my mind. That was until he got up and put the cold barrel of the gun against my back.

"What in the fuck are you two doing? I need some real damn action going on, yah hear me!"

My dick was not cooperating with his demands, and neither was Nokea's dryness. I pulled out of her and touched myself. Attempting to get through this uncomfortable situation, I closed my eyes and thought of Scorpio. My dick hardened again, and once old boy ordered me to continue, I went back inside of Nokea. This time, to keep me hard, she worked with me. Her insides got gushy and she pumped to my rhythm. I didn't know what her stares were about, but they surely made me nervous. I leaned into her ear and apologized to her.

"I'm so sorry for this," I softly said.

"Me too," she responded back.

She turned her head and I lightly kissed a salty tear that rolled down the side of her eye. Nokea picked up the pace and we continued.

The officer heavily breathed and cracked up from time to time. "Give it to her from the back and can she ride? She looks like a woman who knows how to ride," he smirked.

I looked at Nokea, and not saying a word, she got on her hands and knees. I worked her doggy style and my hands touched her silky smooth body to comfort her. I massaged her perky breasts and manipulated her nipples with the soft touches of my fingers. Nokea's pussy was juicy as ever. As I felt myself about to come, I pulled out of her. She looked over at the officer, then straddled the top of me.

"Let's see what you got, gal," he grinned.

Nokea took a moment to look at my hardness, then positioned it to enter her. With each stroke, she gave me pleasure. I did my best to focus elsewhere, but it was so hard with her insides feeling this good. I felt guilty . . . ashamed by what we were forced to do, but I tightened my fist with the anger I felt inside as well.

With Nokea being on top, it gave me a chance to get a clear view of the officer in the chair. He was so into Nokea's hard work, that he closed his eyes to touch himself. Just at the right time, and at the right moment, I flipped Nokea over and got back on top. I sucked her breasts and she moaned with pleasure as I did it. The more turned on we seemed, the more excited the officer got. That's when I made my move. I jumped up, and before he could pull the trigger, I lifted my foot, kicking him hard in his chest. He fell backward in the chair and the gun dropped from his hand. I hurried to pick it up, then aimed the gun at him. He lay on the floor, holding his hand tightly over his chest.

"I . . . I can't breathe," he said.

I lifted my fist, slamming it hard into his jaw. "Good," I yelled and looked at Nokea. "Put on your clothes."

She wasted no time and hurried into her clothes. Once she was dressed, I told her to toss me my jeans. She did and as I stepped into them, the officer made a move for the gun. After all of the racial names he'd called us, I couldn't help but pull the trigger. The bullet went into his upper shoulder and Nokea covered her mouth. She started to cry and I snatched up the rest of my clothes, Nokea's purse and our money on the nightstand. I then took the car keys from the officer's pocket and Nokea and I left.

In a serious panic, we made our way to the police car and I drove off. Nokea was a nervous wreck and couldn't stop crying.

"Do you think he's dead?" she asked.

"Honestly, I don't give a fuck! And you shouldn't either."

Speeding like a bat out of hell, I drove back to my car. It was still parked on the side of the road. I hurried out of the police car and opened the trunk. All along, there was a pump in there, as well as another spare. I wasn't sure if the spare would work, but I put air in my spare tire and had never changed a tire so quickly. I left the police car on the side of the road and Nokea and I quickly made our way to the highway.

Chapter 4

Nokea

Shane's driving was bound to kill us. The roads were still slick and he was in a serious panic. When I suggested that he slow down, he yelled at me. I was devastated too, but he was more than unstable.

"Can we just pull over and chill out for a while?" I asked. "Your hands are shaking and I'm very frightened."

"It ain't everyday that I go around shooting, possibly killing muthafuckas, Nokea. And a cop, too? Damn," he said shaking his head. "I don't know what the hell I've gotten myself into."

"It was self defense, Shane. Since we're miles and miles away from there, can we please stop and get our heads on straight? Besides, that spare tire isn't going to last much longer so let's calm down, get a nice room for the rest of the night and chill."

"I need to get you home, now. We're not stopping again."

I touched his shoulder. "Shane, please. Please do it for me. I don't like how fast you're driving, and sooner or later, I will make it home."

When the exit sign showed a Comfort Inn ahead, Shane listened to me and made the exit. He parked the car and I went inside to get us a room. He stayed in the car. When I came back to it, his head was leaned back on the headrest and his eyes were closed. I tapped the window.

"Let's go inside," I said.

Once we got to the room, I opened the door and Shane locked it behind us. The room had double beds and he lay back on the bed close by the window. He placed his arm on his forehead, closing his eyes again.

"What are we going to do, Nokea?"

"I don't know. But, I know I'd better call Jaylin. He's been calling me like crazy."

Shane sat up and looked at me. "Whatever you do, please do not tell him what happened between us. As a matter of fact, don't tell anybody until I can figure this shit out."

"How am I supposed to keep something like this from him?"

"Do you really think Jaylin is going to understand why we did what we did?"

"But, we were forced to do it! Jaylin would understand that neither one of us wanted to die."

"No, he wouldn't understand. And you're crazy if you think he's going to embrace me with open arms and not throw you out of the fucking house. If he even suspects I was inside of you, forced or not, all hell is going to break loose and you know it."

"But, we have a legitimate explanation. You saved my life back there and there was no doubt in my mind that the officer was going to kill us if we didn't cooperate. In any situation like that, you have to remain cooperative, but it was obvious he didn't have much love for Black people."

"Look, do whatever you want to do. I'm not telling Scorpio shit. When we get to your house, you tell Jaylin I had to get back home. I'm not in the mood to argue with him and I need to find a way out of this mess I've gotten myself into."

My phone rang and startled both of us. I knew it was Jaylin. Before I answered, Shane gave me a serious look.

"Please don't do it. I don't want to see you hurt and you are not going to like the outcome."

"Hello," I answered.

"It's damn near four o'clock in the morning. Where in the fuck have you been?" he yelled. "I've been calling you all damn night Nokea!

Shane's phone is turned off and I don't know what the hell is going on. Don't make me—"

I softly spoke. "Please stop cursing at me like that, okay? Shane caught a flat, we got stranded on a dark road and we just made it to a hotel. I left my phone in the car, so I didn't know you called. Once we got settled, I planned on calling you."

"Bullshit, Nokea! Let me talk to Shane."

After all Shane and I had been through, I was disgusted with Jaylin's behavior. I handed my cell phone to Shane. "You were right," I said. "He's out of control."

Shane got on the phone. "Hello," he said and paused. "Yeah, man. As soon as something opens up, I'm gon' get a tire. I didn't even know my phone was off and Nokea left her phone in the car. We walked about three miles in the cold and couldn't find a gas station nowhere. Finally, a police officer came and took us to this hotel. We're at the Comfort Inn. If you calm down and talk to Nokea for a moment, I'll get you the phone number here."

Shane gave the phone back to me. I took a deep breath and placed the phone on my ear. "Yes," I said.

"I guess you want me to feel sorry for you, but I don't. I plan to keep my peace for now, but we will discuss how you played me off this weekend. That was some cold shit, Nokea. I didn't think you could be so cold."

"And, I didn't think you could be such a liar. Either way, I'm finished discussing my concerns. We'll work things out when I get there."

I gave the phone back to Shane and he gave Jaylin the phone number to the hotel. Once Shane ended the call, he looked over at me. "Now, are you with me or not? Even I couldn't handle news like that and I know Jaylin won't be able to. Let's just stick to the same story, okay?"

I nodded, and tired or not, I had to take a shower. Shane's scent was all over me and I had to wash it off.

Once I finished my lengthy shower, I walked back into the sleeping area. Shane was sitting against the headboard with his shirt off. The top button on his jeans was unbuttoned and his ribbed stomach was sweating. His tired eyes were red. Pure disgust could be seen in his eyes. Wrapped in a towel, I sat on the bed with him. I looked into his eyes, touching the side of his face.

"Don't look so worried. Anybody in that situation would have done the same thing. Whatever happens, I will back you all the way."

His eyelids lowered and he swallowed. "I . . . I didn't want to go inside of you Nokea. Jaylin has been a good friend to me. I don't want him to think I'm just another Stephon. He's already upset about my relationship with Scorpio, and if she found out about this, she . . . she would leave me in a heartbeat. As for the officer, damn, what am I going to do? What if he's dead?"

"Then, we'll have to deal with it. I won't say a word to anyone. Even though it's going to kill me to keep this secret, I know what I have to do."

"Thank you," he said, removing my hand from his face. He scooted down in bed and I got underneath the covers with him. Needing each other's comfort, we lay quietly while Shane held me tightly in his arms.

Sleep was good, even though it was only for a few hours.

"Do you have everything?" Shane asked, looking around the room.

"There wasn't much to get. Let's get out of here and go see about getting a tire."

As soon as we stepped out of the hotel, we heard a siren and panicked. Shane looked at me and I looked at him. We both watched as a police car drove down the highway, passing our exit. Surely, we were relieved.

We drove to a nearby super center and Shane bought a new tire. It took less than an hour for the mechanic to put it on and we were back on the road.

"Are you hungry?" Shane asked.

"I'm starving, but I can wait until you stop at a gas station. A pack of sweet powdered donuts will suit me just fine."

He nodded and kept on driving. He hadn't said much to me, so I looked through his CDs for something soothing to play.

"Is this all you have?" I asked.

"Yes. All I listen to is jazz. If you want to hear Wallace Roney blow his horn this morning, then feel free to slide in just about any CD."

"Well, I'm not in the mood for Wallace, but, uh, can we talk?"

"Talk about what?"

"About what happened?"

"You mean," he cleared his throat.

"Yes. About that."

"Nokea, I'd like to put that as far away from my memory as possible. Talking about it is only going to make matters worse."

"No it won't. Since this is going to be our secret, I want to know how you felt about it."

His voice rose. "I feel horrible, so there! I feel as if I've betrayed my best friend, again. If I could take it back, I would."

"I understand. I feel bad about what happened too, but tell me how you really feel."

Shane looked over at me in disbelief. "Are you trying to fuck with my head? I just told you how I felt. What more do you want?"

"I want the truth. Even though it was a horrible and scary situation, the way you performed said that you didn't mind being where you were. And, your eyes—"

"The only thing you saw in my eyes was madness. Now, why are we going here? Must we sit here and even discuss this?"

"No, but . . . don't you want to know how I felt?"

"With tears in your eyes, I knew how you felt. The look on your face said it all."

"Yes, I was scared, but maybe, the tears in my eyes were because I felt ashamed for wanting to, you know."

"Don't even go there Nokea! We've been down this road before when we kissed. I cannot do this again." Shane spoke sternly and his face was without a smile. "It's over, all right? What happened at that motel stays back there. I don't want to talk about it anymore. Damn you for forcing me into this conversation!"

I continued, wanting to get some things off my chest. "I'll put closure to this conversation, but not before sharing with you my feelings. I . . . I love Jaylin and I will always love him. No matter what, I'll never leave him, and he will never leave me. I had a feeling that one day, somehow, you and I would share what we did. The circumstances weren't great, but the feeling is one I'll never forget. I'm sure you share the same feelings as I do. Feeling that way doesn't mean you don't love Scorpio. It means that we put together a piece of the missing puzzles in our lives, and both of our curiosities about each other have been satisfied."

Shane pulled the car over to the side of the road, turned to me and gave me a disturbing look. "Thanks for sharing, Nokea, but I don't quite see it that way. I think you are an amazingly beautiful and smart woman, but I'm deeply in love with a woman who is all that and then some. What happened back there is—"

I quickly cut him off. "In other words, are you saying you never had any feelings for me? That you never, ever thought about what having sex with me would be like and that the look in your eyes at that motel had no meaning?"

"No, Nokea. I've never had any feelings for you, I never thought about having sex and the look in my eyes . . ."

I grabbed the back of Shane's head to shush him. I moved my face to his, making eye contact.

"You're a liar, but I can see right through you. You never have to speak the truth to me, but that's because, like most men, you're not man enough to tell a woman how you really feel."

I placed my lips on Shane's, forcing my tongue into his mouth. As expected, he worked with me. We smacked lips for quite a while, until Shane reached for the back of my short hair and pulled it back.

"Damn you, Nokea," he whispered. "After this kiss, this is over! We cannot act on our feelings again. Do you understand?"

I nodded and Shane's light tongue turned in my mouth again. His lips were soft like butter. I couldn't help it that my hand roamed inside of his shirt to squeeze his muscles. Finally, we backed away from each other and Shane cleared his throat. I wiped around my wet lips and he quickly sped off.

Chapter 5

Jaylin

I hadn't been this mad at Nokea in a long time. Damn her for not calling me during her stay in St. Louis. I would have never gone to St. Louis without keeping in contact with her. For her to be upset with me about something so stupid proved to me how ignorant she could get.

Surely, I hated to diss her like that, but it was almost 10:00 P.M. and she still hadn't made it home. I got tired of calling and kissing her ass, so my phone calls came to a halt hours ago.

The entire weekend, something just didn't feel right to me. I guess Nokea was right about me feeling something *funny* inside, but I wasn't sure if my semi-attraction for the woman at the airport had me feeling a bit guilty. Yes, the woman was bad, and if I were anything like the man I used to be, I would have jumped on it. Her eyes said that I could have her, but I wasn't going to mess up my happy home. I'd been there, done that before. I don't know what made me keep her phone number. For whatever reason, I felt the need to hold on to it.

When I heard several car doors shut, I didn't move from my bed. I listened for the front door alarm to sound and my eyes focused on the doorway to my bedroom. I heard both Nokea and Shane's voices as they talked to Nanny B and the kids. Shortly after, Nokea appeared in the doorway with Jaylene on her hip. She looked at me and I looked at her. After seeing the angry expression on my face, she put Jaylene down and told her to go over to Nanny B. Jaylene did as she was told and Shane stepped around Nokea, coming into the room.

"Listen," he said, walking up to the bed and slamming his fist against mine. "I gotta head back out, but I wanted to stop in and say what's up."

"You know this is one hell of a favor you did for me," I said, standing to grip his hand. "I appreciate it. At least let me offer you some money for the inconvenience."

"That won't be necessary Jay. Any time I can help out, you know I will."

"I wish you'd stay a while so we can chat, but if getting back home is that urgent, I understand."

"I had planned to stay, but the flat tire incident caused me a bunch of lost time. Some time tomorrow, I'll call you so we can have this discussion we need to have."

I nodded and Shane slammed his hand against mine again. "How's Mackenzie?" I couldn't help but ask because she'd definitely been on my mind.

"She and Scorpio are doing okay. They moved in with me for a few months, but, uh, due to some problems with her pregnancy, you know, she had to terminate it. Afterward, she and Mackenzie moved back home."

For a moment, I stood silently and then looked at Nokea. She cut her eyes at me and walked away. My eyes shifted back to Shane. "Of course, I'm sorry to hear about the baby, but everything happens for a reason."

Shane chuckled. "Yeah, they do. Other than that, we're doing okay."

"It's nice to hear that somebody is. I know Nokea told you what was up. Once I knock her upside her head, we'll be back to normal too."

Shane laughed. "Don't hurt her too bad, man. She's an awesome woman and she loves you very much. Don't forget that, all right?"

"How could I?" I said.

Shirtless and with my gray sweatpants on, I stepped over to the balcony to close the doors.

The wind was kicking up a cool breeze that had the room kind of chilly. I then went to the door and yelled Nokea's name. When she didn't answer, I touched the intercom button and yelled her name louder.

"I take it things are about to get ugly in here," Shane said, walking toward me.

"Very," I replied. "You take it easy and don't forget to give me a call tomorrow. Hopefully, by then, things may have cooled down."

Shane and I walked to the front door and I let him out. He got in his car and I held up the peace sign as he drove away. I went back to our spacious bedroom, and still, Nokea hadn't made her way to me. As I was about to yell her name again, she came into the room and looked at me sitting on the edge of the bed. My hands were clinched together.

"What's your motherfucking problem?" I asked.

"I don't have a problem. If you don't mind, I was spending some time with my children. It's obvious that you want to argue and your tone is not going to encourage me to stand here and listen."

"If you leave this room again, I'm going to hurt you. We have some unfinished business to take care of right now. You've avoided me all weekend and you're not going to avoid me for another damn second."

"I'm not going to give you the attention you feel you need. If reconciling our differences results in you putting your hands on me, then maybe you should leave. Take some time to cool off and step to me like you have some sense."

Nokea was digging herself a deeper hole. When she took it upon herself to turn and walk out the door, I lost it. I jumped up from the bed and went after her. In the hallway, I grabbed her arm, shoving her back into our bedroom. I was so angry. When she charged at me, I tripped her to the floor, slamming the double doors behind me. She sat up on her elbows, staring me down with anger all over her face. Soon, a tear rolled down her cheek and she started to breathe heavily. I stood over her.

"Don't wimp out on me now, Miss Tough-ass. A moment ago, you were talking all kinds of shit! I ain't gon' put my hands on you, but I want to make something perfectly clear to you. If anybody leaves this house, it will be you and not me. I pay the fucking bills here, Nokea! My money bought this house and every piece of furniture in it! Even the clothes on your back belong to me. If you ever, ever disrespect me again, I will have no problem making sure that you are left with nothing." Putting in my final words, I squatted down in front of her, rubbing my goatee. "Hurt don't

always come by using force. My true words can
cause you more pain than you've ever felt before.
I meant everything I said to you. I hope you'd
know by now when not to fuck with me."

Nokea didn't say a word. I stood up, and for
now, this conversation was over. I gave her one
last evil look, before leaving the room and slamming the door behind me.

For the next several days, thing were pretty
quiet around the house. Nokea and I weren't
speaking to each other and I spent my nights in
one of the guestrooms. Even Shane had called
so we could talk about our differences, but with
all that had gone on with me and Nokea, his call
the other day had come at a bad time. I promised
to call him in a few days. When I reached over
to the phone in the guestroom to call him, I was
surprised to hear Scorpio answer his phone.

"Is Shane there?" I asked.

"Jaylin, him and Mackenzie went to get us
something to eat."

"How's she doing?"

"She couldn't be better. Since the last time you
saw her, she's gotten so big. I don't even know if
you'd recognize her."

"Woman, please. Mackenzie is in my heart and memory forever. Legally, she's still my child, you know?"

"I haven't forgotten. But we all know that things worked out for the best."

"If that's how you see it, cool. But, uh . . . has Shane been treating y'all right?"

"Of course. You wouldn't expect anything different from a man of his caliber, would you?"

"I guess not. He told me about the baby. I'm sorry to hear what happened."

"I was too. Now, I understand how you and Nokea felt about y'alls baby. It was a devastating loss for us. I often wonder why things like that have to happen."

"Me too. But, uh, tell Shane to hit me back whenever he gets home, all right?"

"I will, but I have to ask you . . . is everything okay? I know you all too well and your voice—"

I closed my eyes, thinking about my argument with Nokea. "I'm tired, Scorpio. Physically, I'm okay but my mind has been on overload."

"I definitely know how that can be. Get some rest and relax. Hopefully, I'll see you soon."

My eyes popped open. "What?" I smiled.

"I was only kidding. I had to think of a way to make you smile. It sounds like my mission was accomplished."

"It always is, isn't it Scorpio? You shouldn't tease a heartbroken man like that, but the thought of seeing—"

I paused, looking at Nokea in the doorway with her arms folded. "I wasn't sure if I heard her name clearly or not, but are you speaking to your ex-lover in our house?" she asked.

I ignored Nokea. "Scorpio, don't forget to tell Shane to call me, all right?"

"Sure," she said and hung up.

I set the phone down and looked at Nokea. "Did you say something? For several days, you haven't said shit to me so I thought you forgot how to talk."

"I said . . . kiss," she paused, "my," she paused again, "ass!"

She walked away and I yelled. "Don't worry! I'm horny and I was getting around to it!"

For another thirty minutes, I stayed in the guestroom, until I heard a bunch of rambling going on. When I got up, I went into our bedroom and Nokea was in her closet. She had a suitcase lying on the floor and was throwing some of her things inside. I leaned against the doorway, looking at her like she was crazy.

"Where in the hell do you think you're going?"

"Somewhere far away from you. You've gotten too out of line for me and I can't deal with it anymore."

"Suit yourself," I said walking away from the door. I went into the bathroom, dabbed my face with cold water and brushed my teeth. Afterward, I flossed and turned on the water in the shower. I let the water run, and then went back over to my closet to get some clothes. Nokea had closed her suitcase and rolled it out of the closet. I saw the saddened look on her face, but I was still too mad to respond. When LJ came into the room, he asked Nokea where she was going.

"Mommie will call you later, okay?" she said, touching his cheeks.

"Why are you crying?" he asked. He looked at her suitcase and started to tear up. Nokea got mad. "Stop acting like that," she yelled. "I promise you that Mommie will call you later."

"Hold the fuck up," I said, stepping out of the closet. "Don't raise your voice at my child. LJ, go see what Nanna's cooking for breakfast and close the door behind you."

He did as he was told, and without hesitation, Nokea was on her way out.

"Why don't you cut with the bullshit and go somewhere and sit down," I said.

She let go of her suitcase and proudly stepped up to me. She slapped the shit out of me, hard enough to turn my head. Afterward, she removed the diamond wedding ring on her finger

and dropped it down inside of the black sweatpants I wore.

"Go screw yourself Jaylin," she said, turning
to walk away.

I rushed to the door, not realizing how serious
our argument had gotten. I held the door shut
with my hand above her head. "You are not going
to disrupt this family," I said. "Now, I don't know
who or what has gotten into you, but we need to
talk this shit out, right here and right now."

"Nothing you can say will justify your selfish
and hurtful words to me, as well as your conversing over the phone with a woman who has
caused the both of us so many setbacks. The
question is not what has gotten into me, but
what the hell has happened to you? Since we've
been married, you've never treated me like this.
If you don't love me anymore then it's time for
me to go."

"What would make you think that I don't love
you anymore?"

"Replay the last several months of our marriage in your mind, Jaylin. You've been angry with
Shane because of his relationship with Scorpio
and you're starting to take your frustrations out
on me. You're starting to give other women attention now, and when did your good fortune
ever become an issue with us? I don't care about

this house or the lavish furniture in it. This house means nothing to me, if I can't share it peacefully with the man I love. If you think you can live here without my presence, you go right ahead. Your millions and millions of dollars will never provide you with the comfort and support I've given you over the years. And, for the record, if this marriage doesn't work itself out, you'd better be prepared to split your fortune right down the middle. I've earned every bit of it and for me to settle for anything less will not be in my best interest."

Nokea reached for the doorknob and I grabbed her waist. "Look, I know I've been kind of trippin' and I'm sorry." I placed my lips on the back of her head. "I don't know what's been troubling me. Even though I've been upset with Shane, it doesn't mean that I love you any less. I would be devastated if you left me. There's no way for me to stay here without you. No doubt, what's mine is yours. I should have never stepped to you like that. Please forgive me, will you?"

"For almost my entire life, I've been forgiving your mishaps, Jaylin. I hope that if and when the time ever comes, you will have no problem returning the favor."

Nokea stepped away from the door and went into the bathroom. I followed and watched as she got some Kleenex and dabbed her watery eyes. The water was still running in the shower, so I stepped out of my sweatpants and picked up her ring from the floor. I took her hand, sliding the ring back on her finger. I then held her hand and walked her over by the shower with me. She was fully clothed. Once I removed her clothes, I set them on the bathroom's counter. We got into the shower. As the numerous waterfall faucets poured on our naked bodies, I held her close. I felt her hard nipples against my chest and roamed my hands over her curvy wet backside. When I inserted my fingers into her volcano, I added additional rotations to make it erupt. She begged for me to fuck her, turning her back to me so I could aim my hardness at her hole. I was too enthused, until Nokea covered her face and started to cry.

I backed away, turning her around to face me. "Please don't cry," I said, kissing her lips and rubbing her wet hair back with my hands. "I will never hurt you like that again. I love you Nokea. At times, I can be so fucking stupid."

She let out her emotions, while laying her head against my chest. Afterward, she stepped out of the shower and reached for a towel. She wrapped it around her body, leaving the bathroom in a hurry. Yes, I was mad, but I had no one but myself to blame for my disrespect.

Chapter 6

Scorpio

I sat in my contemporary-decorated office at Jay's and couldn't get a thing done. My mind was preoccupied with the thoughts of Shane and our relationship. Yesterday, Shane, Mackenzie and I had a blast. We went snow sledding, went to the movies, and had an awesome dinner at J Bucks. He was becoming everything I dreamed my future husband would be. After our conversation last night, I had a feeling my time was soon to come.

Earlier, Shane told me he had something important to tell me, so I waited at Jay's for him to come. It was already 3:00 P.M., and when I called his house, he didn't answer. I called his cell phone too, but his voice mail picked up. I left a message for him to call me.

Attempting to pass the time, I walked up front and sat with Bernie and one of her customers.

Because of the weather, not too many people were willing to fight the blistering cold. Many of my stylists had even stayed home, but Bernie said that she had money to make and was there to make it.

"Scorpio, I'm just about finished. Give me about thirty more minutes and I'm calling it a day," she said.

"Okay," I said, taking a seat by the window. I gazed out of it, watching the falling snow. It was so pretty. I couldn't decide if I wanted a winter or summer wedding. Also, I didn't know if Shane and I would keep it simple, or if we'd invite all our friends. Knowing Shane, he'd want to keep it simple. I thought of his friendship with Jaylin, and then, my thoughts turned to him.

When we spoke the other day, he sure sounded down. I didn't know what was up with him and Nokea, but from what Shane told me, they were having some minor problems. I wanted to find out what had gone down, but frankly, it really wasn't any of my business. Jaylin had finalized his choice and so had I. He was now a part of my past. Shane had become my future. It took a long time for me to get to this point. I thought my love for Jaylin would never, ever go away. I'd be lying if I said I still didn't think about him from time to time, and it was always difficult for me to forget about the spectacular sex he always dished out.

Bernie's customer had left and time was flying by. Several times, I looked at the clock. It wasn't like Shane to tell me he was going to do something and not do it. Either way, I locked up after Bernie left. When the phone rang, I hurried to my office to answer. It was Shane.

"Baby," he said in a soft tone. "I need for you to do something for me."

His voice didn't sound right to me. "What's the matter? Is everything okay?"

"No it's not. I'm in jail."

My eyes widened and so did my mouth. "In jail? For what?" There was silence. "Shane! In jail for what?" I yelled.

"Attempted murder."

"What?" I yelled. "This is a joke, right? Please tell me this is a joke. I don't have time for games. If you don't want to get married . . ."

"It's no joke. I'm right here in Clayton, but before you make your way over here, I need for you to make some phone calls for me."

I was still in disbelief. I had so many questions, but I knew Shane's time on the phone was limited. "Call who and for what?"

"My bond is two million dollars. I have some money in the bank, but a lot of it is tied up with my company. I only need ten percent. I can swing at least a hundred thousand."

"I have some extra money too, but . . . but please tell me what's going on. Are these false charges or what? Tell me—"

"When I get out of here, I will tell you everything. First, I need the money. Whatever you have, I will give it back to you. The difference, would you mind calling Jaylin to see if he can spot me?"

"I'll get on it now. I love you and I will do whatever it takes to get you out of there."

"Thanks, baby. I love you too."

Once I got off the phone with Shane, I quickly crunched some numbers and he was still forty Gs short. Without Shane's consent, I knew I couldn't pull one hundred thousand dollars from his bank account. I had to ask Jaylin for one hundred and forty thousand and promise to pay him back. I took a deep breath and dialed his number. Just my luck, Nokea answered.

"Hi Nokea. You know that I wouldn't bother Jaylin unless it was important, but can I speak to him, please?"

I couldn't believe she hung up on me. I called back, preparing myself to plead with her.

"Hello," she snapped.

"Nokea, please. Shane has been arrested, I need some help from Jaylin."

Her tone quickly changed. "Arrested? Did he tell you why?" she softly asked. "Whe . . . when did this happen?"

"Today. I really don't know the details, but I just got a phone call from him. His bond is ten percent of two million dollars. We just don't have that kind of money lying around."

"Hold on, Scorpio. Let me go get Jaylin."

Nokea put the phone down. I couldn't remember the last time she'd been that kind to me. I'm sure her concern was for Shane. Jaylin picked up the phone.

"What's going on?" he asked.

"Jaylin, Shane's been arrested. I don't know the details, but he mentioned something about attempted murder. He's short on his bond. I promise you we will repay you every single dime of it back."

"This is a joke, right?"

"No it's not. That's the same thing I said when he called me, but he was serious. If you could have the money wired to my bank, I'll make sure when he's released he'll call and tell you all about it."

"Damn," Jaylin said. "Did he say anything about Stephon or Felicia? He mentioned to me before that he might have a warrant out for messing up Stephon's barbershop that day."

"No he didn't mention a thing about that, but with a two million dollar bond, this sounds more serious than that."

"Two million dollars!" Jaylin yelled. "What the fuck . . ."

"I don't know what's up, but I want him out of jail, now. All I need is one hundred and forty Gs and he'll be free to go."

"Do you want me to transfer the money into his account or yours?"

"Put it in mine, please. It would make it a lot easier."

"Give me your account number. Within the hour, check your account. If you have any problems, let me know. The moment Shane steps out of jail, tell him to call me. Do you know if he's talked to our lawyer, Frick, yet?"

"I hope so, but if he hasn't, I'm sure he will."

"Just in case, I'm going to call him. Wait until Frick calls you and do not take that money to the jailhouse unless he's with you."

"Thanks Jaylin. As always, we owe you."

"Big time," he said.

Before hanging up, I gave Jaylin my account number. Within thirty minutes, the money had hit my account. Frick called about an hour after that. He told me to meet him at the jailhouse. Once I left Jay's and the bank, I hurried to the jailhouse to meet Frick.

It took almost two hours. Finally, Shane was released. I wasn't trying to pull a Whitney Houston and Bobby Brown, but I hurried into Shane's arms. I was so excited to see him. He hugged me tightly and gave me lengthy kisses. Mr. Frick stood close by, waiting until our hugs and kisses were finished.

"Shane," he said. "I need to see you in my office at 9:00 A.M. You and your friend Jaylin have been on a roll this year. I didn't expect for you to get caught up in some mess like this. You and Nokea—"

Shane quickly cut Frick off. "I'll see you in the morning," he said. "We can talk then."

Frick patted Shane on his back and hurried down the steps with his tailored suit on and briefcase in his hand.

"You never told me you had a Richard Gere look-a-like for your attorney," I playfully said, nudging his stomach with my elbow. "And, please tell me what Nokea has to do with this. Mr. Frick mentioned Nokea—what's that all about?"

"Can I go home, get out of these clothes, and then, tell you all about it?"

"Of course," I said.

We held hands and walked to my car. On the drive to Shane's place, he brought up Jaylin.

"So, I guess he came through for me again, huh?"

"Yes, and he didn't hesitate, not one bit. He told me to tell you to call him. When you do, please don't forget to thank him. We have to make sure he gets every bit of his money back."

"Oh, you'd better believe he'll get it back. You will get your money back too."

"Don't worry about me. I just want to know what the hell is going on. I know you didn't attempt to murder nobody, but it would be nice to know why the police think you did."

Shane displayed a worried look. "I assure you that I didn't murder anybody. But, like I said, when I get home, I'll tell you all about it."

Chapter 7

Shane

No doubt, I was fucked! The time I spent in jail, as well as the entire ride to my place, I tried to think of something legitimate to tell Scorpio about that night. She kept pressing me in the car. Even though I told her part of the story, I had in no way told her the truth. I had a feeling the police would catch up with me, but not this soon. I had the day all planned out and it consisted of asking Scorpio to be my wife. Earlier, I'd gone to the jewelry store and picked out a ring. Just as I was on my way to Jay's, the police came to my house. I was arrested and the rest is history. Until Frick showed up, I hadn't said much to the police about what happened that day. I knew what I'd done to the officer was in self defense and I hoped that my side of the story someway or somehow held up.

When we got to my place, I went to my room to get out of my clothes. I stripped down to my white jockey shorts and socks. Scorpio was in the family room, and she seemed a little content with what I had told her in the car. I failed to mention what had happened with Nokea, and I felt bad about the lie I was going to tell if she continued to question me. I stood with the palms of my hands on my dresser. My head was lowered, and I was thinking about all that had happened. My concentration was broken when Scorpio cleared her throat. I turned my head, admiring the beautiful person I was proud to call my woman. She looked downright beautiful in an off the shoulder olive green linen dress. Shame on me for not even noticing how spectacular she looked. Most of her naturally curly hair was pulled back into a clip. Several strands hung on her shoulders. Her body reminded me of Lisa Raye's, but being Black, mixed with Italian, that put Scorpio in a class all by herself. Gorgeous. "Come here," I said. "You are such a sight for sore and tired eyes."

She sauntered over to me, placing her arms on my shoulders. Her hands rubbed the back of my twisties. I turned my head to kiss the inside of her hand.

"Did I ever tell you that you would make an excellent underwear model," she said, rubbing my buffed chest. Her hands scrolled down to my nicely cut abs. Then, she lowered her right hand to my goods.

I wanted to get inside of her so badly, but first, I had to call Jaylin and thank him.

"Baby, let me call Jaylin real quick. Why don't you get comfortable and I'll meet you in the family room in about ten minutes."

"Please hurry. I still got some things on my mind. I'm deeply concerned about what Nokea had to—"

"We'll have our discussion, right after I call Jaylin. I promise."

Scorpio turned around, releasing her long hair from the clip. "Would you take off my necklace and unzip my dress."

Standing closely behind her, I removed her silver necklace and unzipped her dress. To no surprise, she didn't have on any underclothes. I slid my hands inside of her dress, massaging her breasts together.

"It's a shame what you do to me," I whispered in her ear. I licked around it and Scorpio tilted her head to the side.

"No," she said. "I'd say it's a shame what you do to me."

She lowered my hand. Once she wiggled her way out of her dress, she put my hand between her legs. I got anxious and moved her closer to my bed.

"Maybe I should call Jaylin a little later, huh?"

Scorpio kneeled on the bed, looking back at me standing behind her. "Maybe so," she said. "Besides, this *talk* we're about to have could take a while."

As soon as I dropped my shorts, the phone rang. Ignoring it, I touched Scorpio's shapely ass, but she reached for my hand.

"Answer the phone, it might be Jaylin. Besides, if we go for the sex first, I'm afraid you might not want to talk to me later. I really need to know more about what's going on."

Damn, I thought. *Just when I thought I could hit her with something to occupy her mind.* I nodded and Scorpio reached for the phone to answer it.

"It's Jaylin. I'll be in the family room watching TV. Come see me when you're finished, okay?"

I nodded again and placed the phone on my ear.

"Hello," I said.

"All I want to know is who in the hell doesn't know how to follow directions? You or Scorpio?"

"Believe it or not, I was about to call you. I had my hand on the phone and was getting ready to pick it up."

"And, since Scorpio answered the phone, I assume you had your hand on her ass and couldn't quite get to the phone."

I laughed hard. "What, you got cameras in this muthafucka or something?"

"Ha, Ha, nigga. Ain't nothing going on in your household that ain't going on in mine. If you want some tips, you might want to hook up a hidden camera over here. In the meantime, why have you become St. Louis' Most Wanted Criminal?"

"Fool, I've always been St. Louis' most wanted man and I forever will be."

"That's because I moved away. The women there have to settle for what they can get."

Jaylin and I both laughed. "Naw, straight up, though. Thanks for the loan. Soon, I will make sure you get every dime of it back. I have a hundred Gs in the bank. I'll shoot it back to you tomorrow."

"No rush. Just tell me what the hell is up."

"When Nokea and me got stranded, do you remember the police who I told you took us to a hotel?"

"Yeah, I remember."

"Well, that wasn't the truth. At first, he offered to help, but when I declined his offer, he started tripping. He used racial slurs and we got into a scuffle. I fucked him up. When he tried to pull his gun on me, I pistol whipped his ass. Afterward, I left him squirming on the ground and found an air pump in his trunk. I aired up my spare tire and me and Nokea took off. When you called we had just checked into a hotel. Today, from what the police at the station said, the officer is still in the hospital, claiming that I tried to kill him."

"I can't believe you or Nokea didn't mention this incident to me, especially Nokea. With something like that happening, she would've been a nervous wreck and the both of y'all walked in here all cool, calm and collected. Man, that shit don't add up and—"

"I wanted to tell you, Jay, but you and Nokea were going through some shit already. I didn't want to worry you about what had happened. Surely, I thought what had happened was behind me."

"Shane, there ain't no way in hell you pistol whipped a police officer, left him for dead, and you thought the shit was behind you. As for Nokea, she knew better not telling me what happened. I don't care how mad I was, somebody should have told me. She could be in trouble her damn self. I hope like hell Frick helps you work out this shit."

"I hope so too. Please don't be angry with Nokea. I asked her not to tell you because our friendship had already suffered enough. I didn't want you to know that I ran across some difficulties getting her home."

"That's all fine and dandy, but no matter what you suggested, she still should have told me. I wasn't gon' trip. If the fucking fool was shooting you down with racial slurs, then he deserved to get his ass kicked."

"Oh, he definitely got what he deserved. I just hate all of that had to go down with Nokea being there."

Jaylin and I discussed the situation for a while longer, then wrapped up our conversation. He told me if I needed anything else to let him know. He encouraged me to quickly talk to Frick and I couldn't wait until morning to go see him.

Later that night, again, I told Scorpio the same story I'd told Jaylin. To me, it sounded like a fabricated story. I wasn't sure if either of them believed me. For now, it just had to do. I hoped Nokea kept things on the low-low until she spoke to me.

Scorpio wanted to go to Frick's office with me, but I told her I needed to go by myself. Instead, I asked her to take care of some other things for me like wiring some of Jaylin's money back to him and going to the grocery store. She agreed to do it and I felt relieved.

When I got to Frick's office, he immediately invited me in to have a seat. He had a bunch of papers on his desk and cleared them out of the way before he spoke. Being very observant, he glared at me from across his desk.

"Your case is interesting Shane. I need to hear your side of the story. Then, I'll share with you what I know, versus what I don't understand."

I stuck to the same story and repeated it to Frick. He looked at me like I was crazy.

"If you want me to represent you, I need the truth. I don't buy that freaking story, Shane. There are so many things that don't add up. For starters," he said, scrambling through some papers, "I have receipts from two hotels that night. One receipt is from a motel where the victim said you shot him, and you did shoot him. The other is at a hotel almost forty miles away from that one. Are you telling me that you only pistol whipped him and didn't shoot him?"

I lowered my eyes and swallowed. "I . . . yes, I shot him."

Frick took a deep breath. "Why, Shane? I need to know why you shot him, and this time, I want the truth."

"I shot him because he forced Nokea and me to have sexual intercourse. He threatened to kill us if we didn't. At first, I thought he was going to rape Nokea, but he had other plans. He demanded money from us, talked to us like dirt, and held us at gunpoint while we had sex. In self defense, when I was able to rush him, I took the opportunity and did so."

"Why did you feel the need to come in here and lie to me about this? These are some serious charges against you."

"Because I didn't want anybody to know what happened in that room. First of all, I felt . . . felt bad for not being able to protect myself or Nokea. And now, I don't want Jaylin or Scorpio to find out about this. You know how Jaylin gets and Nokea has already been through enough. I'm sure he'll have no problem ending our friendship, but complicating his marriage to Nokea was not my intentions."

"But, it was a situation that no one could have prevented. If you shot this man in self defense, then I'd say Jaylin owes you for saving his wife's life."

"He is not going to see it that way and you know it."

For a moment, Frick sat quietly while in deep thought. "He might not see it that way Shane, but if this case goes to trial, he's going to find out exactly what happened in that room. In the meantime, I have good news, and of course, bad news."

I leaned back in the chair. "Let's hear it."

"The man who you shot was not a police officer. He's a wanted child molester, a con artist and a bank robber. Basically, his rap sheet is three times the size of my dick. I'd say you did the police a favor. They have no idea where he got the police car from, but he'd used it to pull over several victims and rape them. He's being heavily guarded in the hospital. His story is that you attempted to rob him, and when he wouldn't cooperate, you shot him. Because of his criminal record, I doubt that anyone is going to buy his story. But, in an effort to clear your name, you and I have to go to the station and tell the police exactly what happened."

"Okay, that's fine, but what's the bad news."

"The bad news for you is, the detectives are possibly making their way to Nokea's house, as we speak. You and her stories must be on the same page with each other. If they are not, you stand a chance of this case going to trial because no one believes you. You may want to let her know that her attorney should be present. If Jaylin would like for me to send someone there on his wife's behalf—"

"That won't be necessary. I don't want Jaylin getting all worked up over this. I'd rather speak to Nokea first."

Frick picked up his phone. "You're going to have to call her now and encourage her to be honest with the detectives upon arrival."

I covered my face with my hands and rubbed my temples. "Why must we involve Nokea? I . . . the police will believe me. You know they will."

"Considering the background of the individual you shot, they probably will. But, we need to be sure that everything is clear and out in the open. Nokea is the only person who can confirm your story. I'm sorry, Shane, but you've got to call her. Call her now," he ordered.

I took a deep breath and took the phone from Frick's hand. I dialed out and waited for some-one to answer the phone. I hoped like hell that it would be Nokea, but Jaylin answered.

"Hey, man," I said in a dry tone. "I'm at Frick's office. I need to speak to Nokea."

"Sure. Is, uh, everything working out?"

"Everything is going okay. I just found out that the officer was actually a wanted criminal. This is very good news for me. I just need for Nokea to confirm a few things for me."

"I'm sure she won't have a problem with that, but if this is such good news, why are you sound-ing so fucked up?"

"I don't know, Jay. I just wish this shit had never happened. I'm real sorry. I did everything I could to protect Nokea. Maybe it wasn't enough."

"Don't be so hard on yourself. You sound full of fear. With Frick having your back, I don't know why you're tripping."

I couldn't utter another word. Jaylin asked me to hold and Nokea got on the phone.

"Shane," she said. "Are you . . . What's going on?"

"I'm at Frick's office. In an effort to clear my name, I had to tell him the truth. The man who came in on us was a wanted felon. He's saying that I robbed and shot him. Some detectives are on their way to your house. I need for you to tell them the truth about everything."

Nokea was quiet, but then she responded. "Everything?"

"Yes, everything. No need to get into details about our conversation in the car, but everything else needs to be told. I'm sorry. I know this is not going to be easy for you. If you need me, please call me. You know I got your back."

She sighed. "I told you that I wouldn't let you down. Whatever happens, it just happens. Hopefully, Jaylin will understand."

"Don't count on it, but make it clear to him that it was my idea to not tell him the truth, not yours."

"That has no relevance to it at all. I have to go now. I'll talk to you soon."

Nokea hung up and I looked at Frick. "I don't like this one damn bit. I can't even imagine what's about to take place in their home."

"Being dishonest didn't help, Shane. But, under the circumstances, who wouldn't have done what you did?"

I looked away, visualizing what was about to take place.

Chapter 8

Nokea

No doubt, I was in a panic. I was trying to discuss what had happened with Jaylin, but then, the doorbell rang. He left the room and I followed behind as he made his way to the double glass front doors. Nanny B and the kids came from their rooms too. When Jaylin opened the door, I turned to Nanny B.

"Would you mind taking the children to their playroom?" I politely asked. She looked at the three detectives dressed in dark suits. Without any hesitation, she removed LJ and Jaylene from the room. Jaylin invited the detectives in.

"I'm Jaylin Rogers," he said, being very cooperative. He shook their hands. "And, this is my wife, Nokea."

The detectives shook my hand, displayed their badges and told me their names. I offered them a seat and we all stepped down into the sunken great room. Jaylin, however, stood up, leaning against one of the tall, thick white columns with his arms folded. I tried to play it cool, but he definitely could see how nervous I was. Offering me no support, his eyes looked as if they were shooting daggers at me. While on the circular sofa that was spacious enough for everyone to take a seat, I crossed my legs and turned to the detectives. Their eyes roamed the great room and high vaulted ceilings that had four tropical fans hanging from them.

"This is really a nice place," one of them said. "So, this is how the rich and or famous live, huh?"

"We're blessed," is all Jaylin said. He looked at me, but I turned away again.

"Very," the detective said and cleared his throat. His eyes shifted to me and he handed me a picture. "Mrs. Rogers, I'm sure you already know why we're here. We have a convicted felon in custody who we'd like to keep behind bars. He's wanted for child molestation, rape, robbery, assault, and a possible murder in Texas. I understand that you and a companion came in contact with this individual. We'd like to know what happened. He claims that he was robbed and shot by your husband, but Shane Ricardo Alexander is not your husband."

I looked at the picture and gave it back to the detective. "No, Shane is not my husband. He's a very good friend of ours. We did come in contact with this individual, and by all means, he was not the one harmed, we were."

"Do you mind sharing with us what happened?" another detective said.

I swallowed and looked at Jaylin. His eyes did not blink and they were focused on me. Nervous, I massaged my hands together and proceeded to give the detectives my recollection of what had happened that day. "Shane caught a flat tire and exited the highway. He called roadside assistance, but they never showed up. Soon, a man appearing to be a police officer did and he offered to help us. He drove us to a gas station, but it was closed. He then suggested that we stay the night at a motel, and said he'd come back in the morning to help us."

One of the detectives interrupted. "Was the motel his idea or you guys idea?"

"It was his idea because Shane and I didn't know the area well. Since it was getting late, we agreed to have him take us to the motel. Once there, he dropped us off and told us he'd be back in the morning."

The detective interrupted again. "While riding in the car, did you notice anything out of the ordinary? And, once you got out, was there any money exchanged?"

"The car looked like any other police vehicle I'd seen and I didn't notice anything out of the ordinary. As for money, I believe Shane offered the man some money for helping us. I'm not sure how much it was, though."

"Continue," the detective said.

I combed my hair with my fingers and dropped my forehead in my hand. "Once we got into the room, I lay down and Shane went to the bathroom to shower."

"Before you lay down, did you remove your clothes?"

"No . . . I, the only things I removed was my jacket and shirt. The room was muggy, but I kept my bra and pants on. Is . . . is what I had on really necessary?"

The sterner detective spoke up and did so with an attitude. "If it wasn't, we wouldn't have asked. Continue, please."

"I went to sleep and—"

"Alone?"

"Yes, I was in the bed alone. Shane was in a chair. There was a knock on the door and it awakened both of us. When Shane opened the door, the officer came in and pulled his gun on us. He told Shane to close the door and—"

"So, he just busted through the door and pulled out his gun?"

I was getting nervous from the detective's tone. Without even looking at Jaylin, I could feel him looking at me. "The man stepped inside, asked if we were hungry and we told him no, we were resting. Then, that's when he pulled the gun on Shane and told him to close the door."

"You said he pulled the gun on the both of you. Was the gun on you or Shane? Please be specific."

"He aimed the gun at Shane. He then told Shane to go over to the bed and he aimed the gun in both of our direction. Shane asked what he wanted with us and offered the officer more money. Once he tossed Shane his pants, Shane lay his money on the dresser and I put my money on it too."

"Did he ask for your money and how much money was it?"

"I . . . I can't remember if he specifically asked for it, but I hoped that the money would cause him to leave. I can't remember how much it was."

"Continue."

I took another deep breath, swallowing hard. "Anyway, once we set the money on the table, he asked me to, uh, undress. Shane defended me and told him no. He threatened to shoot Shane, until I agreed to it. My . . . my words satisfied him and I removed my clothes."

The officer looked up at Jaylin. "Sir, you might want to step into another room and discuss this with your wife later."

The look on Jaylin's face said it all. He was mad as hell. I knew he was about to explode. "If you don't mind, I'm fine standing right here. Please allow my wife to continue."

The detective looked at me and I continued. "Uh, next, he told me to sit back on the bed and I did. He and Shane started arguing and, uh, the next thing I knew, Shane rushed him. They tussled around for a while and the gun went off. The officer . . . man fell backward because he'd been shot. Shane and I got dressed and then we left."

The detectives looked at each other. The sterner one quickly spoke up. "I know this must be difficult for you, but you have to be honest with us. Did the man in the picture rape you or inappropriately touch you in any way?"

I looked at Jaylin. His eyes had closed and he waited for my response. "No, he did not. He made it clear that he didn't screw Black . . . colored women, and he never touched me."

"Well, then, we have a slight problem, Mrs. Rogers. The motel room was thoroughly inspected and there was evidence of sexual activities in the room, referring to the sheets. Now, I'm sure sex often occurs in motel rooms, but we can have the sheets tested for DNA. I think it would be wise . . . ."

I couldn't even look Jaylin's way. I was down to the wire. I took a hard and hurtful swallow. "Be . . . before Shane shot the officer, he, uh," I slowly turned to Jaylin. "Before I say anything else, I would like to have an attorney present."

Jaylin put his hands into his pockets and stepped down into the great room. "Nah, don't stop now, this shit is getting interesting. He, uh, what Nokea? Finish telling the detectives your version of the story."

"First, I would really like to speak with an attorney."

"Fuck an attorney!" he yelled. "What in the hell happened!"

The detectives didn't even defend me. They wanted answers just like Jaylin did. I dropped my face into my hands and covered my eyes. "He . . . the officer . . . the man, he forced Shane and I to have sex while he watched. I . . . we didn't want to, but we feared for our lives," I sobbed.

Jaylin moved my hand away from my face. He spoke with seething anger. "Why in the fuck didn't you tell me this shit! You betrayed me

Nokea! You lied to me," he paused and turned to the detectives. "Are we done here?"

"No, sir," the detective said. "We have a few more questions, if you don't mind."

"I don't believe this shit," Jaylin chuckled in disbelief. "Take her ass to the station and finish this shit up! I don't give a damn what happens to either one of them!"

He stepped away and I grabbed his arm. "Jaylin, please!"

He snatched away and squeezed his fist. "I swear to God I could kill you right now. Do not touch me!"

"Sir," the detective said, standing up. "I know you're angry, but this seems to have been a very unfortunate situation. We're just here to get to the bottom of this and we are thankful that your wife is being very cooperative with us."

"Well, I'm thankful for having a lying ass and uncooperative wife too! Hurry this shit up and get the fuck out of my house! If you got more questions, take her ass to the station and question her. I don't need to hear anymore of the bullshit."

Jaylin walked away. When the doors to our bedroom slammed, I heard a loud crack. The detectives looked at me.

"Maybe you should come with us and let things cool down for a while. We'd hate for this to escalate into something . . . ."

My whole body was shaking. I didn't know what to do. "Can we please just finish this up later? I will be happy to come to the police station or meet you anywhere you'd like. I . . . I just can't talk about this anymore."

"Will you be willing to take a lie detector test?"

"Of course, whatever it takes. I just need to talk to my husband right now."

The detective standing gave me a card and the other two stood up. "Unfortunately for you, we have to get to the bottom of this. The sooner you can come to the station, the better. No later than tomorrow, okay? If you want an attorney present, feel free to bring one," he said.

I nodded and walked them to the door. Once they left, I headed to our bedroom, but Nanny B stopped me.

"What's going on?" she whispered.

"A lot, Nanny B. Just keep the kids busy in the playroom. You and I will talk later."

"From the looks of it, Jaylin seems pretty upset," she said. "Why don't you stay with the kids for a minute and let me try to calm him down?"

"No, that's okay. This is my battle and I need to take care of it. Thanks, though," I said, and gave her a hug. She hugged me tight. When I loosened our embrace, I went to our bedroom. One of the doors was definitely cracked. When I looked for Jaylin, I saw him standing outside on the balcony. His back was turned and I slowly made my way to him.

"Jaylin . . . ."

"Nokea, do not come any closer to me," he said with his back still turned. "I will toss your ass over this balcony. Please do not challenge me right now."

I stood where I was, which was close by our bed. "Would you please just listen to me before you start making any critical decisions? Neither Shane nor I wanted this to happen. We wanted to tell you, but I knew how angry you'd be. I knew you wouldn't understand that we feared for our lives and we had to do what that man ordered us to do. Don't you know how much it pained me to let another man touch me? Telling you the truth was only going to make matters worse. I know you Jaylin. There was no way you'd understand. An understanding person you are not. Even though I expect for you to be mad at me, don't you know how much I love you? Don't you know that Shane and I did everything that we . . ."

He turned and his eyes were fire red. No doubt, I could see the hurt in them, but he spoke calmly. "Fuck you and Shane, Nokea. The only thing you need to know about me is that I don't give a damn anymore. You are the biggest hypocrite I know. How dare you ridicule me for being a liar when you took the game of lying and ran with it. You didn't tell me about this shit because you wanted Shane and he wanted you. You continuously make me pay for my mistakes in the past, and frankly, I'm fucking tired of it. I am so tired," his voice rose, "of every woman that's been with me, having sex with my damn friends! Now, with you being my wife, you know that shit is unacceptable! There is nothing," he yelled and pointed his finger, "nothing that you can say to me right now to make me understand! Life or death situation or not, you had an obligation to tell me the truth and you didn't! Your stupidity has cost us our marriage. I don't want this shit anymore. I'm tired of going out of my way to please you. I've spent this entire marriage trying to make up my past mistakes to you, and I regret—"

"No, you don't," I said, sitting back on the bed. I was numb. I had so much more to say, but nothing could justify me being dishonest. Jaylin rushed past me and went into his closet. He quickly put on a shirt and a pair of shoes. I tried to be strong, but I couldn't help but scream out loudly to get his attention. "Jaylin, I made a big mistake by not telling you the truth and I'm sorry! Please forgive me. Don't take us down this road again."

He ignored me and headed over to the nightstand. I knew he was going for his keys, so I quickly opened the drawer and took them out.

"Where are you going?" I asked.

"Give me the keys," he ordered.

"No. Not until you tell me where you're going."

"I'm going to go get busy like you did."

His words stung because I could feel the truth behind them. "How many times do I have to tell you that Shane and I—"

"Give me the fucking keys!" he yelled.

"No," I pleaded. I put the keys deep in the pockets of my jeans. "I'm not going to let you do this to us. You have to . . ."

Jaylin's actions turned into raging anger. He pulled on my pocket and didn't stop until I dropped to the floor. He roughly dug into my pocket for the keys. Not wanting him to leave, I forced his hands away. My nails scratched his hand and that's when he caused my head to hit the floor. He lifted me by the collar of my torn shirt. His strength was too much for me to bear and I dangled in his hands like a rag doll.

"You want me to hurt you, don't you?" he yelled.

"I don't want you to go," I cried. "Hurt me or do whatever it is you want to do to let out your frustrations, but don't leave this house under these conditions."

Jaylin threw me back on the bed. He went for the keys in my pocket again and I wiped the sweat from his forehead. Attempting to calm him down, I rubbed my fingers through his curly wet hair and touched the side of his face. "I've never asked for your forgiveness, but I'm asking for it now. Do not leave me and your children like this. We need you Jaylin. From now on, I will be honest with you about everything. I promise."

Just for a moment, I had his attention. He held the keys in his hands and looked down at me on the bed. "Did you enjoy yourself with Shane? Since you're being honest, now, I'd like to know."

"No, I didn't," I whispered.

"Then, why don't I believe you? The evidence on the sheets showed that somebody did. Was it his juices, yours or both?"

"I . . . I don't know what was on . . . ."

He yanked my collar and shook me. "You don't know? You mean to tell me that you don't know if you came or not? Were you wet . . . Did he wet you? How long were the two of you forced to do it?"

"Baby, please stop hurting me. I don't want to discuss this with you being unstable like this."

"Answer my fucking questions, Nokea! I want to know and I want to know now!"

His face was right there with mine. Our eyes were locked together, and the man I loved more than anything in the world was severely crushed. I couldn't stand to frustrate him more, and my dishonesty was more than I could muster. "It was a different feeling, Jaylin. I can't explain how or why I was wet, but I was. Before Shane took action against that man, we had been at it for ten or fifteen minutes. I never came and I doubt that Shane did either. If he did, I'm sure it wasn't inside of me."

Jaylin let loose of my collar and shoved me back on the bed. Not saying another word, he headed for the door.

"You do whatever it is that you have to do," I said. "But, remember, that I still love you. I hope my love counts for something."

He stopped, but didn't turn around. "Your love doesn't account for a damn thing, Nokea. Soon, I will be back to get my kids."

I closed my eyes. When I heard the front door close, I turned on my stomach and seriously broke down.

Chapter 9

Shane

Frick and I had wrapped up my statement at the police station and I was on my way back home. I wasn't sure if Scorpio was there or not, but I felt the need to tell her the truth. I hoped she'd understand why I couldn't be honest until now, but I really wasn't sure. Her personality said she would, but then, since Nokea was "the other woman," I wasn't sure how Scorpio would feel.

Nearly a mile away from my house, my cell phone rang and Jaylin's home number flashed. I wasn't sure if it was him or Nokea, so I picked up to see who it was.

"Shane," Nokea softly said.

"Don't tell me. Please don't tell me things didn't go well."

"They didn't. Jaylin knows what happened and he's gone. He wouldn't even listen to me. I tried to tell him . . ."

Nokea's voice sounded pitiful and I couldn't bear to listen to her. "Nokea, don't be so hard on yourself. Jaylin just needs time to cool off. You and he will work things out. All you can do is give him time."

"Not this time Shane. You didn't see the look in his eyes. He's upset with me and he will never forgive me. He's going to be with someone else, I can feel it."

"That's not going to solve anything, but, uh, just hang tight. I'm sorry that I had to ask you to do that for me, but I had no choice."

"I know, but we should have been honest from the beginning. I don't know if it would have made the difference, and even though Jaylin seems to think that it would, he's more upset about us being together."

"But, we were forced into that situation. What else were we supposed to do? Did you tell him that?"

"Yes, I did. But, he wanted to know more. He asked if I enjoyed it, if I came and the length of our encounter."

Shocked, I pulled the car over. "And you told him? Nokea, please don't tell me that you told him . . . ."

"I told him that it was a different feeling, and even though I was . . . moist, I didn't come. I couldn't lie to him anymore Shane. No matter what I said, he knew how I felt."

"What about our conversation in the car? Did you mention—"

"No, I didn't. But, please don't ask me to lie anymore. I was honest with the detectives and I still have to finish my discussion with them. I might have to take a lie detector test. I will do whatever it takes to clear your name."

"I might have to take one too, but Frick said I really don't have much to worry about. I appreciate you Nokea. I will do anything that you need me to do. Jaylin just needs time and you and I will have to allow him that. I want to explain my side of the story to him too, but right about now, he wouldn't listen to anything I have to say. I'm sure he's going to call me. All I can do is wait to hear from him."

Nokea was quiet. I could tell something else was on her mind. "Have you talked to Scorpio yet?" she asked.

"Not yet, but I'm on my way home. I plan to tell her what happened, but I'm not going to get into too much detail."

"Do . . . do you think Jaylin is on his way there?"

"I'm not sure. That thought hasn't even crossed my mind, but if and when I hear from him, I will let you know. You do the same, all right?"

"Sure," she said.

I told her to hang on to the love they have for one another and gave her a little hope that things would work out. Truthfully, I wasn't sure how things would pan out, but I hoped everything would get back to normal soon.

Once I ended my call with Nokea, I drove home and saw Scorpio's car in my driveway. I was anxious to see her, but I dreaded going inside and telling her the truth. I sat in my car for a while before I gathered up enough nerve to go inside.

When I opened the door, I could smell something cooking. I heard Mary J. Blige on the radio singing her tunes. Scorpio was singing right along with her. I went into the kitchen and saw her standing by the sink. She had tight blue jeans on and an apron covering her pink half shirt. The water was running and it looked like she was cutting up some vegetables. She didn't hear me come in, so I snuck up behind her, wrapping my arms around her waist. She jumped, but smiled when she saw it was me.

"What are you cooking?" I asked while nibbling at her earlobe.

She turned around and put a sliced carrot into my mouth. "Take a guess," she said.

"Uh, I can tell you're making some . . . slaw? But, I have no idea what's in the oven."

"Good," she said, and then reached for the radio to turn down the music. "Then, I'll surprise you. How did your meeting go with Frick? I called you several times, but didn't get an answer."

"I left my phone in the car because I didn't want it to go off while I talked to the police. Frick said I should know something soon, so hopefully, I will."

"So did you tell the police everything that happened? The officer who you hurt . . ."

I stepped away from Scorpio and went to the fridge to get bottled water. "The man who pulled us over wasn't a police officer. He was a convicted felon who was wanted for several other crimes."

"Well, that's good news. Maybe you did the police a favor."

"I'd like to see it that way, but I won't know how things turn out for a few more days."

"I'm sure they'll turn out fine. To me, it sounds like that man was out of line and you did whatever you had to do."

I sipped from the bottled water with all kinds of thoughts in my head. *Should I tell her, or shouldn't I?* Scorpio continued to shred the veggies for the slaw and I interrupted her.

"Say, baby," I said, while standing by the kitchen's door. "How much longer will it be before dinner is ready?"

"About another hour or so. Why?"

"Because I want to show you something in my room."

She smiled. "Uh, you can show that to me later. Right now, I'm trying to cook you a scrumptious dinner."

"I wasn't talking about sex. Seriously, I want to show you something."

Scorpio removed the apron from around her and lay it on the table. She followed me down the hallway to my bedroom.

"Sit on the bed," I asked and kneeled down in front of her. I held her hands together with mine. "The other day, I was on my way to Jay's so I could propose to you. I would love for you to be my wife. The only reason I have not asked for you to marry me is because I need to be honest with you about something. I haven't been completely honest with you about why I went to jail."

"Shane, I hope you didn't do anything . . . ."

"Don't worry. The only reason I went after that man was because he disrespected me. I told you that Nokea and I slept in different rooms, but we didn't. She slept on the bed and I slept in a chair."

"So, what's the big deal? There was no reason for you to lie about something so tedious."

"I know, but I thought you'd be mad. I didn't want to complicate things between us, but, uh, Nokea and me were asleep, and were interrupted by the man who pretended to be an officer. I opened the door and he pulled a gun on me. To make a long story short, baby, he, uh forced me on the bed with Nokea and threatened to kill us if we didn't do what he wanted us to."

Scorpio stared into my eyes and eased her hands away from mine. "Are you telling me—what did he want the two of you to do?"

"He . . . he wanted to watch us have sex. I tried to get at him, but I didn't want Nokea or me to get hurt. When the time was right, that's when I made a move and shot him. Afterward, Nokea and I left and that's why I was arrested."

The look in Scorpio's eyes was killing me. She did not blink once and she placed her hand on her forehead like she was thinking about something. "I can't believe what you're saying to me Shane. This is just too, too much, and even though he forced the two of you to do it, did you?"

"Baby, if we hadn't, we wouldn't be alive. We had to. I know you're not happy about it, but think about what could have happened to us. If you were in that situation, you would have done the same thing."

Scorpio took a deep breath and dropped back on the bed. She looked up at the ceiling and I eased on the bed next to her. "What are you thinking?" I asked. "I . . . I regret what happened and I'm trying like hell to erase the thoughts of that day from my memory. Will you . . . Can you forgive me for not being honest about what happened? It would mean so much to me and I—"

She put her hand up to my face. "Shane, save it. I want to forgive you and I'm sorry that you and Nokea were put into such a life threatening situation." She turned her head and looked at me. A tear rolled from the corner of her eye. "What I'm having a hard time with is you being inside of another woman during our relationship. First, it was Jaylin's ex, Felicia, who forced herself on you. You still don't know if she's pregnant by you. Now, Nokea. Every time this happens, you come up with excuses about why you lied to me. Your encounter with Felicia was hard enough to accept, but this thing with Nokea, you already know how I feel about her. Yet again, she has managed to get a piece of another man I love. I can't sit here and pretend as if this does not have an effect on me."

Scorpio sat up, wiping the falling tears from her eyes. I tried my best to comfort her, but she moved away from me and stood up.

"I know how you feel about Nokea and I assure you that there's nothing for you to worry about. She and I are confused by this too. We knew that our news wasn't going to be easily accepted."

"Well, you both guessed right," she said. "This is not acceptable. After something like this, I don't know how we move forward."

I hurried off my bed and opened my drawer. I pulled out her ring. When I opened the burgundy suede box, her five karat diamond ring flashed at her. I got on one knee and took her hand.

"We move forward by putting this behind us. Trust me, I had no control over the situation, and if I did, it never would have happened. You know how much I love you. For the rest of my life, I want to show you how much I do. I know my timing might not be the best, but I need you now and I want your love forever. Will you accept my proposal and marry me?"

Scorpio continued to look down at me and more tears fell from her eyes. When I tried to place the ring on her finger, she pulled her hand back. "I have wanted this for so, so long. I love you too, Shane, but . . . but under the circumstances, I can . . . cannot accept your ring." She took a hard swallow and broke down on me. I tried to soothe her pain, but she broke away from my embrace and left the room. I followed behind her and watched as she gathered her purse, coat and keys to leave.

"It doesn't have to be like this," I said. "I know you're hurting, but I'm hurting too. You know how much I want this and if a little time is what you need, just ask for it. However, do not end this with me. We've been through too much . . ."

Scorpio opened the front door and left me standing there conversing with myself. Once she drove off, I closed the door and hit the back of my head against the door.

"Damn, damn, damn," was all I could say.

Chapter 10

Scorpio

I was sick to my stomach. Why me? Why did all this crap have to come down on me? Yes, I'd made some mistakes in the past, but why didn't it ever work out with the men I'd fallen in love with? There was always something that stood in the way of my happiness and I'll be damned if her name isn't Nokea.

For the last few days, I hadn't done anything but soaked in my tears. I said I'd never let another man get to me like this, but there I was living the same nightmare I'd lived when Jaylin left me. This time, it had hurt worse because I thought Shane and I had something more special. I would have never expected this from him, and I'd had enough of sweeping shit under the rug just because the man in my life wanted me to. As much as I wanted to, I couldn't forgive Shane, not now, maybe not ever.

That didn't stop him from calling me like crazy. Leslie told him I didn't want to talk, but that encouraged him to show up at my door. When I made it clear to him that I needed some time to think things through, that's when he left me at peace. But hell, there really wasn't much for me to think about. He'd stuck his dick into a woman that I despised. He says sex between them was forced, but I have my own thoughts about what really happened that day. Shane is an excellent lover. There is no way Nokea wasn't excited about him being inside of her, and, vice versa. I had no clue what kind of lover she was, but she didn't become Jaylin's wife just by being pretty. I'm sure she put something on Shane's mind. Even though he says he's forgotten, I seriously doubt it.

As I lay in bed watching TV, my mind kept wandering. I wasn't sure if Jaylin knew what had happened, and if he did, I thought about his reaction. The thought of what Nokea was probably going through made me smile. I knew Jaylin was probably acting a fool. Curious, I reached for my phone and dialed his cell phone number. His phone rang three times, then his voice mail came on. It was late, but I still left a message.

"Hi, this is Scorpio. Whenever you get a moment, call me, okay? I'm at home. Good-bye."

I hung up and lowered myself underneath the covers. I lay my head on the pillow and looked over at Mackenzie beside me. She was sound asleep. I smiled at the thought of her always wanting to sleep in my bed when she had a big and beautiful room of her own. I kissed her cheek. I was so confused about all that had happened. When I couldn't think about it anymore, I closed my eyes to go to sleep.

What seemed to be only a few minutes later, I was awakened by the ringing phone. Just so it wouldn't wake Mackenzie, I reached over to my nightstand and quickly answered in a sleepy voice.

"Did I wake you?" he asked. I recognized his voice and sat up. It was Jaylin.

"I was slowly fading, but I'm up," I said.

"I got your message. What's up?"

His tone was on edge, so I was careful with my words. "I wanted to talk to you. The other day, Shane told me what happened between him and Nokea. I'm confused about how I feel and I wonder how you feel . . ."

"That's a stupid ass question because you know how I feel. Is there anything else?"

"No. Nothing else. Again, I was just curious about your thoughts."

"Well, again, you know me well and this shit ain't sitting right with me. I gotta go, all right?"

Jaylin hung up and I sat in bed listening to the dial tone. Maybe I shouldn't have called him because just that fast, he was capable of stirring up my feelings. I thought about what I could have said wrong, but knowing Jaylin, he was mad at the world and was looking for anybody to take his frustrations out on. During our troubled times together, he reacted the same way. But, the comfort of another woman always seemed to ease some of his pain. I thought about him for a while, and then eased back down in the sheets to go to bed.

I was in a deep and comfortable sleep, until I heard the phone. When I looked at the clock, it was past three o'clock in the morning. I reached for the phone and it fell on the floor. Still in a daze when I bent over to get the phone, I tumbled on the floor.

"Hello," I said angry with the caller.

"No, you didn't," Jaylin chuckled.

"Didn't what?" I said, sitting on the floor beside the bed.

"Did you fall on the floor?"

"Maybe. But I was dreaming and the phone awakened me and scared me."

"Have you checked your head for any lumps?"

"Ha, ha, funny. But, uh, somebody sounds like he's in a better mood. Earlier, you were ready to chop off my head."

"I was tired earlier. You caught me at a bad time."

"Uh, I know what that means. What was her name?"

"Wouldn't you like to know?" Jaylin laughed. "Anyway, what makes you think I was with a female?"

"Come on now, Jaylin. You are highly pissed at Nokea, and if my memory serves me correctly, you always have the last word."

"I'm a changed man, Scorpio. I don't need pussy to calm my nerves, like I did in the past."

"I don't believe that, but if you say so, oh well." There was silence and Jaylin hadn't responded. "Jaylin?"

"What?"

"Are you going to sleep?"

"Nope. I haven't slept in almost two days."

"Where are you and why are you up so late? Lost sleep is no good for you, you know?"

"Shit, I can't sleep. I've been thinking a lot and my thoughts won't let me sleep."

"I know how that is. Would you like to share your thoughts with me? I'm an excellent listener, you know? And besides, I am one person who can actually say I know what you're going through because I'm experiencing the same thing."

"Well, I don't want to talk much about my thoughts because they're not too good. I do feel if I would have taken action when the two of them kissed, maybe this wouldn't have happened. I shouldn't have trusted Shane and Nokea to put that incident behind them. I feel like such a fool for asking him to bring her home."

"Wha . . . what incident and kiss are you talking about? I never knew about the two of them being involved in such a way."

"Sorry. I thought Shane told you about it. He told me that he did and I wasn't aware that you didn't know."

"Are you messing with my head, Jaylin?"

"No, but I wish you were messing with mine." He paused and cleared his throat. "I'm, uh, serious about the kiss, though. Ask Shane. When Nokea came to St. Louis and called herself being there for me while I was in court, she went to Shane's house and some lip action took place. It might have been more than that, but hell, I've been lied to so much that I don't know what to believe."

"Humph, I knew nothing about this. If Shane told you that he told me, he lied. How did you find out about it?"

"Nokea told me. As usual, it was my fault because I had caused her so much turmoil and she turned to another man. I should have put my foot in her ass then, but I swept the shit under the rug and blamed myself."

"What did you . . . I mean, did you confront Shane?"

"Yeah, I did, but he played the victim. Said Nokea stepped to him and he was caught off guard. Maybe so, but, uh, this last incident done took the cake. Both of them lied to me. Nokea confirmed that they had *forced* sex for ten or fifteen minutes and said she enjoyed herself."

"Did she really say that Jaylin? I think you're exaggerating."

"I know my wife, Scorpio, and even though those weren't her exact words, her saying that it felt like 'something different' was enough for me."

"Something different like what?"

"I don't know. Why don't you tell me? What's different about how I make love to you, versus the way Shane does?"

"There's a big difference, but I can't speak for Nokea."

"Then don't speak for Nokea. Speak for yourself."

"The difference is . . . Shane is a gentle lover, and during sex, he knows how to put a woman at ease. You, on the other hand, are aggressive and a woman has to be at her best when she's with you. If not, your sex can be intimidating and a woman can feel easily let down by her performance."

"And, what in the hell is so wrong with being aggressive and encouraging another person to be at their best? If I give you my best, I want the same in return."

"I've never had a problem with that, but some women do."

"Well, honestly, which do you prefer?"

"What I prefer, I haven't had in quite some time. He's been tied up for a while and I've become accustomed to the man I've grown to love."

"So you're settling?"

"To some extent, I guess you can say that. But, settling doesn't mean I haven't been satisfied. As a matter of fact, I'm very satisfied, but I'm disappointed in Shane for not only lying to me about this situation, but always making excuses for his mistakes. I definitely know where you're coming from when you say Nokea does the same."

Jaylin was quiet. I thought he'd gone to sleep until he spoke up. "Hey, I'm getting ready to go, all right? Thanks for listening to me. You know I appreciate it."

"Anytime, Jaylin. But, uh, you never told me where you are."

"I didn't tell you because I don't want you showing up at my door."

"What makes you think I'd show up at your door?"

"Because I've been thinking about showing up at yours."

I smiled. Jaylin was the only man I'd ever be willing to travel back down memory lane with. "Well, right about now, you're definitely welcome. My door is always open for you."

"That's good to know. Maybe I'll see you soon, all right?"

"Maybe so," I said.

Jaylin ended our call and I sat on the floor with the phone in my hand. I hadn't smiled in days and the thoughts of what this could possibly turn into brought an enormous smile to my face.

Chapter 11

Jaylin

I'd been away from my family for almost a week. I didn't think I could stay away from my kids for so long, but I was so angry with Nokea that I couldn't stand to see her. She'd been leaving messages on my phone. She even had the nerve to have Nanny B call me. When LJ left a message for me to call him, I couldn't help but return his call. Of course, Nokea answered.

"Where's my son?" I asked.

"He and Jaylene are outside with Nanny B. When are you coming home?"

"When I get ready to. As far as I'm concerned, I don't have a home right now. That's your house, remember. Instead of half of my assets, you have it all."

"I don't want none of this without you. You've been gone long enough and it's time for you to come home."

"How am I supposed to come home and look at you? I can't even make love to you without thinking about your lies and Shane. You remember how I felt when you had sex with my cousin Stephon and he lied to me about LJ being his child, don't you? Now, I feel the same way again. Don't try to convince me to do something I don't want to do. How dare you force me into a situation I'm not ready for."

"If it's that bad for you, then divorce me. I'm not going to live like this. Not knowing where you are and who you're with is driving me crazy."

"I have no problem divorcing you Nokea. The only reason I haven't taken action thus far is because of my kids. You'd better thank your lucky stars they're still with you. Your tone is about to piss me off. Go get my damn son so I can speak to him."

Nokea hung up on me, but I knew what she was trying to do. She wanted to make me angry so I'd come back to the house, but I wasn't going anywhere. My neighbor had beach front property for sale. When I spoke to him about Nokea's and my issues, he offered to let me stay there. The place was just as immaculate as my house. With all of the luxurious furniture inside, it was as close to home as I could get. The property was less than five miles from my house, but it felt like a million miles away. As comfortable as my surroundings were, I still had a difficult time sleeping.

Since I couldn't sleep, I drove to the mall to look around. I hadn't taken any clothes from the house, so I needed a few things to change into. While I was there, I picked up three pair of silk pajama pants, some underclothes and a few pair of jeans and shirts. Dressed in my loose fitting faded jeans that hung over my leather sandals, I stood in line and waited. The royal blue button down shirt that I wore matched the blue tint in my glasses. I'll be damned if nearly every woman in the place wasn't staring at me. Everybody was smiling and, frankly, I was in no mood to smile back. The sales lady rushed the customer in front of me and hurried him on his way. I set my items on the counter. As soon as I reached for my wallet, this chick bumped me from behind.

"Excuse me," she laughed while hanging on to my arm. "I must have tripped on something. Whatever it was, I'm glad it shoved me in your direction."

Moving my arm, I opened my wallet and set my Black American Express Card on top of the clothes. The cashier picked up my card and rolled her eyes at the woman still standing close by me.

"What is that you're wearing?" she asked.

"Clothes," I responded.

The sales rep interrupted. "Mr. Rogers, do you mind if I see your ID?" I showed her my ID and she smiled. "Thank you."

"I wasn't talking about your clothes, Mr. Rogers. I was talking about your cologne."

"Look, I know what you were talking about, but I'm real busy right now. Besides, no offense, but you're not my type."

She placed her hand on her hip and jerked her head back. "What? Are you gay or something?"

"No, but I'm just not turned on by your approach. Aside from that, you could really use a manicure. Your girlfriend is over there behind the clothes rack scoping you out. Unfortunately, whatever the plan was, it didn't work."

"Whatever," she said. "Your arrogance stinks anyway."

She walked away and the sales rep set my receipt on the counter. "Can you sign this for me, Mr. Rogers?"

I bent down and scribbled my signature. I gave the receipt back to the sales rep and she handed me a garment bag.

"Thank you for your business. I, uh, get off work around seven and my approach is the best I can do for now."

She was somewhat pretty, so I smiled. I did, however, notice her weave extensions that didn't quite match up and the darkness of her lips implied that she was a smoker. I looked at her name tag. "Chloe, I appreciate the offer, but I have plans around eight. Take care, all right?"

She nodded and I walked away. I tossed the garment bag over my shoulder and made my way to the door. As I approached the door, two black ladies walked in, nudging each other.

"Um, um, um," I heard one of them say. "Now, that's my kind of man. Girl, I bet he can tear something up!"

"Tell me about it," the friend whispered. Of course, she couldn't help but stop me. "Aren't you . . . I mean, don't you play in a soap opera or something? I know I've seen your face before, and it was on television."

"No, I've never been on television," I laughed.

"Well, can I just shake your hand for looking so darn good? My friend and I are pretty impressed. Go ahead and represent for the Black man. Baby, you got the game and gone with it."

I held out my hand and she shook it. Her friend did too. As she shook my hand, she took her other hand and squeezed my biceps. "Nice," she said. "Oh, so nice."

Like always, I was flattered by the attention. "Thanks for the compliment, ladies. I gotta go, though. Have a good day."

"You bet we will," they said, standing and watching as I walked away.

I made my way to my Hummer. As soon as I got inside, my cell phone rang. I hung the garment bag in the back seat and reached for my phone clipped to my jeans. The number was from my house and I really wasn't in the mood to talk to Nokea. I thought about LJ calling me back, so I opened my phone and answered. Thank God, it was him.

"What's up?" I said, excited to hear his voice.

"Daddy, I wanna go outside and ride my motorbike. Mommie said I had to wait until you were here. When are you coming home?"

"You wanna what?"

"Ride my motorbike."

"Get your language together. There's no such word as wanna. It's . . . Daddy, I would like to go outside and ride my motorbike."

"Daddy, I would like to go outside and ride my motorbike. Can I?"

"You can ride it when I get there. Give me a few days, all right? Then, you can ride it all day long."

"You promise?"

"Yes, I promise."

"Daddy, how come you say wanna and I can't say wanna?"

"Because I'm your daddy and I require that you speak the English language correctly."

"But, you don't. You always say wanna and I speak how you speak."

"LJ, do you *wanna* get in trouble?"

"No."

"I didn't think so. Stop challenging me and do like I tell you to, all right? I will never tell you to do anything that will steer you in the wrong direction. My advice will always help you, got it?"

"Yes."

"Good. In the meantime, I love you and I will see you soon. Give Jaylene a big kiss for me, okay?"

"Okay."

"And?"

"And, I love you too Daddy."

I smiled and hung up. Thinking for a moment, my thoughts were interrupted when I heard a horn blow. I looked in my side mirror and saw a white woman waiting on me to pull out. She had to be waiting for quite some time, but the sound of her horn was working me. I even put my truck in reverse. Although the reverse lights came on, I still hadn't moved. The woman was pissed. I watched as she put her Mercedes in park and got out of the car. She boldly stepped up to my window and I lowered it.

"Is there a problem," I said, gazing at her from behind my glasses. She was at a loss for words.

"Uh, I was just," she paused and squinted. She then covered her mouth. "Oh my God! It's you, isn't it? You're that . . . that movie star!" She happily jumped around and reached into her purse. Excited, she gave me a pen and piece of paper. "Would you mind autographing this paper for me? My friends and I love your show."

I didn't even bother to explain. I scribbled my name and handed the paper and pen back to her. "Thank you," she excitedly said. "You are even more handsome in person, and my friends are not going to believe this!"

"I can't either," I said. "But, uh, I really need to get going. Can you back up your car so I can get out?"

"Sure," she said. She snapped a picture of me with her cell phone and headed back to her car. When I pulled out, she blew the horn and waved at me.

I stopped to get a bite to eat before returning to my neighbor's house. After I hung my new clothes in the closet, I removed my shirt and turned down all the lights. I turned on the radio and it played soothing jazz throughout the entire house. Only for a moment, I stood at the back of the house and viewed the ocean's scenery through the tall glass windows. Just to take in the fresh air, I pushed a button that slid the glass windows over and opened up to the outside. I made a mental note to someway or somehow add this little accessory to my house.

Intending to get some kind of rest for the night, I went into the bathroom and turned on the waterfall faucets to the marble octagon shaped tub. The tub was not only deep, but extremely relaxing. I clicked on the forty inch plasma built into the marble wall and started to watch television. From the cool breeze stirring around the room, and the soothing water and music, I started to fade.

What seemed to be only minutes later, my vision blurred when I heard someone call my name.

"What?" I asked, not seeing who it was. Soon, Scorpio came into the bathroom with a pink towel wrapped around her naked body. Her long hair was full of bouncing curls and the sight of her not only shocked me, but it put a semi smile on my face.

"What are you doing here?" I asked. "How . . . how did you know where I was?"

She stepped toward me and dropped the towel. "I'm here because I knew you needed me. And, you'll never have to tell me where you are. When I want you, I'll always find you."

She got into the tub with me, laying her body on top of mine. I wasn't sure how I felt about this, but when she took my hand and placed it on her apple bottom ass, my dick instantly grew. She rubbed her wet body against me and brought her beautiful face close to mine.

"Do you want this?" she whispered. "I don't want you to do anything that you're going to regret."

I still couldn't say a word, as I was in disbelief. Scorpio seductively smiled at me and her eyes lowered to my lips. She covered my mouth with hers and when our tongues intertwined, I indulged myself. Her lips had a sweet taste. Wanting . . . needing each other, both of our fingers combed through each other's hair.

"Tell me I'm not dreaming," I said. "Please tell me I'm not."

"I can show you better than I can tell you."

Scorpio got out of the water and the suds and water dripped down her body. The tips of her long hair were wet and she pulled her hair over to one shoulder. My eyes focused on the gap between her legs and her perky thick breasts. She motioned with her index finger, telling me to come to her. Anxious for her, I got out of the tub and followed her into the main room by the opened windows. She lay back on a huge Jaipur area rug that covered the hardwood floors. Her legs fell apart. It was such a pretty sight. I wanted so badly to taste her. After so many years of thinking about her, now was my opportunity.

"Do you know how long I've wanted to do this?" I said, massaging her body with stimulating body oil.

She poured her legs over my shoulders, getting into position. "No, Jaylin. Do you have any idea how long I've waited for this? I want to feel you everywhere I can possibly feel you. Explore my body parts and do whatever it is you want. I need this . . . damn, I need you."

With those words being said, I feasted upon her insides for a while, and then explored her body like she asked. This went on for quite some time, until she straddled my lap to ride me. She looked down at me breathing heavily and leaned in to me. As she kissed me, her wet hair fell over my face.

"I can't stop telling you how much I love you, Jaylin."

*"I love you too, baby. I love you so much. I'm
sorry for what I did to you."*

*"I'm sorry for hurting you too. Come home.
Please come home. I . . . We need you."*

"I need you too," I said.

*Scorpio sat up. When I looked at her, I'll be
damned if it wasn't Nokea. She smiled at me
and wiped the tears from her eyes.*

In a sweat, I quickly sat up and rubbed my
eyes. When I opened them, I was sitting in the
tub filled with cold water. The music was still
playing and the TV was still on. I looked around
and there was no Scorpio or Nokea in sight.
What a fucked up dream was all I could think.
My dick was hard as ever, but I had a solution for
that little problem.

Chilly, I got out of the water and dried myself.
I wrapped the towel around my waist and went
into the main room by the windows. I looked at
the area rug, thinking about my dream. I smiled,
pushing the button to close the glass windows.
Afterward, I poured myself a shot of Remy. Once
that was gone, I poured another one. I gulped it
down, put on my jeans and reached for my keys
on the table. Before leaving, I downed another
shot of Remy for the road.

I was buzzed, weaving in and out of traffic at
one o'clock in the morning. There weren't too

many cars on the road, but there were enough. Either way, I managed to make my way home and quietly crept into the house. When I went to Jaylene's room, she wasn't there. I checked Nanny B's room that was on a different level and Jaylene was in bed with her. I didn't want to wake them, so I made my way to LJ's room. He was sound asleep. I leaned down and gave him a kiss on his cheek. I rubbed his soft hair like mine and stood for a minute thinking about him. The room slightly spun, so I closed my eyes and rubbed them with the tips of my fingers. Once I cleared my thoughts, I left LJ's room and went to my bedroom. Shirtless and only in my jeans, I stood beside my bed, looking at Nokea. It was good to know that one of us was resting well. Her light snores said that she had no problem sleeping. I searched her body with my eyes. She wore a cream silk nightgown with very thin straps. The lace parts of it covered her breasts and the gown's length was right at her thighs. I stared at her for a few more minutes, and then unhooked the belt on my jeans. They fell to my ankles and I stepped out of them. I then leaned over Nokea, removing her straps from her shoulder and lightly pecking it with my lips. I eased over the lace part of her gown, exposing her right breast. How beautiful it was, and it invited me to it. A few times, I plucked her nipple with my mouth, then twirled my soaking wet tongue around it. When I felt Nokea move I got on the bed and lay on top of her. She was startled and lifted my face to make sure it was me.

"Jaylin," she said in a sleepy voice. "What are you doing?"

"What does it look like I'm doing?" I continued to suck her right breast and made my way to the other one. When I massaged them together with my hands, Nokea put an arch in her back, moaning for more pleasure. She wasted no time reaching for my dick to put it in her. Her insides were a slippery slope, and giving it to me just how I liked it, Nokea wrapped her legs around my back. Her pussy was delivering a clear message that it missed me and wanted me to come home soon. I, however, barely moved, and when she grabbed my face to kiss me, I avoided her kiss, but continued to give her breasts the attention. Still, there was so much going on inside of me and my stomach was turning in knots. She couldn't see my face, but I was full of emotions. Physically I was there, but mentally, my mind was fucked up. I removed Nokea's legs from around me and placed them high on my shoulders. I plunged deep into her, slamming myself against her as if I were hammering a piece of meat. She tried to lower her legs, but I had a tight grip on them.

"Jaylin," she said while taking strained breaths. "That . . . It hurts my stomach. And your grip . . . it's too tight."

I pretty much ignored Nokea. I loosened my grip, but not by much. I continued at my pace, and when she tried to kiss me again, I wouldn't let her. She stopped the motion and pushed her hands against my chest.

"Put my legs down, now," she demanded.

"I'm not finished yet."

"Oh, yes you are," she said. "Now, get up."

I was in the midst of coming and wasn't about to pull out. Nokea felt my release inside of her and pushed me off her. She reached for the light on the nightstand and looked at me.

"What is wrong with you? Have you been drinking?"

I got off the bed and snatched up my jeans from the floor. "No, I have not been drinking."

"Quit lying. I smell alcohol all over you. Please don't come into our home like this again."

"You're the one who asked me to come home. Now, you don't want me here. Make up your mind Nokea, or is Shane on his way here to take my place?"

Nokea turned her back to me. "I'm not going to entertain your comments. You are drunk and you have no idea what you're talking about. Call me when you're sober, and there are serious consequences for drinking and driving. You wouldn't want to cause anymore problems for this family, would you?"

I stepped into my jeans and zipped them. As I slid the belt back into the hoops of my jeans, I looked at Nokea. "That pussy was awfully wet. By any chance, did you serve things up for Shane like that?"

Nokea turned around and snapped her finger. "As a matter of fact, I did. How could I not? After all, he excited the hell out of me. It was way more excitement than the lame sex you just put down and if you continue to throw up Shane in my face, I'll have no problem hurting your feelings."

I chuckled and leaned down over Nokea to give her a kiss. She put her hand up in my face. "Save it. Your breath stinks and so does your attitude. Don't come back here until you get your mess together."

"Okay," I nodded. "See, you didn't want me to have sex with anybody else, and even though I'm mad at you, I . . . I still respected your wishes. I was in need for some loving so I came to my wife. Now, what is a man supposed to do, if his wife shows him no love?"

"Jaylin, at this point, I don't care what you do or who you do it with. You are living somewhere in your own little world and you haven't even called me in over a week. I'm not going to beg for your forgiveness anymore. Whatever happens, it just happens."

"You're right, Nokea. Whatever happens, it just happens." I touched her ass and squeezed it. "I'll see you soon."

I stumbled to the door and left. Somehow, I made it back to my neighbor's house. When I got there, I dropped back on the bed. The room spun some more and I reached over to the phone and dialed out. It was almost four thirty in the morning, but I knew she'd answer her phone.

"Did I wake you?" I asked Scorpio.

"Jay . . . Jaylin, what is it? Of course you're waking me up, and possibly, the rest of my family too."

"Have you worked things out with Shane yet?"

"No, I haven't. We're not speaking right now, but I plan to discuss some things with him soon."

I paused and Scorpio called my name.

"Whaaaat?" I slurred.

"What is up with you? You've been drinking, haven't you?"

"A li'l bit. But, uh, do . . . do you still love me?"

"It's obvious that you've been drinking more than just a li'l bit."

"Don't avoid my question. I just had this amazing dream and you could not stop telling me how much you loved me."

"Sounds interesting. And, uh, what else took place in this dream of yours? I'm sure if I told you how much I loved you, then you must have been doing something worthy of my love."

"Woman, without getting a hard on, I can't begin to tell you about my dream."

"Well, calm yourself and tell me about it."

"I will, but you gotta promise me something."

"What's that?"

"That if I tell you about it, and my dick starts to rise, promise me that you'll take care of it for me."

"How am I supposed to know if and when your dick rises?"

"Because I'm gon' let you in on it."

"I don't trust you to be honest. Let's hear about this dream and we can pretty much go from there."

I laughed and started to tell Scorpio about my dream. She was real quiet, and by the time I finished, my hardness was in my hands.

"You mean to tell me, I gave you permission to explore me like that?" she asked.

"Every single inch of you. Like I said, I explored you to the fullest. And, baby, it was spectacular. You should have been there."

"Damn, by the sounds of it, I wish I was. Even though your dream sounded so enticing, it doesn't come close to the dream I had the other night."

"So, you dreaming too, huh?"

"Regularly. I can't control my dreams, but how do you feel about making some of this a reality?"

"After tonight, I feel damn good about it. What you trying to say?"

"I don't know, Jaylin. I really don't understand why we're doing this to ourselves, because, at the end of the day, you and Nokea are going to remain together."

"Maybe so, and you and Shane might stay together too. For now, though, I'm going to take advantage of this situation and do what I want to do. That's talk to you when I feel like it, and if we can agree on a location, I'd love to see you."

"See me? Is that all you want to do is see me?"

"Don't make me get specific."

"Why not? You've never had a problem expressing yourself before."

"Scorpio, I, Jaylin Jerome Rogers, want to fuck you so badly. I'm talking hours or possibly days of ongoing sex until we both are exhausted.

Do you remember all the sex we used to have, and all the love making and sweating we did in the shower? My favorites were our intimate moments on the balcony where I bent that ass over and wore it out from behind. What about that time we did it in the rain and inside of the car? Those were some good ass times and . . ."

I listened to the dial tone, as Scorpio must have hung up on me. When I called back, she answered.

"Don't take me back to the past like that Jaylin. I know you're going through some things and I'm dealing with my issues too, but this can't be the right thing for either of us. I remember everything about our relationship and those thoughts stay with me a lot. Are you prepared to go back to what we used to have? If so, I'm making it clear to you that Nokea better get ready for the fight of her life. I'll play for keeps, Jaylin, and this time, you will not control the outcome. Just think about us hooking up, and if your mind is made up, call me in a few days and tell me my destination."

Scorpio hung up. I lay back on the bed thinking hard about what I intended to do.

Chapter 12

Scorpio

Jaylin really had me hyped! I was attempting to sort through my feelings for Shane, but with Jaylin calling me it had me looking at things a little differently. At this point, I felt as if I had nothing to lose. To me, I had already lost Shane, and under the circumstances, there was no way for me to continue our relationship. A part of me thought that I could get over the incident between him and Nokea, but when Jaylin told me Shane and Nokea had previously kissed, that was a bad sign. I pretended as if Jaylin's words didn't bother me, but I stayed up all night thinking about this kiss between Nokea and Shane. He hadn't mentioned one word about it, and with all the secretive shit that was going on with him, I didn't expect him to be honest.

Either way, today, I was ready to confront him. I'd held my peace long enough and it wasn't fair for me to keep him dangling on a string, knowing I wanted closure. So, while at Jay's, I picked up the phone and dialed his number. I figured he was probably at home working, so I called his office phone. After two rings, he answered.

"Shane, it's me. Would you like to meet somewhere later so we can talk?"

"Meet for what Scorpio? If you have something to say, go ahead and say it. There's no need to waste my gas and time if all you intend to do is end this with me."

"How do you know what I've decided? You act as if I should forgive you for everything you do. I'm sorry, but it's not going down like that this time."

"I figured it wouldn't, especially since I'm sure you've already spoken to Jaylin. This is the perfect opportunity for the two of you to patch things up. Now that I'm out, he's in again, right?"

"How dare you blame Jaylin for your lies. He has nothing to do with this and you need to take responsibility for the damage you've cost our relationship. Do you think I have fool written across my forehead? Well, sorry, but I don't. First, you lied to me about your life long booty call chick, Amber, not calling you anymore. Then by *accident* you put your dick inside of Felicia. Now, you and Nokea were forced to have sex, but

I guess you and her were forced to kiss at your place, too."

"Yeah, you've been talking to Jaylin. And, if you two hot motherfu—idiots wouldn't have started this shit, then maybe Nokea and I wouldn't feel the need to be there for each other."

"So, the two of you have been there for each other, huh? Well, you can keep on being there for each other, Shane, and that's why you can take your ring and stick it where the sun doesn't shine."

"This conversation is so fucking stupid! Why did you call here, Scorpio? The only thing you wanted to do was throw Nokea and Jaylin up in my face."

"You're darn right I did, especially Nokea. You pretend that you don't have feelings for her and you do. If you had moved to Florida, God help us all! I truly believe that your decision was based on you wanting to connect with her. Be honest about it, damn!"

"You do sound like a fool. How many times am I going to have to tell you that Nokea and I were on the verge of losing our lives? You or Jaylin's stupid asses don't give a shit. If the two of you were in the same situation, nobody would have had to force nothing! I'm not going to let you raise my blood pressure and stress me out. If you want to end this, then do it! Don't call here trying to convince me that I've been such a terrible man to you, especially when you know I'm the best man you ever had. So, free yourself so you can go back to Jaylin. When he disses you, don't come running back to me because I will not be willing or able to clean up his mess again."

"Stop letting Jaylin's name flow freely from your mouth. Was Jaylin there when you kissed Nokea? Was he there when you put your dick inside of her? For fifteen long minutes, I might add, you were inside of her. And, there is no way that you didn't enjoy the feel of her. You could have done something to free yourself from that man, Shane, but you didn't want to. When Jaylin called and asked you to pick her up from the airport, you broke out of your house like a bat out of hell. There was a winter storm and warnings were up all over the place. You rushed me home like I meant nothing to you, and ran off to get your queen. Then out of guilt, you called and lied to me about your sleeping arrangements. How?"

"Okay, Scorpio. I'm going to put this shit to rest, once and for all. You want the truth, so here it is. Yes, somewhere along the line, Nokea and I developed some feelings for each other. Even though we were forced to have sex, I liked . . . loved it. On the drive to her house, we discussed our feelings. We wound up pulling over to the side of the road and lip-locked with each other. Afterward, we agreed not to act upon our feelings and move on with our lives. Unlike you and Jaylin, we have not contacted each other or even discussed hooking up. We're going through some shit too, but we're not searching for ways to make this situation more complicated than what it already is. I know Jaylin, and I definitely know you. If y'all haven't already had sex, the plan is in the making. Go ahead and do what he wants you to do, and don't call my fucking house anymore with no bullshit about how you want to talk! Right now, I'm talked the hell out and you don't have to end this shit 'cause I just did!"

Shane hung up and I lightly put my phone on the receiver. To hell with him. I knew I was right about his feelings for Nokea. After all I've done for him, having any kinds of feelings for her was a stab in my back. I was so angry. I never wanted to see or hear from Shane again.

Chapter 13

Nokea

For the last three consecutive nights, Jaylin showed up drunk as hell and had sex with me. The first time, I didn't know how bitter he was, and the second time, he kissed me and told me he wanted to work things out. Afterward, he left. When he came back last night, he choked up and told me how painful this was for him to accept. I couldn't help but feel sorry for him and I tried to comfort him as best as I could. Again, he abruptly left. I was so confused about what to do. He was becoming more and more unstable and having sex with me was not the answer to our problems. To me, it made him even more upset. I had to put an end to this and do it soon.

As I lay in bed, Nanny B came into the room. First, she looked around and then she looked at me.

"Is LJ in here with you?" she asked.

"No. I thought he was in the room with you."

I got out of bed and we looked around for LJ. He was nowhere to be found. We were both rushing around the house and outside looking for LJ. There were many openings to our house, and I feared that LJ had gone out to the beach by the water. He liked to work out with Jaylin, so I hurried to Jaylin's work out room to see if LJ was there. He wasn't, so I checked the loft areas, the wine cellar, the sauna, along with the kid's playroom again. Nanny B had checked all six bedrooms and she looked for him in the up and downstairs kitchens. Last night, I knew Jaylin had left alone, but before I called the police, I quickly called his phone. Thank God, he answered.

My breathing was heavy. "Jaylin, is LJ with you?"

"Yes."

I closed my eyes, thanking God. "Why didn't you tell me you were taking him with you? And, you were drunk last night! How could you risk his life like that?"

"Nokea, don't call here yelling at me like you've lost your damn mind. This is my son and I take him wherever the hell I want to."

"I never said you couldn't, but you will not take him from this house without telling me.

And, to risk his life because you won't grow up and be a man is unacceptable."

"I'm gon' let your remark slide. When you get through with all of your bullshit talk, he's safely here with me. I will bring him back whenever I get ready to."

I dropped the phone and Nanny B picked it up. "Jaylin, you listen to me good. Now, I've been real patient with you and Nokea's mess, but when you involve these kids, you involve me. You do not take LJ from this house without telling somebody something. With all that's happening in this world, we almost lost it! If you're drinking and driving with your son in the car, you should be ashamed of yourself. I don't know what's gotten into you, but whatever it is, you need to not let your kids suffer." Nanny B paused and listened to Jaylin for a long while. I could hear his loud voice through the phone. The click from him hanging up was even louder. "That's your husband," she said. "For better or worse, you married him. Right about now, I sure as hell would like to put my hands around his neck and choke him!"

Nanny B shook her head and walked off into the kitchen. I was frustrated too and feeling as if I hadn't protected my kids. I stopped in Jaylene's room to get her. I carried her into my bedroom

and sat her on the bed with me. I colored in a
coloring book with her. After I read a story to
her, I turned to the Cartoon Network channel
on TV. She was tuned in. As she was occupied,
I reached for the cordless phone to call Shane. I
hadn't talked to him for a while and I wanted to
find out if there was any news on his case. When
he answered the phone, he sounded dry.

"Did I reach you at a bad time?" I asked.

"Sorry, I thought you were Jaylin. I'm not prepared to talk to him yet."

"I'm surprised that he hasn't been in touch
with you. I just knew you'd be the first . . . Maybe
second person he'd call. I'm sure Scorpio might
have been the first."

"Well, I'm not going to argue with you there,
and from speaking with her earlier, they've definitely been in touch."

Shane's validation went to the pit of my stomach. I had been speculating all along, but knowing that Jaylin had been talking to Scorpio made
me numb. But, what could I do? I knew Jaylin
would run to Scorpio. It wasn't as if it was a surprise. "So, uh, how have you been? I hope better
than me because your life couldn't be any worse
than mine."

"I'm pissed Nokea, but I'm not going to allow
Scorpio's decision to end our relationship be the

end of the world for me. Relationships come and go. I gave her all that I could. Yes, I made some mistakes, but I never claimed to be perfect. She was waiting for me to fuck up. She and Jaylin both are blowing this incident out of proportion."

"I agree with you, but nobody likes to be lied to, especially by the ones who say they love you. That doesn't give Jaylin the right to treat me as he has. Right about now I am so angry with him. Sorry, though, I really didn't call to discuss my problems. I wanted to know how your case is progressing."

"Earlier, I talked to Frick and the charges against me were dropped. They might need me to testify against the man, but Frick said he'd be in touch."

"I'm happy to hear that. The other day, I met with a few detectives who stopped by our house. I told them my side of the story and they said they'd be in touch too. If I have to testify, you know I will. That man needs to pay for what he did to us, and for what he did to those other people too. The more I think about it, we could have gotten seriously hurt."

"I agree. And I'm grateful for how everything turned out."

"Me too," I said. Afterward, there was complete silence, until Shane cleared his throat.

"Well, I gotta get back to work Nokea. Call me any time, all right?"

"Same here. But, would you do me a favor?"

"Of course."

"Keep an eye on Scorpio. If she and Jaylin connect again, I'm ending this. There's no way for me to find out what's happening in St. Louis, but if you find out anything, let me know, okay?"

"I'll do what I can, but I want you to do me a favor too."

"Anything."

"Be strong. Don't let Jaylin mistreat you and stand up to him. Jaylin is a man that has to be challenged. Whatever happens, you'd better put forth your best fight. You know him better than I do. If you think about the troubled times y'all had, you always got him to react when you took control of the situation."

"You're so right, but it's hard for me because I'm not a confrontational person. That's why you and Jaylin are good friends. You're confrontational and he enjoys going toe-to-toe with you."

"When he's ready, I'm sure he's going to confront me. I'm going to be very honest with him about my feelings, just like I was with Scorpio. After that, he can do whatever."

"It's always a pleasure speaking to you. I'll be in touch, okay?"

Shane hung up and his words made me feel so much better. He was right about Jaylin. From this moment on, some things were about to change.

Chapter 14

Jaylin

LJ and I had a good time together. I watched him on his motorbike, we went to the movies, the beach, and I drove around the city in my Hummer. He'd been with me all day, and not once did he ask for Nokea. How dare she and Nanny B call and criticize me for wanting to spend time with my son. They were lucky that I hadn't taken both of my kids and left the fucking country.

On the drive home I explained to LJ that I needed some time for myself. I promised to come back for him. When we got home, he gave me a squeezing hug and kiss. I opened the door and he hurried inside. He went straight to the kitchen where Nanny B was and I followed behind him.

"Nanna," he said, jumping into her arms. She picked him up and tightly embraced him. She didn't even look at me. When I asked where Jaylene was, Nanny B shrugged her shoulders.

"Are you upset with me or something?" I asked.

"Very. I don't like how you spoke to me over the phone. I'm too old for this mess Jaylin. Things have been good. Nobody needs any of the stress that's been going on around here lately."

"You don't even know what's going on. You're always siding with Nokea. I'm sure she half-ass told you her side of the story."

"I'm not siding with anyone, but at least Nokea knows how to speak to me. You're out of control and leaving here like this is ridiculous."

I stared at Nanny B, wanting to go the hell off. "Whatever. I apologize for my tone, but I will not apologize for anything else."

"Your apology is not accepted."

That fast, I was irritated. "Well, too got damn . . . too bad then. What else do you want me to do?"

"For starters, you'd better get that mouth of yours together. I'm not Nokea, and if need be, I will put you back in place where you belong. Don't make me disrespect you in front of your child, and at this point, I will."

I looked at LJ who was still snuggled up with Nanny B. I wanted to put her in her damn place, but instead, I snickered and left the kitchen. She wasn't worth my time. When I looked into Jaylene's room, she wasn't there. I then went into my bedroom. She and Nokea were on the bed. Jaylene reached for me and I picked her up.

"Hello, precious," I said.

She said hi and placed her small hands on the sides of my face. She then puckered her lips and gave me a kiss. My heart melted. I hugged her tight. I knew she'd seen me do that to Nokea a million times and I looked over at her.

"Did anybody call?" I asked.

"Nope," she said. I zoned in on her clothes lying on the bed. I watched as she held a bottle of fingernail polish in her hand, carefully polishing her toenails.

"Where's LJ at?" she asked.

"He's in the kitchen with Cruella."

Dressed in her pink silk pajama shorts and white half tank, Nokea got up and left the room. I put Jaylene down and she followed behind Nokea.

I stayed in my room and fell back on the bed. The Cartoon Network channel wasn't my cup of tea, so I reached for the remote to change the channel. As I flipped through the channels, I looked at the sexy red dress set across the bed. I then turned to the cordless phone on the dresser and picked it up. Just for the hell of it, I pressed the redial button. The phone rang several times, and then Shane picked up. I hung up on him and held the phone in my hand.

By the time Nokea came back into the room, I had put the phone down and was still lying across the bed. She went into the bathroom and started to curl her hair. A huge part of me wanted to fuck her up, but I remained cool. I entered the bathroom, but Nokea ignored me, continuing to style her hair.

"Where are you going?" I asked.

"Claire who lives up the street is giving a candle party and she invited me to it."

"What time are you leaving?"

"As soon as I get ready."

"What are your plans after that?"

"I don't have any plans after that."

"Then what time are you coming home?"

She lowered the curling iron and huffed. "Why do you want to know? So I can be here when you come in for your nightly sex session?"

"No, I just thought you might have some plans with Shane. The red dress is a li'l jazzy for a candle party, ain't it?"

She stared at me as if I were pitiful. "I had a feeling where this was going. You just won't let it go, will you?"

"When's the last time you talked to him?"

"I can't remember."

I walked over to the phone, picking it up. Nokea knew what I was getting ready to do, so she stepped out of the bathroom and tried to take the phone.

"Would you stop this?" she yelled.

I bit down hard on my lip and rubbed my goatee. "Again, when is the last time you talked to Shane?"

She ignored me, turning back around and moving toward the bathroom. I yelled her name. When she turned around hollering, "What?" I threw the phone into the wall beside her. It broke into pieces. Nokea ducked out of the way. I pointed my finger at her.

"Don't be calling that muthafucka in my house again! As for the candle party, you got until midnight, Cinderella, to wrap shit up! If you're not home by then, you can expect trouble."

Nokea blinked and shook her head. "I'm really starting to dislike you Jaylin. As long as you're away, I'll call whoever I want to call. Pertaining to the party, wait up for me, Prince Charming. Stay your butt right here and you'll see if I show up."

She went into the bathroom, but I grabbed her arm, squeezing it tight. "You want me to hurt you, don't you?"

"Physically, I wish you would. Maybe it would make you feel better. Mentally, you're tearing me up. I'm not sure if you can do any more harm than you already have."

She snatched her arm away, went into the bathroom and closed the doors. I went into the other room, said good-bye to my kids and left.

When I got back to my neighbor's house, I sat back on the chaise in the living room and watched the football game. The Rams were still my favorite team, but since they were out of the play-offs, I quickly became an Indianapolis Colts fan.

The time was flying by. I kept watching the clock. As soon as it turned midnight, I called home. The voice mail came on. I didn't want to keep calling back and wake the kids. I contemplated hard on getting up and going to see what was up. By the time 1:00 A.M. came, I could no longer sit still. I drove to my house, went inside and Nokea wasn't there. I drove down the street to Claire's house and mostly all of the lights in her house were out. I had a feeling that Nokea was going to test me, but now was not the time to play games with me. I drove back to my neighbor's house and didn't even trip. When I sat back on the chaise in the living room, I dialed out on the phone and called Scorpio. Leslie answered and said that she was still at Jay's, so I hung up and called there. An unknown voice answered.

"Scorpio Valentino," I said.

The person who answered asked me to hold. Shortly, Scorpio answered the phone.

"What in the hell are you still doing at work?" I asked.

"Jaylin, sometimes Jay's is opened until two or three in the morning. This is still early for us. The question is, why are you calling me in the wee hours of the morning? It took you long enough to call me back, so I guess that means you've made up your mind."

"I want you to come see me."

"When?"

"Now."

"Jaylin, I can't come right now. You have to give me at least twenty-four hours notice."

"Then, come tomorrow night. I'll pay for your ticket and have my driver, Ebay, pick you up from the airport."

"You know what I don't understand?"

"What?"

"You can have nearly any woman you want. I'm sure there are plenty of beautiful women in Florida. Why me?"

"Because I don't want to be with just any woman. What I want, only you can give me."

"If I come, you and I are not having sex. Mentally, I don't think you're ready for that and neither am I."

"Then, why are you willing to come?"

"Because I miss you. I want to see you and I know I'm capable of making you smile. Besides, we've always been good friends. A face-to-face talk might help this situation we're in."

"Well, I got a better suggestion that might help this situation we're in. It's right between your legs . . . ."

"Jaylin, I'm serious. I'm not coming there so we can have sex. I'm a different kind of woman. It's not going down like it did in the past."

"All right, but just come. I'll book your flight and call you back with the details."

"See you soon," she said.

I hung up and went to the computer to book her flight. It was booked for nine A.M. I called her back with the time.

"Nine o'clock," she yelled. "I told you I needed twenty-four hours notice. Besides, you said tomorrow night."

"It was the only flight available for tomorrow."

"You are such a liar. There's no way I can make it by nine A.M."

"Come on now, baby, damn. Why you making this shit so difficult? I booked an early flight 'cause I can't wait to see you. I can't wait until tomorrow night."

"You're working me Jaylin. Once I get to the airport, my ride better be there."

"I ain't worked you yet. Ebay will be holding up a sign that says, 'On my way to Jaylin's crib.'"

"Wait a minute. I'm not coming to your house, am I?"

"Naw, baby, I'm chilling elsewhere. You'll see when you get here."

"Bye Jaylin."

I hung up and lay back on the chaise. *Nokea knows better than to fuck with me*, I thought. *I hope she ain't forgotten what I'm about. If she has, I have no problem refreshing her memory.*

I could barely sleep last night. First and foremost, the thoughts of Nokea drove me crazy, but I was too upset to think about her all night. I knew if I called the house and she wasn't there, there was no telling what I would do. Then, I couldn't wait to see Scorpio and share with her what was on my mind. Ebay was already on his way to the airport to get her. Just as I got out of the shower, he told me they were on their way here.

I waited patiently in the living room wearing my satin brown pajama pants that tie around my waist. My house shoes were on my feet, and a cup of coffee sat beside me. I occupied myself with the newspaper to pass by the time. It wasn't long before I heard Ebay's Jeep pull up. I already told him the door would be opened. My eyes stayed focused on the door. A few minutes later, Ebay opened the door, holding it for Scorpio. She came inside. Her eyes connected with mine. She smiled, but the only thing I could do was stare at how fine she looked. Her hair was full of fluffy loose curls that hung past her shoulders. She wore a sexy black top that had a low v-neck in the front and barely covered the thick meat on her breasts. Two thin silver necklaces lay between her breasts. Her dark denim, hip hugging jeans were held in place by a silver belt. As she held out her arms and walked over to me, her stilettos clicked on the marble floor. I glanced at the gap between her legs. All I could think about was how badly I wanted to get inside of her. Certainly, my dick was already on the rise and couldn't contain itself much longer.

Chapter 15

Scorpio

What in the hell was I doing here, I thought, as I made my way over to Jaylin. I struggled all morning with coming here and I promised myself that I wouldn't give in to him, unless I got what I wanted. After seeing him, I was already feeling as if my coming here was a big mistake. All he had on was a pair of satin pajama pants that hung low in the front, revealing his minimal smooth and sexy hair above his goods. His abs were tight, and I'll be damned if that monstrous dick of his wasn't poking through his pants. It was obvious that he'd just gotten out of the shower. His chest was a bit wet and his healthy curly hair lay beautifully on his head. The stare of his grey eyes is what broke me. When he licked his bottom lip and rubbed his goatee, I knew my plan was destined to fail. *Damn*, I thought, as he tightly embraced me and I felt his hardness press against me. Taking a deep breath, I backed up.

"Now, are you happy that I'm here?" I smiled.

"Yes," he said, slightly touching himself. "We are elated that you're here."

Jaylin picked up his wallet from the table and stepped up to Ebay who was still standing by the door with my luggage.

He handed Ebay some money. "Would you take her luggage upstairs to the master bedroom for me?"

Ebay nodded and headed off to the bedroom. I stood in the humungous living room accessorized with the most expensive looking contemporary furniture I'd ever seen. A square white leather sectional took up most of the room, and a triangle shaped glass table, in the middle of the sectional, sat on a white rug. Two leather chaises were separated by a fireplace that had a plasma television above it. As I stood in awe looking at the rest of the house, Jaylin snuck up behind me. He wrapped his arms around my waist.

"You like it, don't you?" he asked.

"Oh, I love it. This isn't your house, is it?"

"Nope. I live about four or five miles down the road."

"Does your house look like this?"

"Somewhat. My house has some of the same amenities, but this bad boy cost about eleven million dollars."

I stepped away from his embrace. "Eleven what? It's nice, but I don't see eleven million up in here."

Once Ebay left, Jaylin took me by the hand and walked me around to show me the mansion. The kitchen was decked out with stainless steel everything. On the lower levels, all four bedrooms had private bathrooms. There was an indoor swimming pool, a basketball court, and a movie room for entertainment. The crystal staircase that led to the upstairs master bathroom was unlike anything I'd ever seen. It had an octagon-shaped marble tub, his and hers showers, a television built into the wall, and beveled glass mirrors covered the walls. His and hers closets were close by the bathroom and the space was ridiculous. The best part of the house was the tinted glass windows that secured the back of the house. When Jaylin pushed a button, some of the windows slid over to view the palm trees and sandy white beaches. I was at lost for words.

"This . . . this is worth every bit of eleven million dollars. Who owns this place, Donald Trump?"

"Naw, it's my neighbor's place. He's letting me chill here until things cool down."

"If this is just a chill spot, I'd hate to see his house. I knew you were living well, Jaylin, but I had no idea you had it going on like this."

"Never underestimate me, Scorpio. You know that money has never been an issue with me."

While Jaylin stood by the sliding glass windows and looked out, I stood on the rug with my arms folded. "So, how much are you really worth? You spend money like crazy and with all the money you give away, I don't understand why you're not broke."

Jaylin smirked and walked up to me. He put his arms around my waist and pulled me to him. "It's called investing, Scorpio. I've been investing my money since I was eighteen years old. I continue to let my investments work for me. Since I moved here, I've dipped into some of the most profitable real estate opportunities. Some have already paid off and some will pay off over time. Either way, I'm cool. I'm always looking for more ways to make money, and for me, the sky is the limit."

Jaylin leaned in for a kiss. How could I resist him? I closed my eyes and enjoyed the moment. That moment turned into minutes of intense kissing. It had been a long time since we'd indulged ourselves in such a way and the feeling felt so, so right.

Jaylin backed up, looking me in the eyes. "Do you remember what I told you about my dream?" I nodded. "Well, you're standing on the rug where all the action took place. I don't know about you, but I'm ready to make my dream a reality."

I placed my finger on Jaylin's lips and lightly wiped my lip gloss from them. "Not right now, okay? I have so much that I want to discuss with you. If we only exercise our time together by having sex, I'll never be able to tell you what's on my mind. So, what other plans do you have for us today? You have me for the next three days. I hope you've planned something exciting for us to do."

"Baby, I have planned the ultimate vacation for you. If we start fucking now, we can possibly wrap this thing up by the time you get ready to go. We are wasting valuable time standing here talking. If you think that you can step up in here looking as good as you do, and I ain't gettin' none of that, then you are out of your mind. You knew damn well what time it was and that's why you're dressed like that. Titties all pretty and shit. Skin glowing and sweet perfume lighting this muthafucka up! I ain't had time to check that ass out like I want to, but," Jaylin gripped my ass and squeezed it. "Um, um, um . . . girl! Only if you knew."

His sexiness always made me smile, but of course, I had some concerns. "Only if I knew what, Jaylin? That I wouldn't be here if you weren't upset with Nokea? This is why you and I have to talk. Trust me, I am just as anxious for your loving too, but like I said to you over the phone, I'm not going to lose out this time around. Whatever you start, you'd better make sure you can finish it."

Jaylin let go of his hold around me. My words silenced him and he walked back over by the windows to close them. Once they were closed, he headed upstairs.

"I'm going to go put on my swimming trunks. My neighbor called earlier and said that somebody was stopping by to look at the house. They should be here soon."

I nodded and followed Jaylin upstairs. While he put on his trunks, I took my luggage into the closet and hung up the few pieces of clothing I'd brought. I put my accessories in the bathroom and Jaylin peeked his head in the door.

"Did you bring a swimming suit?" he asked. He had on a pair of navy swimming trunks.

"You know I did. Are you in the mood to go swimming?"

"I don't do much swimming, but the scenery is awesome. Get changed so we can go to the beach."

Jaylin left the bathroom, and since black always went well with my light skin, I changed into my two-piece fishnet bikini. To partially cover my good parts, I tied a sheer wrap around my waist. I teased my long hair with my fingers and slid some M•A•C glossy lipstick on my lips. Afterward, I left the bathroom to find Jaylin. From upstairs, I looked over the rails and saw him sitting on the chaise in the living room. He seemed to be in deep, deep thought and didn't hear when I called his name. When I loudly cleared my throat, that's when he turned his head, looking up at me. He smiled.

"Come on down," he said. "The couple who wants to see the house should be here in a minute. Once they leave, the day and house belong to us."

I made my way downstairs and Jaylin couldn't stop staring at me. I knew he wanted me badly, but I was so afraid of letting my guard down. I'd already been hurt enough by him, but it was so hard for me to keep him out of my life.

Just as I stepped into the living room, the doorbell rang. Jaylin quickly stepped up to me and took my hand.

"You look beautiful," he said, kissing me on the cheek. "You're my wife, we're moving out in about a month, and we've shared so many good memories here. You hate to let the place go, but we're moving on to bigger and better things."

"What?" I said.

"Just follow my lead and agree with everything I say."

The doorbell rang again, and looking like the happy couple, Jaylin and I stepped to the door. When he opened it, there was a lady who introduced herself as Sally, the real estate agent, and the couple she introduced as Mr. and Mrs. Delgotto. We all shook hands and they entered the house. I was very uncomfortable with what I had on, but Mr. Delgotto couldn't keep his eyes off me. The smell of money was all over him and he was casually dressed in khakis and a well pressed Hawaiian shirt. I saw Jaylin check out his Gucci glasses and diamond filled Rolex. As for his wife, she looked like a movie star. She had on a white suit that fit her petite waistline to a tee. Dolce & Gabanna black shades covered her eyes and her D&G bag was clutched underneath her arm. Her body was tanned, and even though her long black hair was beautiful, it wasn't as bouncing and behaving as mine. She slowly removed her glasses, revealing her olive green eyes.

"This is gorgeous," she said, ignoring us and stepping toward the living room. Her husband followed and agreed.

With his arm around my waist, Jaylin spoke up. "We were getting ready to go for a swim.

Take a good look around and if you have any questions, my wife and I will be around back."

The real estate agent nodded and headed toward the couple to do her thing. Jaylin and I exited through the glass doors. Instead of walking to the beach, he suggested that we stay close by the house until they left.

Passing the time, we sat on the balcony and talked. "Did you see the watch that fool had on?" Jaylin asked. "That sucker was bad, even badder than some of mine."

"It was rather nice. I didn't think a Rolex came with that many diamonds."

"He probably had it special made."

"Maybe so. And Mrs. Delgotto, she was working it too."

"Yeah, she was clean, but he's the one with the money."

"Why do you say that? She's the one who looks like a movie star. What makes you think she's not the one with the money?"

"I know these kinds of things, Scorpio. If you peeped that ring on her finger, then you would know that she didn't purchase it for herself."

"I didn't even notice the ring. I was too busy checking out the purse and her shoes. And that perfume she had on, I need to find out what it was. It had a peculiar, yet awesome smell to it. Did you smell it?"

"I was too busy smelling you. Mr. Delgotto was too. I wanted to punch his ass for looking at you like that." Jaylin paused and looked inside. "Cool out, here they come."

The Delgottos and the agent stepped onto the balcony with us. Mrs. Delgotto looked at me. "You have very exquisite taste."

Jaylin couldn't help but cut in. "She married me, didn't she?"

Everybody chuckled.

"Does the furniture come with the house?" she asked.

I looked at Jaylin for an answer. "For the right price it does. That's something we'll have to discuss."

The Delgottos and the agent stepped off the balcony and made their way down to the beach. Jaylin rushed into the house and I saw him talking on the phone. Once they returned, everyone went back inside. He ended his call, turning his attention to the Delgottos.

"So, what do you think?" he said, rubbing his hands together.

The Delgottos looked at each other. The husband spoke up. "We love it. But, I'm not sure about the price."

"Well, there's not much I can do about that," Jaylin shrugged. "This piece of property is worth way more than fifteen million dollars and my wife and I have already lowered the price before. We're not prepared to do it again."

"I thought it was only eleven million?" Mrs. Delgotto said. "Does that price include the furniture?"

"I'm afraid it doesn't. The furniture will have to be negotiated," Jaylin said.

The agent flipped through her organizer. "The specs on this house say that the sale price is eleven million. I see nothing about it being fifteen million."

Jaylin asked to see her spec sheets and he looked them over. "There must be a typo. Like I said, we're not selling the house for less than fifteen million."

"That's just too much," Mr. Delgotto arrogantly said. "Honey, let's go."

She looked around again and then looked at her husband. Her eyes had the nerve to water. Jaylin glanced at me, smiled and turned his head.

"Sweetheart, this is just too beautiful to let go. Out of all the places we've looked at, this is definitely the one. You know how I am when I have my heart set on something."

I couldn't believe that a tear had rolled down her face and she wiped it with her perfectly manicured fingernail. Mr. Delgotto looked at Jaylin.

"Fourteen?" he asked.

"No can do." Jaylin stood his ground. "Again, there will be no negotiations, and not to be blunt, but if you're not interested, I have someone else coming to look at the property soon."

Mr. Delgotto looked at his weeping wife, and then at the agent. "Let's go back to the office and work up a contract. Take it off the market before someone else gets it."

Mrs. Delgotto smiled and threw her arms around her husband's neck to hug him. She looked over his shoulder at Jaylin. "Thank you," she whispered.

Jaylin nodded. Once everyone shook hands, they left. Immediately following, Jaylin asked me to be patient and told me to make myself at home. He spent the next few hours on the phone. When he finished his business, he was one happy camper.

"That's what the fuck I'm talking about," he said, sitting next to me on the couch.

"You are a crook," I laughed. "You drove up the price because you knew those people could afford it."

"And? It happens all the time and my neighbor is ecstatic about what I did. I will be highly rewarded. That was the fastest and easiest three million dollars I've ever made."

"Well, what can I say? You definitely know how to make money. I'm impressed."

Jaylin smiled, but he seemed to have something on his mind. I kind of knew what, but when he said it, his words really stung.

"I can't wait to tell Nok . . .," he paused and looked at me. "You don't want to hear about this, do you?"

"No, I don't. I'm happy for you, though, okay?"

"I know. Now, let's go outside."

Jaylin and I spent several hours on the beach. We took a long walk and got massages from two very experienced masseuses. Once the sun went down, we spread out beach towels and lay on the sand. I relaxed on my stomach while he lay sideways holding my waist. I hated to admit it, but I was falling for him all over again. When he asked why I was so quiet, I had to tell him.

"You know what being in your presence does to me. This all seems like a dream and I'm afraid to wake up."

"Well, this definitely ain't no dream," he said, touching my butt. "I know how you feel, but let's not make this so complicated. Can we just enjoy each other's company without all of the doubts and fear of what might happen?"

"That's so easy for you to say. There's no doubt that my relationship with Shane might be over. But, I can't say the same for you and Nokea."

Jaylin lay on his back, looking up at the sky. "What is it that you want from me Scorpio? I'm not exactly sure what you want, and I know that you came here to tell me."

"I want what I've always wanted and that's for us to be together. I want to share a home like this with you, and I want a blood child with you. I want you to love me like you love Nokea. If I can't have those things, Jaylin, then I need to cease this friendship between us once and for all."

Jaylin slightly turned his head in my direction. He moved my blowing hair away from my face. "Baby, the last thing I want to do is lie to you about my feelings. There is no way possible for me to give you those things right now. Nokea and I are having a very difficult time and I don't know what the future holds for us. But, I just can't stop making myself love her and love you. You know how I feel—"

"I am so tired of hearing you say that! Since I've known you, you've been saying that 'you know how I feel,' quote. After so many years, when things don't work out, you have to be willing to try something different. I'm just asking you to try something different with me."

Jaylin lay quietly for a moment. Then he turned his body to the side. He rubbed my back, untying my bikini top. The strings fell to my sides and he asked me to turn around.

Instead, I stood up and held the bikini top close to my chest. "If I take off my top, we're going to have sex. I told you that ain't happening so I wish you'd stop asking."

I walked off and Jaylin stood up. He sped up to catch me, but I started running. Once he caught up to me, I was near the house and almost out of breath. He pulled my bikini top away from my breasts and looked at them.

"Stop playing this game with me, all right? Let's go inside and make love," he suggested.

"How can two people who don't love each other make love? One person's love is never enough."

"Give me a chance and I'll show you."

We went inside. While in the bedroom, I continued my resistance. I changed into my silk short gown. Jaylin was upset that I put on something to cover up. He lay naked in bed and barely held me as I lay on his chest.

"I can't believe you're going to do this to me," he said. "Look at how hard my dick is."

I was already looking at it, as it lay on his stomach extending past his navel. "Go to sleep, Jaylin," I whispered. "I'm tired."

Definitely, I was tired, but Jaylin must have been tired too. Before I shut down, I watched as he took several lengthy breaths in and out. Soon, I heard him snoring. I lifted my head from his chest and saw he was out. I smiled and thought . . . *one day down and two more to go.*

The next day went by quickly. Jaylin and I had so much fun playing scrabble, slow dancing, getting cozy in the theatre room and spending numerous hours on the beach. The long boat ride took up most of the day, and around 11:00 P.M., we headed back to the house. We'd both been drinking and I was a bit tipsy. Jaylin held me close and escorted me inside. He walked me up to the bedroom and lay me on the bed.

"I am so, so tired," I said. "Would you mind getting my nightgown for me?"

Jaylin didn't hesitate. He hadn't pressured me all day about sex. Once I removed my bikini, he helped me into my nightgown. He said that he wasn't tired, and told me if I needed him, he would be downstairs watching television. I nodded and lay across the bed. I remembered thinking this was my last night with him, but I still had one more day to go. I smiled before dozing off.

Several hours had passed and I quickly woke up. I felt a slight pain in my stomach, but the other feeling was more than a good one. While resting on my stomach, I slowly opened my eyes, turning my head to the side. Jaylin's lips met up with my ear and he whispered. "Either yell out rape, or let me slide in further. Whatever you decide, I'll roll with it."

The feeling of his hard dick inside of me, and his hands circling my ass was the best feeling ever. I closed my eyes, fighting my feelings. "Rape," I whispered and swallowed. Jaylin slowly eased himself out of me and my eyelids fluttered. I bit down on my bottom lip and could hear him go down the steps. For a while, I lay on the bed with my eyes opened. My insides were dripping and I needed to feel more of him. I got up and headed for the stairs to find him. I could see him sitting naked on the chaise with a serious look on his face. He'd made himself a drink and held the glass in his hand. I walked down the stairs, but sat on the middle step.

"Jaylin," I said, interrupting his thoughts.

His head quickly turned in my direction. There was no smile on his face. "What?"

"Are you upset with me?"

"No."

"Then, why are you looking as if you're bothered by something?"

"Because, you're getting ready to ask me too many questions. You know what I want, but you insist on depriving me. It doesn't make sense and I . . . I don't feel like a bunch of talking right now."

"Neither do I," I said. I stood, pulling the gown over my head and showing off my near flawless body that he admired so much. My ass was still plump and my perfect perky breasts could easily earn me a spot on the top ten sexiest black women alive. I sat on the steps, slowly separating my legs so Jaylin could see my well shaven slit. I squeezed my coochie lips with my fingers, then sunk them deep inside me. I sucked in my bottom lip, taking deep breaths while eyeballing Jaylin.

"Don't look so sad. You know what belongs to you so come over here and get it." I continued to work my insides, and Jaylin's eyes did not move from looking in between my legs. He finally took another drink from his glass. When he cleared his throat, he lay the drink on the table. With swagga in his walk, he came up the steps naked, relieving my fingers and replacing them with his.

"You know can't nobody work that pussy better than me," he said.

I couldn't agree with him more. As I slightly backed away from the feeling, he leaned me back on the steps. I'd never seen him look into my eyes so seriously. As he wrapped my legs around his waist, my insides awaited him. He navigated his nine plus inches inside, busting me wide open with his thickness. No doubt, it had been a long time since my *bottom* had been tampered with and he'd been the only man who was capable of filling me up. I spewed every curse word in the book. It was a motherfucking shame how good this man made me feel. Damn him for doing this to me. I never understood how or why him being inside of me made me feel like I was the love of his life. A part of me wanted to cry, but through us searching deep into each other's eyes, he knew how I felt, and I knew how he felt as well. At that moment, I couldn't help but tell him how much I loved him. With tears in my eyes, I knew I'd spoken the truth. He hadn't said much, but the way he plunged into me, he knew damn well he was making me his all over again. My breasts were tight and felt as if they wanted to bust as he sucked and squeezed them like balloons. Jaylin was doing his job well, and in an effort to make him never forget, I had to step up my game. I loosened my legs from around his waist, and showing my flexibility, I relaxed my legs on his shoulders.

"That's right, baby," he whispered. "You know how to set that pussy up for me, don't you?"

Jaylin's words were bringing me to a convulsion like state. Needing more room, I crawled backward up the steps, making more room at the top for us to *spread our love*. He lay on his back, welcoming my straddled legs across him. I took lengthy strokes on top, slamming my ass down hard on his midsection. He fired back on his end, pumping everything he had up into me. With sweat dripping from our bodies, the room filled with an erotic sexual scent that he and I both enjoyed.

Throughout it all, though, Jaylin remained quieter than usual. I wasn't sure what was up with him, but I wasn't about to ask. His hands roamed all over my body. He dug his fingers into my butt cheeks and I could feel his dick thumping.

"Ahhhh, shit," he strained. "Get up, baby, I'm about to come."

Of course I didn't listen, and after a few more jolts on my end, he gave me what I wanted. His juices filled my insides, and rushed into me like falling rain. He wasn't done with me yet. As I followed him to the "magic" rug in his dream, he explored me just as he'd mentioned over the phone.

It started with him rubbing some exotic oils on my body that gave me a warming sensation and increased my sexual appetite for him even more. I was oily all over and his hands massaged deeply into my skin, especially near my inner thighs. I was so ready for him to go inside of me, but he obviously needed a moment to touch what he'd been missing.

"Sexy, sexy, sexy," he confirmed, continuing to rub me all over. I turned on my stomach, and as his hands massaged my butt cheeks, pulling them apart, I couldn't wait any longer. I directed his fingers to my hot spot, just so he could feel how anxious I was.

"Damn," was all he could say after sinking his fingers into me. "That pussy ready . . . more than ready, ain't it?"

I nodded. Jaylin lay behind me, lifting my leg and stretching it over his hip. My pussy was clearly exposed, and my curvy, heart-shaped butt rested against his hardness. With his fingers, Jaylin softly rubbed my clit like he was stroking a violin. My moans were like music to his ears, implying that we'd gotten off to a phenomenal start. His dick sunk into my wetness, causing my mouth to open and water even more. I closed my eyes, taking deep breaths with every lengthy stroke he gave me. Like always, his sex was fierce, forcing me to give it my all. He couldn't keep his eyes off my jiggling ass in motion. When he dropped his head back in pleasure, I turned my head to the side. I gripped the back of his head, bringing it forward so I could touch my lips with his. "Mm-mmm," I moaned, tasting his tongue and pecking his lips. "I want my around the clock dick back, baby. Please tell me what I can do to keep *this* in my possession. I'm not letting you go again and if you think we're going to stop fucking like this anytime soon you're crazy."

The more I spoke, the more aggressive Jaylin got. His dick was a force that couldn't be reckoned with. As thick cream built up between my legs, the sounds of satisfying sex filled the room. Jaylin still hadn't said much, but I couldn't help but to keep on expressing myself.

"I . . . I, we've waited so long for this. I need to know how you feel. Tell me how this pussy feels, baby. Is it still how you like it? You fill me up perfectly and ca . . . can't you feel how well you fit inside of me? All of you . . . every inch, and your thickness . . . damn, your thickness. Are you loving this as much as I am?" He continued to have his way with me from behind and wouldn't answer me. I bounced my ass hard against him, moaning his name every chance I got. "Jaaaay-lin, Jay-Baby, please talk to me. Don't stop fucking me like this. As painful as this feels, this is good pain, baby, damn good pain! Ohhhh, how I've missed this. Tell me how much you missed this. Tell me how badly you want to do this forever. This dick . . . I swear this dick just makes me crazy! Am I crazy for wanting you so much . . . tell me. Talk to me, and tell me why we can't let this go. Whyyyyyy?"

Jaylin stirred up my insides even more and my pussy was a slippery wet mess. I was hooked. Once I let out another well overdue explosion, I rolled on my stomach. Jaylin lay over me, releasing his juices onto my butt. We both took deep breaths. He moved my hair away from the back of my neck, kissing it. "How could I not love the hell out of this," he whispered. "And, my dick makes you crazy because that pussy does the same to me. Now, to answer your questions about how I feel," he rubbed my butt cheeks again, turning me over to look at him. He placed tender kisses on my stomach and stopped when he reached my goods. "I feel like . . . like sexing you every damn day of my life. Baby, I love this connection between us and . . . damn, your pussy. How does it perform for me like that? You know better messing with my mind like this."

"What can I say, other than I'm in love and so turned on by you. Since we've waited so long to do this, there's a major build up inside of me."

Jaylin laughed and asked me to turn over. I did and he licked his tongue where his name used to be tattooed on my butt. "You know what I'm about to ask you, don't you?" he said.

"Yes, I know, but I don't know why my butt is so shapely, and plump, and workable . . . ."

Jaylin smacked my ass hard and we burst into laughter. I turned around and tightened my legs around his waist. "I removed your name because I thought we'd never see this day again. I never thought I'd feel you like this, and I'm so afraid. I'm afraid of what tomorrow will bring and—"

"Tomorrow is going to bring about good things," he said, gearing up to go at it again. "And the day after that will bring even better things. Let's not worry about the future. All that matters is what we're sharing right here, at this moment, this day and this time." He paused, shaking his head as he observed his insertions. "Umph, umph, umph. This shit is a crime, baby, it's a crime! If you the least bit feel what I'm feeling, then your time should be focused on how this sweet and creamy pretty pussy of yours can get the best performance that it can out of me. Time is of the essence, and I'm not in the mood to waste any more of our time."

"You're right," was all I could say. "Definitely, time is not on our side so it's up to us to spend our time together wisely."

***

That night led to me extend my vacation. We had sexed our way through another two days, and I was damn happy about it. Whether it was on the beach, in the shower, back on the rug, on the stairs again, or in the bedroom, we could never get enough of each other. Simply put, I was not ready to go home. I was so upset that once my time was up Nokea would have him back in her possession. At any time, she could make love to him, and she could wake up to his handsome face every single morning. She had access to his money and their children guaranteed her a lifetime with him. The thoughts of it made me crazy. For any woman to have Jaylin Jerome Rogers the way she had him was so unfair.

In less than two hours, Ebay was on his way to get me. Jaylin and I were getting through our last good-byes in the bathtub which was filled with bubbles. He was at one end and I sat at the other.

"Now, what am I supposed to do without you here?" he asked.

"You don't ever have to be without me, Jaylin. All you have to do is say the word. I hope you think about this, like you said you would, and you'd better keep in touch with me."

"I will. But first, you know I gotta straighten some things out, right?"

I nodded and there was a moment of silence.

"Jaylin, what was the best sex you ever had? I want the truth too."

"Truthfully, the best sex I ever had was . . . I remember three occasions. They all run close together."

"And?"

"The best sex I ever had was . . . my first time making love to Nokea and she was a virgin. It wasn't that it was the greatest, but in my heart it was. The second time was that night I proposed to you. That was the best and I've never been able to forget it. Third, it's kind of a toss-up. Either it was the night Nokea came to Florida to find me, or what I experienced with you a few nights ago. You put a hurting on my dick and I don't know how it's going to recover."

I laughed. "You are crazy, but thanks for being honest."

"Always. Now, what about you?"

"No doubt, the other night is at the top of my list, and another time would be the first time I met you. Sex at your house that day was unforgettable. Other than that, the first time Shane and I had sex was great and the sex we had during a limo ride might rank number two."

"So, how are you feeling about Shane now? I want you to end it, for good and none of that break up to make up shit either. Do it as soon as you get back to St. Louis. Can you promise me that you'll end it?"

"I don't want to make you any promises, especially if you can't make me any."

Jaylin was serious, but he wasn't willing to give an inch. "Do it for me," he said. "I want the relationship over with for good, Scorpio. You and he had no business hooking up."

"I . . . I don't know what I'm going to do . . . ."

"End it!" His voice rose. "Tell that muthafucka it's over and be done with it."

I cut my eyes at him and looked away. It wasn't fair for him to demand something from me when he hadn't spoken about his intentions with Nokea, not one time.

"No matter what happens between Nokea and me," he said softly. "I still want you to end it with Shane. The thought of him being with you and making love to you always drove me insane. What could you possibly want with him, after sharing these several days and nights with me?"

"I could reverse that question back to you and ask that you refer to Nokea, but I won't."

"Then don't. Besides, I know your position regarding Nokea and me, but this conversation is about you and Shane. Open your eyes, Scorpio, and see your relationship with him for what it truly was. It was your way of getting back at me, nothing more and nothing less."

"I disagree, and like you once said, love doesn't disappear overnight. Since I've been here, I haven't thought much about Shane. I don't know if I'm discouraged because of his lies, or if I was never really in love with him."

"It doesn't take a rocket scientist to figure that out. It's time to do the right thing."

"I have to ask, but what about Nokea? During our time together, have you thought much about her? A few times, I've seen you spaced out and I wondered . . . ."

"Yeah, well, I've been thinking about her. Not all good thoughts, but she's definitely been on my mind."

"Before I left St. Louis, Shane told me that during their drive home that day, Nokea and he discussed their feelings for each other. He said their feelings were confirmed, and after they shared an overdue kiss, they agreed that pursuing each other wouldn't be in anyone's best interest. Did Nokea mention anything like that to you?"

Jaylin's eyebrows rose, so I could tell he was mad. "Nothing. She said nothing like that to me, but when I asked her about what took place at the motel, in a sarcastic way she said that she

enjoyed it. Bottom line, I know what time it is.
That's why I'm here. I can't wait to see or talk to
Mr. Shane, but there's a time and place for every-
thing. Our day is definitely coming."

Instantly, the thoughts of Nokea put Jaylin in
his own world. When he was angry, he always
performed at his best, so I made my way to his
side of the tub. I wanted to relieve his mind from
the brought upon stress, so I asked him to sit on
top of the tub. After he did, I massaged his goodness with both hands, occasionally covering the
tip of his head with my mouth. My jaws were
sucked in and every time he went to the back of
my throat, his fingers tightened in my hair. "Te . . .
tell me that it'll be over," he said softly. "Scorpio,
promise me that you will never again make Shane
feel what I've felt these last several days."

I removed his goods from my wet mouth and
looked up at him. As far as I was concerned, it
was already over, but at first, I didn't want to
confirm it for Jaylin. Now that we'd hooked back
up, things were definitely going to be different.
"It's over. You have my word that I will never be
with him again."

Those words put a smile on Jaylin's face. I got
back to work, but I remembered how difficult it
was to make him come like this. Still, I put forth
my very best effort. When he held a tight grip on

my hair, I knew I was in business. He let loose and I didn't let a drop of his lava drip from my mouth. I swallowed, and while Jaylin calmed himself, he held my head steady.

"Yo . . . you must pay for that," he barely uttered.

I definitely knew how, and when he escorted me to the bed, I paid dearly.

Nearly an hour later, I got dressed and gathered my things to go. Jaylin helped me pack, and when Ebay came to get me, again, I hated to go. While standing at the door, I tightly embraced Jaylin and we shared a lengthy kiss.

"Don't forget to keep in touch," I said. "And next time you have this desire for me, you're coming to St. Louis. Hopefully, that'll be soon."

"I hope so too," he said.

On that note, I stepped away from him to exit. He reached for my hand, pulling me in for another hug.

"I'll never forget you coming all this way to see me, Scorpio. You are truly a special woman, no matter what happens. You know I got love for you, right?"

I nodded. I wasn't sure if I'd ever see Jaylin again. I knew how he felt about me, but was it enough love to separate himself from Nokea? No doubt, he'd gotten what he wanted from me, only time would tell if I'd get everything I wanted from him.

Chapter 16

Nokea

This was unbelievable. The other day, Shane called with very bad news. He told me Scorpio had taken a flight out of St. Louis to Florida. We didn't say much else to each other, but both of us were stunned!

Since then, I hadn't heard from Jaylin. I knew he was upset with me about disappearing that night, but I purposely did so, just so I could see how far he would go. I definitely knew the man I married and I accepted that. I would never tell anyone that I didn't know what I had gotten myself into because I'd sound like a fool. No matter who got hurt, Jaylin was always going to be Jaylin. Whenever he was hurt, other people always had to feel his pain right along with him. What I didn't expect, though, was for him to neglect me and his children for this long. For me, that was a true wake-up call. Even though I knew Scorpio was here, I hadn't a clue where they were. I definitely wasn't going to go look for him. I waited for days, until he finally showed up.

I was helping Nanny B clean up the kitchen, while LJ and Jaylene were down for their naps. Nanny B knew how devastated I was, but I asked that she give me some space and let me deal with this situation as best I could. All she did was continue to make excuses for Jaylin's behavior. She talked about all he'd been through and all the changes he'd made. Personally, I didn't give a care about any of the changes he'd made. The only thing that his changes proved to me was, that with a snap of my finger, he could always resort back to the person he was before.

As I took the plates out of the dishwasher and put them into the cabinets, I heard the front door alarm sound. It was two o'clock in the afternoon, and when I looked to see who it was, Jaylin walked in the kitchen. He was casually dressed in blue jeans shorts, sandals and a football jersey. He couldn't look at me for two seconds before his eyes quickly shot in another direction. He picked up the mail and thumbed through it.

"Is this all the mail we got?" he asked.

Neither Nanny B or I said a word.

"Is anybody talking in this muthafucka?" he yelled.

Nanny B just stared at him and I left the kitchen. I heard her say something to him, but I couldn't quite make it out. I returned to our bedroom. Minutes later, Jaylin came through the door. I looked in his eyes again, and I still got the same response. Guilt was written all over his face. The thought of what obviously transpired between him and Scorpio made me want to throw up. I rushed to the bathroom, shut the door behind me and did just that. As I hugged my stomach and leaned over the toilet, Jaylin knocked on the door.

"Are you all right?" he asked.

I didn't say a word. I threw up some more, and then cleaned myself up. I looked in the mirror and wanted to cry so badly. A big part of me wanted to believe that Jaylin would never cheat on me. Even though he'd done so in the past, I truly thought being married to him would be different. I couldn't stand the sight of him. I took a few more minutes to gather myself, and then left the bathroom. Jaylin was sitting back in the chair next to our bed with his eyes closed.

"I'm coming back home tonight. I had time to think about some things and we need to talk," he said.

"I'm not ready for you to come home yet and there's not too much more that we can discuss."

Jaylin sat up, gripping his hands together. "Nokea, how much longer is this going to go on? I'm not gon' come in here every day arguing with you. You've had your fun by staying out all damn night. It's about time you got back to being a wife and mother."

In disbelief, I stood with my mouth hanging open. "You haven't even been here every day for us to argue and I've always done my best as a wife and mother. It's not something I have to get back to. You're the one who has to adjust to the change. Wherever you were, I hope your time away did you some good. I'm sure it did, and without going into any details, you will pay dearly for what you've done to me."

"Whatever, Nokea. Without all the mumbo jumbo, face it, Daddy's home. Make sure your boyfriend ain't ringing my phone and try to keep your feelings for him under control, all right?"

One good slap across his face would've made me feel good, but I wasn't going to go there. Lord knows I wanted to walk out on him, but that took careful preparation. I never thought I would feel so disgusted by the sight of him. Just knowing . . . thinking about him with Scorpio, sparked a mad rage inside of me. For now, all I could say to him was, "Welcome back, Jaylin."

* * *

What else could I say, other than living in this house was like living in hell. I couldn't stand to be around Jaylin. At night, it was so hard to sleep next to him without wanting to choke the mess out of him. The more I ignored him, the angrier he got. He continued with his smart remarks about Shane, but I let him have his little fun. I had no plans of telling him that I knew Scorpio was here, but I had a feeling he'd already known I knew it.

As for sex, please. Last night, for the first time since he'd been home, he tried to sweet talk me. He wrapped his arm around me, told me he was sorry and that he loved me. At times, I thought Jaylin needed some Prozac. He was on one minute and off the next. Then again, I probably needed some strong medication for putting up with his mess too.

Jaylene and I were in the playroom painting some pictures. LJ was at the grocery store with Nanny B, and the last time I checked, Jaylin was still asleep. As I was getting ready to clean up the mess we'd made, Jaylin came into the room and sat on the floor with us. He looked at the pictures we painted of our family and told Jaylene how pretty they were. He put her on his back, pretending to be a horse. She was laughing her butt off, and seeing her smile, definitely made me smile. Once Jaylin got tired, he lay flat on his stomach and took deep breaths. She kept telling him more, but he told her later. Of course, that caused her to cry and he picked her up and carried her into another room. I stayed behind, continuing to clean up the mess. Once I was finished, I went into the kitchen where they were, and saw that Jaylin had given her a huge bowl of chocolate ice cream to keep her quiet.

"Jaylin, she already had breakfast. Ice cream is for lunch or dinner."

"But she told me she wanted some ice cream, so I gave her some. It's no big deal."

Since chocolate was all over her face, I wet a paper towel and walked over to her to wipe it off. Jaylin sat close by her. After I wiped her mouth, he reached for my hips and pulled me back to his lap.

"I gotta tell you something," he said.

"What?" I said, feeling uncomfortable.

"While I was away, I got in on a profitable real estate deal. Once the deal is closed, we stand to make three million dollars. The deal is expected to close sometime next week and I was wondering if you'd like to take a vacation somewhere? Anywhere? We need some time alone. Anywhere you'd like to go, Paris, Hawaii, Africa . . . Wherever, we can go."

I wanted to tell him he could go to hell, but instead I stood up and responded, "Let me think about it and I'll let you know."

He grabbed my waist again and put me back on his lap. "I missed you while I was away," he said. "I know I've said and done some hurtful things to you, but I can't get my anger under control. I just wish that incident with you and Shane would have never taken place. I want you to understand how hard it was for me to swallow. By all means, it doesn't justify my behavior, but if you're willing, I'd love for our healing process to begin. We got some work to do and I'm ready to start whenever you are."

I shrugged, really not caring much about our marriage. I was there for my kids and I had been thinking hard about what I needed to do. "That's fine. Whatever works."

I got off his lap and picked up Jaylene. Jaylin stood up, gave her a kiss and then put his lips on mine. I backed up and touched his chest.

"Not right now, okay? Like you, I have some things I need to sort through."

"It's just a kiss Nokea. I can't even kiss my wife?"

I quickly pecked his lips and left the kitchen.

Nearly an hour later, I started to wonder what was taking Nanny B and LJ so long at the grocery store. When the doorbell rang, I rushed to the door. A florist stood outside with dozens and dozens of red roses.

"Nokea Rogers?" he asked.

I nodded and widened the door for him to bring the roses inside. They were very beautiful and I thanked him. Once I closed the door, I picked up the flowers and placed them on the round glass table in the foyer. I reached for the card and read it.

> This is so awkward, as I never thought we'd get to this point in our marriage. I don't know where to begin in correcting the pain I've caused you. I've missed your smile and I hope these flowers brighten your day. Love Jaylin.

I stuck the card back into the envelope, thinking about my failing marriage. My thoughts were interrupted by Nanny B and LJ coming through the door. Immediately, Nanny B noticed the flowers.

"Oooo, those are pretty. Where did you get them from?"

"Jaylin had them delivered."

She tooted her lips and headed to the kitchen with LJ. When I left the foyer, I saw Jaylin standing by our bedroom doors. He awaited a reaction from me, but all I did was hug and thank him.

"Did you like them?" he asked.

"They're nice," I said, going into our bedroom. He followed.

"Look, I don't like to see you like this. You're distant, quiet, and I'm willing to do what I can to make things right," he said.

I sat on the bed and began to express myself. "I don't know if you can make things right, and I don't know if I can either. Yes, I can see that my lies caused major damage, but instead of dealing with them, as I've dealt with yours so many times before, why did you allow things to go this far?"

"I needed space," he said, walking over to the bed and sitting next to me. "If I had stayed here, things would have been worse."

"So, you just run off and do whatever? Then, you think it's okay to come back here and things are supposed to get back to normal?"

"This marriage isn't perfect Nokea. It will never be perfect. We had a disagreement, and now, it's time to work through it."

I wanted to tell him that I knew about Scorpio being here, but it didn't seem like the appropriate time. More than anything, I wanted him to tell me, but surely he would not.

"Whether you agree with me or not," I said. "We had more than a disagreement. It's been kind of a reality check for me. As angry as you've been, I never thought you could stay away from me and the kids for so long."

"You act like I was gone for months or something. Didn't I call here almost every day? I stopped by several nights, and some nights, you didn't even know I was here."

"Well, tomorrow, the kids and I are checking out of here for a few days. I'm taking them to see my parents. I've been subpoenaed to be a witness in court against the man who posed as an officer and forced Shane and me—"

"So, fuck me, right? Do you think I'm going to let you go to St. Louis without me?"

"What are you so worried about? I'd like to see this man behind bars for a very long time and so would Shane. Whether anyone likes it or not, we have to do what is necessary."

"I'm doing what's necessary too. What time do we leave?"

"My plane departs at seven o'clock in the morning. There are no more seats available, and the next flight out of Miami isn't until eleven."

"Then, cancel your flight and leave with me at eleven."

"I can't do that. I'm supposed to be in court no later than two. Once you get off the plane, you can meet me there. If you do show up, please do not embarrass me and I do not want you to say anything to Shane. You know I'll have to speak about what happened that day, so I don't know why you'd want to come, especially if the situation bothers you so much."

"I'll keep my cool. I just want to be there for you, okay?"

"I hope so, and if you get yourself in any legal trouble while you're in St. Louis, I'm telling you ahead of time that the kids and I are coming home."

He kissed my cheek. "I'll be on my best behavior. I promise."

Chapter 17

Shane

I couldn't even explain what the hell was going on with me. Inside, I was mad as hell, but my anger didn't stop me from moving forward. Once I found out Scorpio had booked a flight to Florida, I didn't have much else to say to anyone. At Nokea's request, I called and told her about Scorpio's little trip, just so she wouldn't be left in the dark about all that was going on. Through a little investigation of my own, I found out Scorpio extended her stay in Florida and that was enough to break my heart.

I decided not to return the phone call she left the other day, and when she stopped by my house, I couldn't even open the door. Basically, what in the hell did she have to say to me? I wasn't about to listen to how many mistakes I'd made, when Scorpio knows damn well she never, ever, shook Jaylin from her heart. I do believe she loved me, but Jaylin has a tight hold on her and vice versa.

Either way, I was out of this mess. I wasn't in the mood for Jaylin's bullshit. I decided to take the high road and focus on Shane and Shane only. I made my business my priority and things have been going well. Last week, I picked up two new accounts and was paid a nice sum of money for my design with the Mayor's Group. I made sure Jaylin was paid back every dime of his money. Scorpio's money was transferred back into her account too. In her message, she thanked me for returning the money and sounded as if she really cared.

Yesterday, I removed her ring from my drawer. I spent hours looking at it and thinking . . . what if? What if I had married her without realizing her constant desires for Jaylin? For that, I was grateful things turned out as they had. Instead of keeping the ring in my possession, I went to my mother's house and gave it to her. She was disappointed things didn't work out between Scorpio and me. She told me she'd wear it until I found the woman who was right for me.

For now, though, I wasn't looking to be in a committed relationship. All I needed was a woman I could have fun with, without all the attachments. For the time being, my standby, Amber, was back in the picture. I could always rely on our companionship to help me get through troubled times. Last night, she and I kicked up a good conversation. If I didn't have to prepare myself for court, I probably would have gone to see her today. I told her I'd stop by soon. Like always, she made it clear that she was anxious to see me.

Late last night, Nokea called and told me Jaylin was coming to St. Louis with her. She asked me to keep it cool. I told her that I wasn't the one she needed to worry about. I made it clear that I wasn't tripping off Jaylin. As far as I was concerned, everything was everything. As my friend, he knew how I felt about Scorpio, but that didn't stop him from wanting to put his dick inside of her. Yes, I had feelings for Nokea, but if we had never been forced, I doubt that sex between us would have ever happened. I think I was more upset with Scorpio, simply because she took her ass to Florida to see him. Even if he would have come here to see her, Scorpio didn't know where to draw the line. Any future drama he brought to her would be well deserved.

According to Nokea's latest phone call, she was in St. Louis and the kids were with her parents. When I asked where Jaylin was, she said he was coming in on a later flight. Since the courthouse was in a small jurisdiction that neither one of us knew much about, Nokea asked if she could follow me. Just so she didn't get lost, I agreed. She told me she was on her way to my house. After my shower, I started to get dressed. I couldn't step in the courtroom with jeans on, so I wore my Kenneth Cole jacket, with a gray vest and white crisp shirt underneath. As soon as I stepped into my pants, I heard a car door shut. I hurried into my black leather shoes, not wanting Nokea to wait long. I straightened my goatee with the tips of my fingers and added some shine to my twisties. As the doorbell rang, I quickly splashed my face with aftershave. I hurried to the door and invited Nokea in. She looked magnificent. She wore a light tan suit with a dark brown silk blouse underneath. Her accessories were gold and her layered haircut was cut to perfection. Normally, the front of her hair was spiked, but this time, bangs covered her forehead and barely covered one eye. I couldn't help but stare at how pretty she was. When she stepped inside, I shot a glance at her curvaceous hips and butt that were well fitted in her short pencil skirt.

"You can have a seat in the living room. All I have to do is get my coffee, my wallet and find my keys."

I walked off to my bedroom to get my wallet and keys. On my way to get my coffee, I asked Nokea if she wanted some.

"No thanks, Shane, but before we go, come here and sit down for a minute."

Since Nokea was sitting in my chair, I sat on the couch next to it. She turned to me, nervously rubbing her hands together. Obviously, she had something on her mind and I gave her all of my attention.

Her voice was soft. "I . . . These past several weeks have been very difficult for me. I feel lost and the way Jaylin has reacted to all of this has tremendously damaged me. I wanted you to know that I don't regret what happened between us. The only reason I'm testifying today is because of what this man did to his other victims. I know for a fact that Jaylin was intimate with Scorpio. I have this dying need inside of me to make things right. I need for you to help me do so."

"I'm not sure what you have in mind."

"I paid for a mistake that was beyond my control. A lie from me should not have resulted in what my husband did. And since it did, I need a reason to have been so deeply betrayed. I'm asking that you make love to me and do it without being forced."

I dropped my head into my hands, closing my eyes. I was getting frustrated with this shit. "Nokea, why do we all keep doing this? What good is going to come out of you and me having sex? More headaches will follow and I am not up to continuous arguments with Jaylin. I can't believe you just asked me that."

A tear rolled down her pretty face, and it tore my ass up. "Shane, I'm hurting. I need to make this right. I am so tired of being the nice girl. It's time that I do what I want, and I want to continue what we started at the motel."

"So, in other words, you want to use me to get back at Jaylin?"

"No, that's not what I'm saying. For once, I want to let my hair down and do something I've always wanted to do, just like Jaylin does when he's angry. I want to know what it feels like to do something so out of character and not worry about the consequences."

I sat back on the couch, shaking my head. "And what about what I want Nokea? My feelings are tied up in this shit and nobody seems to give a fuck. Do you think I can just have sex with you, without any attachments? Jaylin might be good at that shit, but it's not my style. I can't turn myself on and off like that."

Nokea wiped her watered down eyes. She pulled off her jacket, placing it on the arm of the couch. "I understand how you feel, but why must we continue to deprive ourselves? Scorpio and Jaylin didn't. If I can cope with my feelings, I know you can too. Let's just make this right, please?"

Nokea had me thinking hard about what Scorpio and Jaylin had done to us. This would be sweet, sweet revenge, but I couldn't seem to get with it. Invading my thoughts, Nokea stood up and proceeded to undo her blouse. I couldn't say much of anything. After she exposed her plump and pretty breasts, she stepped out of her shoes and faced me. I spread my arm on top of the couch, looked at her hard nipples and felt defeated. I shook my head from side to side and softly spoke.

"What about Jaylin, Nokea?"

"What is it that you want to know? They . . . he and Scorpio played us and this will be our secret, okay?"

She hiked up her skirt and straddled my lap. After looking at her breasts again, I dropped my head back, closing my eyes. Nokea took my hand and placed it on her upper hip. I felt her thong, and when she let go of my hand, I kept it in place. My hand eased around to her curvy and smooth backside, causing my dick to poke through my pants.

"Damn, Nokea," I said, raising my head. "This is so fucked up!"

"No it's not, and, there's no way you're going to feel that way when this is over."

She placed her arms on my shoulders, leaning in to kiss me. Her soft lips and sweet smell drew me in even more. I couldn't help but think how lucky Jaylin was. Then again, so was I. As we kissed, my hands worked her ass and my fingers swiped her slit. Through her thong, I felt her moistness and it sure as hell turned me on. Thinking of nothing else but getting inside of her, I slowly directed her back on the couch. We were pressed for time, so I moved her skirt up a bit higher and pulled off her thong. I couldn't believe that Nokea had willingly opened her legs for me. Like at the motel, her pussy was so sexy and inviting. The wet look of it made my mouth water. I quickly came out of my jacket and lowered my pants underneath my butt. I hurried to put on a condom. When Nokea grabbed my ass to push me in further, I couldn't help but tear that pussy up. With every stroke, I looked into her eyes and she gazed into mine.

"Now, this . . . this isn't bad, is it?" she insisted, while holding tightly around my neck. I sucked her breasts and kept up with my rhythm down below, not saying a word. My actions answered her question, but they weren't good enough for Nokea. She lifted my head away from her breasts.

"I . . . I want all of your clothes off Shane. I need to feel your sexy body next to mine. Stop holding back and do this shit," she gritted.

"We don't have time . . . ."

Ignoring me, Nokea reached for my pants to pull them all the way down. I stood up to step out of them, rushing out of the rest of my clothes as well. She rushed out of her clothes too, but when she lay back on the couch, I looked at her naked body and had a change of heart.

"Like you said, if we're going to do this, we need to do this right. Come here," I said.

Nokea stood in front of me and I easily lifted her petite body. She straddled my waist and we intensely kissed as I carried her down the hallway to my bedroom. Having much more space to work with, I lay her on my bed, giving her exactly what she—I wanted.

Definitely, time was not on our side. Before leaving for court, we attempted to clean up, but wound up spending thirty extra minutes in the shower. We rushed to my car, and tried to redeem ourselves on the way to the courtroom. By the time we got there, I'd say things were pretty obvious. Nokea's hair wasn't intact like it normally was, her makeup was all gone and both of our clothes had wrinkles. The only excuse we had was the rain, but I wasn't sure if that would save us. What was so fucked up was Jaylin had beaten us there. I walked in first, and Nokea followed only a few minutes behind me. When she looked at Jaylin, the look on her face said it all. I wasn't sure what his thoughts were, but maybe it was me feeling . . . knowing what had gone down.

Even though we were late, things were delayed. Once Nokea, Frick and I talked to the prosecutor, I sat up front with Frick. Nokea sat in the far back with Jaylin. My mind was all over the place. I felt like I was on the verge of an anxiety attack. I was so anxious for this shit to be over with so I could leave.

Finally, the man in question came out with an orange jumpsuit on. Cuffs were on his wrists and ankles and his face was badly bruised. When he looked at me, he held his head down low. I kind of felt sorry for the motherfucker, but as I looked at all the hurt people in the courtroom, I was happy about testifying so he'd get what he deserved.

The trial dragged on and on. I had hoped they would call me to testify before Nokea, and surely enough, they did. I was sworn in and took the stand. Immediately, my eyes looked to the back of the courtroom and connected with Nokea's, then Jaylin's. He already looked pissed. I knew when I started to tell my story, things would get worse. I focused my eyes on the prosecutor who started to ask questions.

At first, things were going smoothly. However, somewhere down the line, my mind confused what had happened today with what had happened at the motel. Several times, I asked the prosecutor to repeat himself and my pausing didn't help much either. I kept visualizing the sweat Nokea and I kicked up today, and my testimony was all over the place. I guess I did okay, but when Nokea took the stand, she was thorough and very credible. She painted the defendant as the true criminal that he was and didn't appear nervous at all. As she explained what had happened, she continued to look at Jaylin, and at times, she looked at me. At one point during her testimony, I heard the door open and Jaylin walked out. Minutes later, he came back, and when I turned around, his eyes connected with mine.

Frick tapped my shoulder and I lowered my head so he could whisper in my ear.

"She's good," he whispered.

"Tell me about it," I said, not referring to her testimony. "Very, very good."

Finally, the trial wrapped up for the day. Or at least, my and Nokea's jobs were finished. Jaylin and Nokea stood up to leave and so did Frick and I. We actually made our way to the exit doors before Jaylin and Nokea did.

Frick walked up to Jaylin and shook his hand. "I had no idea you would be here," Frick said.

"I gotta be here to support my wife, don't I?" Jaylin replied.

"Yes. And, that was a courageous thing Shane did for himself and Nokea. Things could have turned out a lot worse, you know?"

"Maybe," Jaylin shrugged, turning to me. He held out his hand. "What's up, brotha can't get no love?"

I reached out for his hand. "I wasn't sure how you felt, Jay. Just trying to give you some time to sort things out."

His grip got a little bit tighter, so I pulled away. "Hey, you, uh, got time for a drink later?" he asked.

"I might. Give me a holla on my cell."

"Will do. Definitely will do."

Not knowing if I'd see Nokea anytime soon, I carefully wrapped my arms around her and gave her a hug.

"Take care, all right?" I said.

"You too, Shane."

We held each other for a few more seconds, then broke our embrace. Afterward, I left. Frick stayed around and chatted with Jaylin.

As expected, when I received a phone call from Jaylin, it was less than an hour later. I hadn't even made it home yet, but I could tell he was anxious to talk. We agreed to meet at CJ's in Clayton. I told him I was on my way and we both hung up.

Traffic was a bit crammed. When I got to CJ's, Jaylin was already there. He was sitting at a small table for two, talking on his cell phone. Suited up in his dark pin-striped suit, I noticed two women sitting behind him going crazy. When I walked up, they smiled at me and I took a seat. Jaylin ended his call and the lady behind him tapped his shoulder.

"Excuse me, but my girlfriend would really like to—"

"Not right now, all right? I'm in the middle of something," Jaylin arrogantly said.

. She looked at me, sort of rolled her eyes and turned around.

Jaylin picked up the menu, looking it over.

"I thought you only wanted to have a drink," I said. "Have we changed our plans?"

"If I took a seat at the table, instead of the bar, then I guess our plans must have changed. Besides, I'm hungry. How about you?"

"I'm all right. I ate very well earlier and I'm still a little full."

Jaylin looked at me and chuckled. "Now, why did I read a little bit more into that comment, Shane? I got the impression that you weren't talking about being full from food."

"Maybe, it's just your mind playing tricks on you. I was definitely speaking of getting full from my breakfast this morning. Besides, what I liked to *eat* was recently served to you. After nearly five long days with you, I know you're very full, aren't you?"

"Yeah, Shane, but there's always room in my body for more. I assume you're talking about my time with Scorpio, right?"

"Hey, let's not beat around the bush. You know that's what I'm talking about. I can't seem to understand how a man like you can live with himself. How can you look in the mirror and be satisfied with who you are?"

Jaylin gave me a serious look, making himself clear. "Shane, I'm more than satisfied with who I am. But, uh, I didn't ask you to come here so we could discuss Scorpio. Since you brought her up, though, what can I say? As usual, the pussy was finger licking good, and the excellent head she gave me hasn't been accomplished by any woman I know. I've told you, for a very long time, that Scorpio will never love another man the way she loves me. Always, at the snap of my finger, she'll be there for me. Don't blame me if you failed to face reality and got caught up. You shouldn't have ever tampered with my leftovers. Backstabbing me has never paid off for anyone. Now, I'm sorry if your feelings got bruised, but you set yourself up for the downfall, my brotha."

I wanted so badly to tell him about me and Nokea, but I couldn't even play her like that. I quickly brushed his remarks off and decided to take the high road. "Whatever, Jaylin. Maybe I did set myself up, but hey, it was fun while it lasted. We live and learn, don't we?"

The waiter interrupted us to take our orders. Keeping it simple, I ordered hot wings and a beer. Jaylin ordered a steak burger with fries, and was working on his second glass of Remy.

After taking a sip, he put the glass on the table. "Yes, Shane, we do live and learn. More than anyone, I'm ecstatic about the outcome of your relationship with Scorpio. But I am saddened by what I saw today. I saw with my own eyes, that my wife seriously got some feelings for you. In addition to that, the late appearance in court really shook me up."

"Why's that? We got lost trying to find the place, and the rain delayed us."

"Maybe so, 'cause I got lost too, but let me tell you something that I know about my wife. Nokea is very particular about how she looks. Her hair is always in order, her clothes are neat and the time she spends on her makeup drives me crazy. There are not too many places she goes looking as she did in the courtroom today. Can . . . can I tell you where I'm going with this, or do you already have an idea?"

"No, I don't know, but like I said, guilt can be a muthafucka, you know?"

Jaylin hopped out of his seat and grabbed my collar. "Don't bullshit me, nigga! Did you fuck my wife today?"

Several people turned to look in our direction, but once Jaylin let loose of my collar, they looked away. I calmly dropped back in my seat, and so did he. I straightened my collar and gave him a stern look. "You need to calm the fuck down. Now, if you want to shake something up in here, we can. I'm damn mad about you and Scorpio. Even though I want to put my foot in your ass, she was the one who messed up a good thing. So, no, I did not fuck your wife today. Nor have I ever, or intended to, go inside of Nokea. When she came to my house today, we stayed there five minutes and left. During those five minutes, she briefly shared with me her feelings from your actions and was really shaken up. She cried so much that she washed the makeup from her face, and as for her hair, the rain must have wrestled with it. I encouraged her to be strong and told her everything would work itself out. Even though I knew Scorpio had gone to see you, I didn't say a word to Nokea about it. She's been through enough already. I have no desire to continuously inflict pain on her like that. I'll leave that up to you, as you seem to be doing a damn good job of it already. I just don't understand how you can risk losing a woman like her, for a woman like Scorpio."

"You are so full of shit, Shane. Months ago, Scorpio was the best damn thing that happened to you. Now, Nokea is the prize winner. For the record, my dick took a risk. When my wife lied to me about her encounter with you, my dick suspected something was up. It went on a search for the only woman who was capable of making it heal. It had fun, and fucking was the only way to calm my ass down. When *it* needed a little love and tender care, *it* went home."

"So, let me get this straight. Are you implying that Nokea is not capable of fucking you like Scorpio does? If so, I think you're out of your mind."

"Unless you've seriously got it on with Nokea, then how in the hell would you know how the two of them compare?"

"I . . . I'm only assuming. From what you've told me about Nokea, I knew she was capable of doing something right, especially if you married her. Therefore, I can assume that she's a better lover than Scorpio. Not from my experience, but rather from what you yourself told me."

"That's right, clean your shit up. Nokea is a better lover, but when I'm angry to the extent that I was, I need to fuck. Scorpio worked out just fine, and if anybody knows that to be true, I'm sure it's you."

"So . . . I'm still unclear. You got with Scorpio because?"

He snapped. "Because every chance I get, I make love to my wife. During the process, all I think about is how much I love her and how precious she is to me. On the other hand, when I fall on hard times, I can fuck Scorpio, whenever, wherever or however I want to! During those times, I'm thinking just that. If you don't understand what I'm talking about, then that's too damn bad."

"Oh, I understand. I understand very well, Jay. You use people to get what you want from them, and you have no consideration for their feelings. You know the thought of that shit really bothers me, but, uh, ain't nothing I can do about it now."

"I apologize for shaking up your feelings, but it's obvious that no one considered mine. Scorpio, she knows what it is that I feel for her. I don't have to explain myself to you or to anyone. Now, getting back to today, my gut thinks something happened between you and Nokea. I'm really not sure what, but because I don't believe Nokea would give away what belongs to me, that's why I'm not gon' trip. But, let me say this . . . if I ever find out anything differently, you'd better have a safe and secure place for her at your place. She knows how precious she is to me and you know how I feel about her as well. I've accepted this incident between the two of you, but the idea of y'all having feelings for each other is way, way out there. As my friend, once again, I need for you to pack up your feelings and lay them elsewhere. Nokea is off limits."

"Scorpio too, right?"

"Exactly. It's nice to know we're finally on the same page."

"Well, damn, Jay. I'd say you really have this thing under control. Like you've always wanted, you have both of your women back in your possession. I hope you'll somehow manage to work out the mess you've created. All I can say is good luck and I wish the three of you well."

I stood up, and before I left, I stepped over to Jaylin's side of the table. I leaned down and spoke to him. "They're taking too long with my food and drink, so I gotta go. Until we chat again, do me a favor." Jaylin looked up at me. "Don't underestimate Nokea. She's a very smart woman. She's not as stupid as you think she is. Scorpio gon' always be Scorpio and your dick will continue to make her turn flips. Just maybe Nokea too, but whether you realize it or not, she's got more power than you think she has. I'd hate to see you blow a good thing. If you do, there are plenty of men waiting or hoping that you'll fuck up. I being one of them. Good friend or not, pretty-ass women with spectacular pussies seem to fuck us up every time. For now, let the past stay in the past. I hope like hell we don't continue to let these women come between our friendship."

Jaylin stood up and reached in his pocket. He laid a fifty dollar bill on the table and took a sip from the glass of Remy. "I don't appreciate waiting this long in restaurants either, and you don't have to tell me about Nokea because I already know. I know that she'd better not find out about Scorpio, and I know you better not have lied to me about your activities for the day. As long as everything checks out, Shane, I agree with you. We cool as a fan and I owe you for *protecting* Nokea at that motel."

Jaylin held out his hand and I gripped it. We patted each other's backs and headed for the door. His rental car was parked close by the door. My car was parked in the garage.

"Where are you headed?" I asked. "Are you and Nokea going back home or are y'all staying in St. Louis?"

"We got some serious making up to do, so after I go make this important stop, we're heading back out tonight. The kids are staying with her parents for two weeks. I don't know how in the hell her parents got me to agree to that shit."

"Well, be safe. If you need anything, holla."

"Same here," he said, getting into his car. I went into the parking garage and Jaylin drove away.

Chapter 18

Jaylin

Honestly, I didn't know what to believe. My gut was telling me one thing, but Nokea and Shane had said the same thing about their delay with getting to court. Thing is, I wasn't sure if it was my guilt that had gotten the best of me, or if something had really gone down between them.

While on the drive to her parents' house earlier, Nokea assured me that no matter how bad things had gotten between us, turning to another man was not the answer for her. She admitted to doing that with Stephon and talked about how many problems her decision to kick it with him had brought to us. She did say that Shane provided her with some encouraging words, and whatever words he'd said to her, they seemed to give her hope for our marriage. No doubt, I was pleased about that.

As for my dealings with Scorpio, there was no other way to put it, other than admit I was out of my mind! I had no justifiable excuse for all the sex I'd had with her. The only thing I could admit to was how much I enjoyed it. I don't know why or how I'd gotten myself into this situation, but I was in too deep and couldn't change a thing that had happened. I hated like hell to disappoint Scorpio, but there was no way in hell I'd leave Nokea for anybody. By any means necessary, we were going to work things out. I was sure it would take some time, but I planned to deal with her distance until she decided to come around. I understood her distance very well and I was upset with myself for saying some of the things I'd said to her. Not only that, but I'd definitely crossed the line. By having sex with Scorpio, I opened up old wounds and I prayed like hell that Nokea never, ever found out. I planned to take that secret to my grave. I wasn't about to lose my wife and kids over this mistake. Before I went home, though, I had to set the record straight with Scorpio. I wanted to see her face to face, explain what I truly felt and tell her how I could not give her what she wanted.

As expected for a Friday, Jay's was crowded. I saw Scorpio's Thunderbird out front. I had to park almost a block away. Before getting out of the car, I checked myself in the mirror, and adjusted my baby blue silk tie. My dark blue suit was already working for me. As I looked at the time on my Rolex, I realized that I didn't have much time to discuss my decision with Scorpio. Yes, I could have called her, but as good as she'd been to me, it was only fair that it happened this way.

As soon as I opened the door, I already knew what to expect. Every eye was on me and Jay's got extremely quiet. That was until Jamaica, a woman I'd met before, ran up to me. She threw her arms around me.

"It was so nice of you to come back for me. Tell me, please tell me that you're not here looking for *that thing*," she joked.

"Jaylin Rogers," said a voice to my right. I looked over, and sitting in a chair was a chick I'd dated in college named Erin. Well, maybe not dated, but fucked a few times.

Before I could say a word, Jamaica looked at Erin. "Do you know my man?"

"Sorry," she laughed and got out of her chair. "But your man has a wife."

I gave Erin a hug. "What's up, Ms. Lady? I haven't seen you in a long time."

"I haven't seen you in a long time either, but I heard Nokea whisked you away."

"That was then and this is now," Jamaica play-fully said, attempting to get my attention. She continued. "Listen, Jaylin. Can I somehow get to know you like errrbody else has? I thought we had a connection?"

"And we do, baby. Just, uh, go get the boss lady for me and you and I will chat later."

Jamaica kept flirting so the other stylist, Bernie, told me to go on back to Scorpio's office. I gave Erin another hug, telling her to take care.

Once I made my way back to Scorpio's office, I stood in the doorway, looking in at her. She was focused on some papers on her desk and seemed occupied. Her hair was pulled back into a clip and a few strands dangled on her face. Always looking sexy, she wore a mustard, off–the-shoulder fitted sweater dress and was barefoot. Her shoes were on the floor beside her and her legs were crossed. When the intercom buzzed, she hit the button.

"Yes, Bernie."

"Did you see who's here?"

"No, but I'm busy. If it's somebody looking for me, take a message."

"Jaylin's on his way back there."

Scorpio's eyes widened. "Who?"

"If you're busy, I can always come back," I said, leaning against the doorway.

She looked up at me and stared. Of course, a smile followed. "I underestimated you. I didn't think you'd come so soon," she said, lifting her finger from the intercom button.

"I had a sense of urgency to see you," I said, walking into her office. Scorpio stood up and walked around her desk. Her sweater dress fit every curve she had and she was working the hell out of her dress. I wasn't sure how I was going to break my unfortunate news to her, especially since I was already turned on by her.

"Before you come any closer, just do me a favor and turn around," I said.

She laughed and turned. Her back faced me and she slightly turned her head to the side. "Am I good," she said.

I walked up, standing close behind her. I moved a piece of her curled hair behind her ear and whispered in it. "Good, you are. But, don't settle for good, when I consider you to be so much more than that. What's the word I'm looking for?"

"Spectacular?"

"Oh, so much more than that, too."

She turned around. "Well, whatever it is, I don't have time to think about it right now. How about just showing me how good/spectacular you think I am."

Shiiit, what was a man supposed to do! I had all of this in front of me and I intended to make good use of it. I wrapped my arms around Scorpio, touching the small of her back. My hands eased to another soft place and Scorpio put her arms on my shoulders. We looked at each other's lips, and then, they met up.

"Ummmm," I said, after a lengthy kiss. "You are on point with that shit. Good kisser, good lover, good dick su—"

Scorpio placed her hand over my mouth. "All of which I'm sure you came here for."

I smiled and walked over to the sofa in her office. After I took off my jacket and loosened my tie, I sat back, resting one of my legs on the sofa and one on the floor. I placed my right arm on top of the sofa and looked at Scorpio leaned against her desk.

"Well, make yourself at home," she said. "You look awfully comfortable."

"I am and why shouldn't I feel at home whenever I come to Jay's? This place has memories of me written all over it, doesn't it?"

"Maybe. But, right now, I want to know the purpose for your visit. Do you have good or bad news for me?"

"I can't tell you while you're standing over there. I need for you to come over here so I can tell you."

Scorpio came over by me and put her knee between my legs. She leaned over me, which caused me to lean further back.

"My mind has been deluged with nothing but thoughts of you," she admitted. "Help me understand this connection I have with you. Is it strictly sex for you or do you want—can we have more?"

Scorpio's pretty eyes were right there with mine. "Baby, I would love to offer you so much more, but I am in the most fucked up position that I've ever been in before. I . . ."

Scorpio's phone buzzed and saved me. I thought she was going to get up to see who the caller was but her eyes stayed glued to mine. "No matter what you've decided, I still love you. I'll just have to live with your decision," she said.

Her words and the look in her eyes killed me inside. I held the sides of her face and went for her lips. She straddled herself wider on top of me and maneuvered her arms out of her dress. Once she lowered the top part of her dress, she sat up on me and removed her hair clip. She teased her hair with her fingers and I held the sides of her breasts with my hands. I softly touched her nipples and dreaded what I was about to say. "Baby, you don't know how sorry I am . . . ."

"Shhh," she said. "Let me get up and close the door."

Before getting up, she leaned in for another kiss. That's when someone behind us cleared their throat. Scorpio quickly turned, and I rose up to look over her shoulder.

"You have two seconds to get off my trifling husband. As for you, Jaylin," Nokea took a hard swallow and I swore I saw fire burning in her eyes. "Please explain to me what in the hell you're doing here!"

I slowly sat up, having very little to say. Scorpio pulled up the top of her dress and got off me. She folded her arms and, gloating, she turned to Nokea.

"Who let you in here?" she asked.

Nokea ignored Scorpio and continued to look at me. I stood up, reached for my suit jacket and lay it across my arm. "Let's go," I said. "I'm not getting ready to talk about this right here so let's go."

"I can't think of a better place to discuss this," Nokea said. "If you won't tell me, I'm sure Scorpio can enlighten me on what's going on."

"What does it look like to you?" Scorpio snapped. "You have eyes and I hope you use them to see."

"Look," I said. "I'm not going to stand here and do this! I said, let's go!"

Nokea pointed her finger at me, confirming every word she spoke. "Jaylin, let me tell you something . . . if you walk out of that door, and leave me to fight your battle, you'd better walk out for good. I want to know right here, and right now, what the hell is going on?"

"Not a damn thing. I stopped by to say what's up and that's it."

"That's it, huh? To me, and my eyes do provide twenty-twenty vision, it looked like a whole lot more to it than just that."

Scorpio dropped her arms and rolled her eyes. She spoke out, as she made her way over to her desk. "This is just so fucking stupid. I wish you'd be honest with her so she can step up out of here."

"By all means, somebody please be honest with me. If Jaylin isn't man enough to do it, then you tell me what I should know. You sound very eager, and this would be the perfect opportunity for you to share."

I could see Scorpio's anxiousness to tell Nokea something. Certainly, I couldn't let that happen.

I looked at Nokea. "Look, I came here because I made a mistake. I don't want to stand here and talk about it right now, but if you'd let me explain, I promise to tell you everything when we get home."

"Have you had sex with her, and did you come here to have sex with her again?" Nokea asked.

"I do . . . do not want to go into details right now."

Nokea turned to Scorpio. "During the course of our marriage, have you had sex with Jaylin?"

Scorpio stood behind her desk, folded her arms again, and spoke with assurance. "Within the last two weeks, a total of eleven times. Today would have made twelve."

Wowww, Scorpio's response did not sit right with me or Nokea. I looked at Scorpio in disbelief. "Why?" I said. "Why you gotta go out like that? Let me handle this, all right?"

"Eleven times," Nokea said, shaking her head. She questioned Scorpio again. "Did you come to Florida to see Jaylin?"

"Yes. I spent five eventful days and four long nights with him."

"I'm out of here," I said. "Y'all can sit here and discuss this . . ."

Nokea was enraged. "Are you going to defend your fucking self, Jaylin? Is what Scorpio telling me the truth? Must I hear the truth from another woman, and not my own husband! Since when did you become such a coward? Man up and lay your mess on the line!"

"Don't talk to me in that tone, Nokea! I'm trying to spare some fucking feelings up in here, but since y'all wanna get this shit out in the open, then let's. I was angry and Scorpio was there for me. You were at home trying to work through your feelings for Shane and you didn't understand the pain I was going through! I can't sweep no shit like what happened between you and him under the rug. I needed time to heal. Unfortunately, my inability to cope caused me to consult with another woman." I looked at Scorpio. "I wasn't trying to hurt anybody, but the reason I stopped by here was to tell you that I could never give you the things you asked for. I hope that you find happiness with another man, other than Shane, and don't miss out on your happiness because of me. I will never choose another woman over my family and it's no secret how much Nokea means to me." I looked back at Nokea. "Now, I hope you're satisfied—can we please go?"

"Oh, you don't know what it takes to satisfy me," Nokea said. "How dare you stand there so arrogant and full of yourself after putting me through this mess again! I'm far from being satisfied, Jaylin, and I hope you've carefully thought this through. I'm leaving and I will see you whenever you get home."

Nokea made her way to the door. She couldn't quite make it out as so many people stood by the door listening. I turned to Scorpio and she had fury in her eyes.

"I knew you were going to do this to me. All you wanted to do was break up Shane and me so you could have your way. Mission accomplished, Jaylin. Now, go take good care of your wife and leave me the hell alone."

I could still see people by the door, so I closed it. I looked back at Scorpio. "I might have assisted with breaking up you and Shane, but you helped with that too. You knew I was not going to leave—"

"Like hell, Jaylin," she screamed and darted her finger at me. "You misled me, again! You made love to me like you wanted to be with me forever. You expressed over and over how much you needed me! The connection that you have with me says that something is definitely there. But, you pretend that Nokea is the best thing that's happened to you, and without her, you can hardly see straight! How do you do it, Jaylin? How can you be so fake like that? I wish like hell I could be fake too, but I don't operate like that."

"You did so when you were with Shane, but I'm not going there. Listen, I got some deep-ass feelings for you and there's no denying that. I just can't walk out on my wife and kids for some good pussy. I love other things about you too, Scorpio, but our connection is very sexual. We can't make it work on that. If I could, I would, but I can't."

"You keep saying that our connection is sexual, but that's because you refuse to face reality. You cheated on your precious wife and risked losing your children out of your love for me and not for my pussy. You missed what we shared, Jaylin. You couldn't wait for Nokea to disrupt y'alls marriage so you could run right back to me. If it were all about a piece of ass, you could have gotten that anywhere. Many women would have opened their legs up to you, but you wanted me! That in itself accounts for some love buried deep inside of you. If what I'm saying don't jive with what you feel, then walk your ass out of that door and never look back. Besides, I'm sure your wife is heartbroken and needs you. As for me, I should have known better, but you'd better believe that I'm going to be all right."

"I'm sure that Nokea needs me too. Even though part of what you've said might be true, I love no one like I love her. Losing her would make me a very miserable and unhappy man. That's not the kind of person you deserve to have in your life. Now, unfortunately, I gotta go. Stay sweet and focus on the good times."

"To hell with the good times. What good does it do me to think about them? Why don't you think about them, and while you're thinking, think about getting the hell out of my office. Now!"

I stood, giving Scorpio a long stare. I couldn't blame her one bit for being angry, but for now, all I could do was turn and walk out the door.

Chapter 19

Scorpio

After all that had happened, I was almost too embarrassed to leave my office. I knew everybody had heard what had gone down. Trying to maintain my composure, I put on my game face and headed up front. All eyes were on me, as everybody wanted to hear the scoop.

"You have got to tell us what all of that was about!" Bernie said.

"Didn't everybody hear?" I responded.

"Nope," Jamaica said. "All we know is . . . you went to Florida, fucked Jaylin eleven times, he came here to fuck you again, and his wife showed up. We tried to call back there and warn you, but Nokea insisted that she knew where your office was."

"Well thanks. If she had come in here with a gun, I would have had so much to be thankful for, right? Y'all sent her right on back, knowing Jaylin was back there with me."

"Don't be upset with us," Jamaica added. "You shouldn't be messing with that woman's husband no way. He fine and all, but that dick done had you hooked for way too long. It couldn't be all that."

A chick close by cleared her throat. "I don't know Scorpio too well, but I can vouch for Jaylin. During our college years, he was the daily talk on campus. Everybody was trying to get screwed by him, but he was real particular. I got lucky at a party and I haven't forgotten about that brotha since. He was damn good and the size of that thing and what he can do with it . . . girl!"

Bernie and Jamaica looked at each other, laughed and spoke in unison. "We know!"

"Well, it was something else," she continued. "When I heard he'd gotten married, I was disappointed. I was sure we'd someway or somehow hook up again. I had no idea that he'd been seeing you Scorpio."

"How couldn't you know?" Bernie said. "We talk about him a lot around here, and if the name of this place isn't a clue, I don't know what is."

The chick covered her mouth. "I didn't even think about that. What a small, small world. His wife, though, she's real pretty. I heard about some chick named Nokea who he grew up with, but I never saw her. When I did, I expected her to be as pretty as she is."

"She cute," Jamaica said. "But, Scorpio got her beat by a long shot."

"Thank you, Jamaica," I said. "I think so too."

"She cute, I'm cute, we all cute, but she's the one who's married to him. Besides, does being beautiful even matter anymore?" the chick said.

"Not at all," Bernie said. "But, a man like Jaylin brings about too much heart and headache. From what little I do know, you gotta be a strong woman to put up with him. And let's not talk about being married to him. I'm sure it's not all peaches and cream."

"Girl, please," Jamaica said. "The only aching and pain coming from my marriage to him would be from me lying on my back for so long. If I was married to him, as long as he satisfied me and dished out his money, he could do whatever he wanted to. What I can't seem to figure out is," Jamaica looked at me, "if you were gone for five days, how much screwing did y'all do? Y'all must have been at it while y'all were sleeping too. You can't squeeze eleven times in five days, you just can't do it!"

"It averaged out to a little over twice a day, and the more I think about it, it might have been even more than that. If you don't mind, we had some major catching up to do."

"Was it worth it," Bernie asked. "What about your dignity and respect for another woman's husband? Was running back to Jaylin worth losing Shane? Sorry, but you know I had to go there."

"I didn't lose Shane because of Jaylin. It didn't work out between us because he continuously lied to me."

"And, Jaylin has always been such a saint, right?" Bernie said. "You and I will talk later, but you know I'm highly upset with you."

"I know, and I should have known better. It doesn't sting that much now, but it's going to sting later."

Not wanting to discuss what had happened any longer, I walked off to my office. I closed the door and looked over at the couch where Jaylin and I were. Disgusted with him, but more so myself, I took a deep breath and bit the tip of my fingernail.

Damn, I thought. *How did I ever let this happen to me again?*

Chapter 20

Nokea

By the time I left Jay's, I couldn't even think straight. I wanted to go somewhere far, far away, but what was I running away from? Instead, I went back to my parents' house, kissed my kids good-bye and told everyone I'd see them in two weeks. After that, I headed for the airport to go home. I had no clue where Jaylin was and I surely didn't care. I wanted him to go away and leave me at peace.

No doubt, I was devastated when I saw Scorpio on top of him. Just to know that he would have had sex with her again was shocking. What in the hell was he thinking? I knew Jaylin had some suspicions about Shane and me, because Shane told me about their conversation at CJ's. Shane also told me that he and Jaylin wrapped up their meeting quickly. Since Jaylin was already in Clayton, I had a feeling he'd stop at

Jay's. My suspicions were correct, but I hadn't anticipated walking in on what I did.

As for Scorpio, why did I hate her so much? I wanted to hurt her so badly, but for now, my issues lay with Jaylin. The only thing that kept me a bit at ease was my thoughts of Shane. I got much pleasure out of what we'd done. My time with him was unforgettable. We agreed to never share our secret with anyone. I trusted him and he trusted me. I even thought about going back to his house for the night, but all I wanted to do was go home.

As I sat at the airport waiting for my plane's departure, I picked up my phone to tell Shane good bye.

"I just wanted to tell you that I'm on my way back home. I wanted to stop by, but I didn't know how you'd feel about it," I said.

"Nokea, you're always welcome here. But I do want you to do your best and try to work things out with Jaylin. I know you're angry about a lot of things, but be smart about your choices. Don't let them hurt you in the long run."

"Are you saying what we did wasn't a smart thing to do? I feel very good about what happened between us. I don't regret it. Do you?"

"Not at all. If I had to do it all over again, I wouldn't do it any differently."

I took a deep breath, as Shane's response was good to know. "After I finished speaking to you earlier, you know I went to Jay's don't you?"

"Why?"

"Because I knew Jaylin would be there. I can't even tell you what I walked in on."

"Don't tell me. I don't want to know, but I would like to know what Jaylin's response was."

"Shane, you know how arrogant and stubborn my husband is. He played it off like he was there to inform Scorpio that he wasn't going to leave me. Even though he said it to her, it was one big act. I left. Have you ever been so deeply tired of a situation that your body felt numb and you couldn't react?"

"Naw, but I'm sorry you had to experience that. I don't know what to say."

"No need for you to apologize. I'm a big girl and I'm going to handle this."

Shane laughed.

"What's so funny?" I asked.

"I was just reminiscing about you. You go ahead and handle your business. I have faith that you will do it well. Have a safe trip home and don't call me when you get there. I don't want Jaylin throwing another phone at you. Call only if you need me."

I agreed to only call Shane if I needed him. After giving our good-byes, we ended our call. Afterward, I looked up and saw Jaylin heading my way. I guess he managed to wrap up his visit with Scorpio and decided to make his departure. He held his cell phone to his ear and I turned my head to look away.

He walked up to me, placing his cell phone on my ear. "It's your mother," he said.

I held the phone and my mother asked if I was okay.

"Mama, I'm fine. I told you I was. I don't know why you keep asking."

"Because a mother knows her child, Nokea. I talked to Jaylin too. I hope the two of you aren't being untruthful with me."

"If anything was going on that I couldn't handle, I'd let you know. I'm okay, all right?"

"Only if you say so. I love you, and your father and I are really enjoying our grandbabies. It's nice not to have to travel to Florida and see them. You know, you can always come back home."

"Mama, I'm fine. I know where my home is and I love you too. Kiss my babies for me. I'll call you when I get home."

My mother and I hung up and I gave the phone back to Jaylin.

He held my hand. "Your mother is worried about us. I am too. Should I be?"

I eased my hand away from his and walked away. I wasn't up to speaking to him in the airport, so I stayed in a gift shop until they announced our plane's departure. Once they did, I got on the plane. Ignoring Jaylin was difficult because I had to sit right next to him. I sat by the window, using every opportunity to look out and avoid him. He reached for my hand to hold it, then leaned his head on my shoulder. I moved it away.

"I'm tired," he said. "Can I use your shoulder to rest my head?"

"My shoulder hurts, just like the rest of my body." I paused. "Eleven times, Jaylin? Did it take that many times?"

I knew that would cause him to loosen his hand from mine and sit up straight. "She exaggerated, Nokea. You can't believe everything you hear."

"But, surely, I can believe everything I see, right?"

He had nothing to say and I turned to look out the window. Once the plane took off, I started thinking about my amazing day with Shane. I wasn't sure how I was going to work through all of this, but I knew some changes had to be made. I couldn't let Jaylin think it was okay for him to cheat on me. If I did nothing about it, I knew he was the kind of man who would take advantage. He'd shown me that today, by going to Jay's, even after he told me he wanted to begin the healing process. Yeah, right. He was playing me for a fool and I didn't like it. As I thought about all we'd been through, the thoughts of it brought tears to my eyes. I thought of Shane's words, "be strong," but how could I be? How could I be strong after we'd both betrayed each other? Did I even have the right to be mad at Jaylin? Of course I did. He knew better than to hook back up with Scorpio, but if it hadn't been her, it would have been someone else. That's just Jaylin's style. Had I been a fool for thinking our marriage would change him? I knew he was going to do everything possible to make me stay with his program. Well, the program was about to change. I had so many things that I could do, but they could only be done over time. I'd definitely come out of this with some kind of victory and it was high time that I did.

While in deep thought, a few tears rolled down my face as I stared out the window. I wiped them and Jaylin called my name.

"What?" I said, continuing to look out the window.

He reached for my face and tried to turn it. "Are you crying?" he asked.

"No," I said, still not turning my head.

He let my face go and took my hand again. He kissed the back of it. "I know you don't want to hear anything I have to say right now, and I know my words mean very little to you, but I didn't mean to hurt you. I hate to see you cry. Haven't I done my best to keep you happy? I made a mistake, baby, and I'm sorry."

I closed my eyes and the thought of Scorpio on top of him was in my head. The way he was comfortably lying back on the couch with her breasts staring him in the face was gut-wrenching. I thought about the many places sex between them could have taken place and it made me sick to my stomach. I felt myself getting ready to throw up, so I got up and stepped over Jaylin. I headed to the bathroom in first class. As soon as I got there, I vomited. I cleaned up and splashed water on my face. After patting it down with a napkin, I left the bathroom and returned to my seat.

"Are you okay?" Jaylin said, moving out of my way.

I took my seat. "I'm fine. This ride is just making me sick. I can't wait to get home."

Almost three hours later, Jaylin and I returned home. Nanny B wasn't there. When I asked Jaylin if he knew where she was, he told me that he'd arranged for us to be alone for the next two weeks. I got a glass of water from the fridge and made my way to our bedroom. Before going to bed, I gathered my things to take a shower. Jaylin stayed in the kitchen to call my parents and let them know we made it home. Once he finished, he stood in the bathroom with me.

"Your mother wants you to call her," he said.

"For what?" I asked, and then turned on the shower.

"She wants to make sure you're okay."

"I told her I was fine."

"But, I understand her concern. You've been awfully quiet. I'm worried about you too."

"Jaylin, if you were so worried about me, you wouldn't have done this to us. You knew what this would do to us, but this is the kind of marriage you wanted. If you're expecting me to lose it over this, I'm numb right now. I haven't accepted all that's happened. Don't expect much from me right now, please."

I stepped into the shower and Jaylin watched as I lathered myself. I didn't even care that he watched, as long as he didn't get in with me. Once I finished, he opened the shower's door and handed me a towel. Normally, he'd dry me off, but I wasn't in the mood for it. I dried myself and slid into my lime green lace nightgown. Jaylin could see all of my good parts and he couldn't stop looking at me.

"I'm going to take a shower too. When I get out, would you like to watch a movie?"

"If I'm still awake. By the time you finish, I might be asleep."

"Then, I'll hurry."

Jaylin went into the bathroom. I opened the doors to the balcony to let the soothing breezes and noise of the ocean come in. For a while, I stood on the balcony, looking at the amazing scenery. I saw a couple on the beach holding hands and thought about the many nights Jaylin and I had taken walks and wound up making love. I tried hard to think positive thoughts, but then, the thoughts of him making love to Scorpio crossed my mind again. Did he make love to her like he does to me? Did he tell her how much he loves her? Why her? Why did he always have to go back to her? What was it about me that wasn't enough for him? I felt . . . terrible. I wanted to wake up from this bad dream, but couldn't. As I stood on the balcony wiping my tears, Jaylin came up and turned me to him. He was naked and held my body against his. He then kissed my forehead.

"I know this is easier said than done, but please don't do this to yourself or to us. I assure you that we'll get through this. I will never put us in a situation like this again."

I didn't believe one word he said, but I wanted some answers. "What is it about her, Jaylin? Why can't you let her go? If you can't, leave me, please. I don't want to be in this if you continue to love her."

"Nokea, I have never loved Scorpio. The only woman I've ever loved is you and nobody will ever take your place. I'm not going to leave you and you're not going to leave me. If I have to spend the rest of my life making this up to you, I will. I'm sorry, baby. Don't make me watch you hurt like this. It was a selfish thing I did. You know I've always had a tough time dealing with my pain."

Jaylin held me tighter. Once I calmed down, I broke away from our embrace. I went into our bedroom and lay sideways in our bed. Jaylin lay behind me, holding my hands together with his. I was worn from our discussion, but felt very comfortable.

"I love you," he said. He kissed the back of my head, and I guess, waited for me to return the love. I didn't feel like responding, but I did pray for God to help me get through this.

Chapter 21

Jaylin

What can I say, other than I fucked up! Even though a tiny part of me felt as if my actions were justified, I never thought I was capable of bringing so much turmoil to my marriage. I felt horrible inside and to see Nokea so torn really made me feel bad for what I'd done. My selfishness was a muthafucka, but at the time, I surely felt as if I was doing what was best for me.

And Scorpio? She was just as pissed about the whole damn thing. I wasn't trying to break it down to her like that, but when she started running off at the mouth to Nokea, that shit made me mad. She didn't have to tell Nokea we'd had sex eleven times. She could have said one or two times and been done with it. I guess I can be a bit thankful that her numbers were way off. I knew damn well we'd done it more than eleven times and I had the after effects to prove it. I hadn't really thought about any pussy since then, and when I stopped by Jay's, I wasn't intending to go there for sex. Truly, I wanted to share my decision with Scorpio and try to end things on a positive note. So much for that. When I saw Nokea, my heart jumped right into my stomach. I felt her pain. It really looked as if Scorpio and me were about to set some shit off. As always, Nokea handled her business well. No matter what the situation was, she never showed her ass. I knew she wanted to mess me up, and possibly Scorpio too, but being the woman she was, deep down, she knew what belonged to her. That's why I love my wife. She's a classy lady. I have to give her credit for putting up with me.

By morning, I hadn't gotten much sleep. I lay in bed with my arms wrapped around Nokea while she lay on my shoulder. Looking at how pretty she was, I moved her bangs away from her forehead and kissed it several times. The television was on, so I flipped through the channels with the remote and stopped to watch the news. A few minutes later, Nokea slowly opened her puffy eyes and looked up at me.

"What time is it?" she asked, noticing the bright sun cracking through the opened doors to the balcony.

"Almost eight o'clock. Do you have something to do today?"

"Nothing," she said, laying her head back on my shoulder. Her eyes faded again. Once she went back to sleep, I eased out of bed without waking her. I went to the kitchen to make us breakfast. As soon as I got there, I noticed my cell phone on the kitchen's island. The light was blinking so I knew I had a message waiting. I saw that Scorpio had called me at one fifteen in the morning. I checked my voice mail and heard her message.

I just had to call and tell you what a cruel person I think you are. And as cruel as you may be, I could kick myself for loving you so much. You might not think that I got much out of the deal, but just being with you for those days was, I guess, more than I could ask for. I'm hoping there's a possibility that I gain more from our time together, but only a few more weeks will tell. Yes, I'm speaking of having your child and I worked hard to make that happen. So did you, and even though you might be angry about this possibility, remember, it was a risk you were willing to take. Don't expect to hear from me anytime soon, and eventually, you know I'll be in touch.

Scorpio ended her call and I deleted her message. I couldn't tell if she was fucking with me or not, but I did take a big, big risk. I'd thought about using a condom, but I was so caught up and excited about being inside of her again that I decided against it. As I thought for a moment about all the juices I put inside of her, I picked up the phone to call Shane. I knew he had some of the answers to my questions.

"Damn," he answered in a sleepy voice. "I hadn't expected you to call me any time soon. I guess I'm forgiven?"

"Hell, naw, so shut the fuck up. Are you awake, though?"

"Barely. I just got to bed around five in the morning, what's up?"

"I need to ask you a few things."

"If it's about me and Nokea, what did I tell you?"

"Naw, it's not about you and Nokea. I got some suspicions about that shit, but maybe it's just me tripping. I want to know the last time you and Scorpio had sex."

"The day I got out of jail, why?"

"I'm just checking. I know you ain't trying to hear this, but I rocked the boat without a jimmy on. I'm trying to make sure everything's cool, that's all."

"No, I'm not trying to hear that Jay, and what you and Scorpio do or did is not my business anymore."

"Look, don't be bitter about this shit, all right? I know how you felt about Scorpio, but you knew how I felt about her too. You once told me that you couldn't control who's in your heart and I accepted that. Well, my dick made some choices this time, and even though I'm not delighted about my choices, I can't change a thing that's happened."

"Believe me, I'm gon' shake this shit as quickly as I can. Still, I'm a bit shocked by how quickly Scorpio ran back to you. Nobody understands the hold you have on her better than her."

"I understand it, and many times, love makes you do some crazy things. I was her first love, Shane, and Scorpio will never forget me. Now, though, I do need a favor from you."

"I'm almost afraid to ask."

"Just be there—be nice to her. Don't be hard on her for the choice she made and, uh, keep me posted on things."

"You mean, keep you posted if she pops up pregnant?"

"You're a smart man, Shane. I knew I could count on you. Would you happen to know when her next period is expected?"

"How would I know that shit?"

"Because I keep up with Nokea's like clockwork. When you're in a relationship, these things are important."

Shane laughed. "She's expected to come on next week. I'm not sure if we'll keep in touch that much, but whatever I find out, maybe I'll let you know."

"Thank you. I hope I can count on you to let Scorpio find happiness with another man."

"Only if I can count on you to be the man who your wife deserves. I will never touch Scorpio again. What could have been will never be."

"I'm putting forth my best efforts to make shit right with my wife. I admit, I fucked up, big time. I hope like hell we recover from this shit. If I lose Nokea, man, I know I will have lost a good thing."

"I'm glad you recognize that. Y'all will get through this, only because of the love you share. In a week or two, I'll be in touch to let you know what's up."

"Cool. You know I appreciate it and if you're bothered by my accusations about you and Nokea, I apologize for those too. I feel as though she . . . somebody's not telling me everything. I will not be mad if she found comfort in another man through all of this. I just want to know."

"Negro, you must think I'm a fool. You would go crazy if Nokea had been with me or anybody else and you know it. There's no way you would be able to handle what you dished out to her.

Luckily for you, Nokea is not capable of bringing that kind of hurt to you. You can believe whatever it is that you'd like, but instead of looking for an outlet for what you've done, you'd better focus on trying to do what you can to make things right. No doubt, she's been through a lot, Jay. She doesn't need to hear about your bullshit assumptions about me and her. What happened at that motel was unfortunate, but you have my word, it never went any further than that."

"I hope not Shane. I truly hope that you and Nokea didn't pursue your feelings for one another. I could barely deal with your relationship with Scorpio, but you know Nokea is a lot different. The thought of her being with anyone else just kills me. I'm not making excuses for what I did, but it was the only way for me to escape my harsh feelings. Scorpio put me at ease. Being able to discuss and release my frustrations really helped me. I hate she got disappointed again, but didn't we all?"

"Yeah, we did. Now, it's time to pick up the pieces and see how we can put them back together."

"I'm starting with breakfast in bed for my wife. Hopefully, I'll get lucky by the end of the week and things will start to take a turn. Pray for me, dog, all right?"

"No doubt."

"Good. Now, walk me through how to make French toast. Since Nanny B ain't here, I'm trying to impress Nokea. I know there's some seasoning salt around here somewhere."

"Seasoning salt? For what?"

"The French toast, fool."

"Ah, I think you might want to ditch the seasoning salt and go with some cinnamon. That will work a lot better."

"Cinnamon?" I said while looking through the seasoning rack. I reached for it. "Got it! You damn sure all right with me. Now what?"

Shane laughed and walked me through preparing the French toast. Once I got things started, I thanked him and hung up. I turned on the radio and kicked up "Made to Love You" by Gerald Levert. I sang and hummed the lyrics, thinking of Nokea.

Breakfast was finished, so I put everything on a tray, and grabbed a sunflower that was in a vase on the table. Nokea was still asleep so I mumbled her name to wake her. She cracked her eyes and then widened them when she saw me. She sat up in bed and stretched her arms.

"What's this?" she said, as I lay the tray in front of her.

I removed the flower from my mouth and handed it to her. She took the flower. "Thanks, but I can do without a plastic flower. I need a flower with good fragrance to wake me."

"I got you," I said, leaving the room. I went outside through the kitchen and picked a flower from Nanny B's flower garden. I went back into the bedroom, giving the flower to Nokea.

"This is the best I can do for right now," I said.

She took the flower from my hand and sniffed it. "Thanks," she said, placing it on the tray with her food.

"Move your legs up so I can lie sideways on the bed," I said.

Nokea sat Yoga style and I lay sideways in front of her so I could feed her. I held the fork and picked up a piece of the cut French toast.

"Your mouth is going to water so badly for more of this. Open wide."

She opened her mouth and once I put the French toast in she chewed. She nodded with approval. "Okay, not bad. But, who told you how to make French toast? Did you get a hold of one of Nanny B's recipes?"

"Baby, French toast is simple. Who needs a recipe?"

"You do. You rarely cook and I—"

"Okay, I ain't gon' lie. I called Shane and he hooked me up."

"Are you serious?" she smiled. "Shane told you how to cook French toast?"

I fell back on the bed, looking up at the ceiling. "Thank you, Jesus, she smiled! I can't believe she smiled. Even though I had to mention Shane in order for her to do it, I feel blessed."

I sat back up and Nokea rolled her eyes at me.

"Sorry," I said. "But, I had to go there. I was only kidding, though, all right?"

I reached for the fork again, but Nokea took it from me. "I think I can do this," she said. "Your efforts are well appreciated. Since you fixed your plate too, why don't you join me?"

"I am. But, after I fed you, I wanted you to feed me."

Nokea looked at my plate and forked up a piece of the French toast. She put it in my mouth and I chewed. "Damn, that's delicious. You gon' owe me big time for slaving in the kitchen like that."

Not saying a word, she scooped up some cheese eggs with a spoon and fed those to me too. I took the spoon from my mouth and scooped up some eggs on her plate. She looked at the spoonful of eggs and smiled again.

"That spoon was in your mouth, wasn't it?" she said. "I don't think I can use that spoon."

I put the spoonful of eggs in my mouth and removed the tray from her lap. I put it on the floor, dropping the spoon on the tray. I lay over Nokea and she stretched her legs so I could get comfortable. I looked down at her.

"So are you implying that my mouth is contagious," I asked.

"No," she whispered. "I was implying that the spoon was."

"That's right, baby, clean up your words. For the record, you are stuck with these lips. They got too much love for you, and like it or not, they're here to stay."

I leaned in and placed my lips on Nokea's. At first, she was hesitant, but then she went with the flow. Her hands held the sides of my face, and when her fingers teased the back of my hair, I felt slightly relieved. I took things a bit further and pecked down the side of her neck, making my way to her breasts. When I tried to lower the thin strap on her shoulder, she lightly pushed me back.

"Not now. Give me time, okay?"

I looked into her still puffy eyes, placing tender kisses on them. "Take all the time you need. I'll be right here. I'm not going anywhere, I promise."

She nodded and her petite body remained underneath me. We made such an attractive couple. I was starting to feel as if we were making progress. We kissed again, and as I started to get more into it, Nokea stopped me.

"I have to go to the bathroom," she said.

I rose up and she got out of bed. Still dressed in her lace nightgown, my eyes dropped to her visible ass and sexy body underneath. I wanted to make love to her so badly, but I had to be patient. She closed the bathroom door, but I could hear her coughing. After a few more coughs, I listened to the water run for a while.

"What was up with that?" I asked as she came out of the bathroom.

"After using the bathroom, I brushed my teeth."

"I'm talking about the coughing. That's the third time you've thrown up. You're not pregnant, are you?"

Nokea walked over to the bed and sat on it. "No, I'm not."

"How do you know? Have you taken a pregnancy test?"

"No, but I can't be. The doctor said the chances of me getting pregnant again were slim, and quite frankly, I don't want another child."

My eyebrows rose. This was breaking news to me. "I can't believe you just said that. You know how much I . . . We've wanted another baby. Why the sudden change?"

She looked at me with a blank stare. "Because I don't want another child, Jaylin. Two is enough."

"Like hell. You promised me another child and we never gave up hope after what the doctors said. You even said that you were willing to keep trying until it happened."

"Yeah, well, I don't feel that way anymore."

I was getting angry, so I had to calm myself. "Why and when did this change take place? Does it have anything to do with what has happened between us?"

"Jaylin, look, I don't want another child. What more is there left to be said. If I am pregnant, I don't know what I'm going to do."

"What!" I yelled. "I know damn well what you're going to do. You gon' have our baby, that's what."

"Don't raise your voice and demand anything from me. You're in no position to tell me what I should or should not do with my own body. If I don't want a baby, I don't have to have it."

This was a touchy subject for me and it was hard for me to hold my peace. "Now, you know what? You're about to piss me off. The only reason you would not want to have this baby is if it were not mine." I paused and my thoughts made me frown. "Did Shane come inside of you at that motel? You both said he didn't, but baby, please don't lie to me. If he did, I need to know."

"No he did not," she spoke with assurance. "I didn't start throwing up until a week after your midnight drunken visits. I've been sick ever since and I would hate to have made a child with you during that time."

"Well, you know how potent my mad sperm can be. It gets me every time. Both LJ and Jaylene were conceived that way."

"No they were not. LJ was conceived during sex at my house, and I was the one mad because, prior to that, I'd seen you and Scorpio having sex in the shower. Jaylene was conceived the first night I came here and we were both happy about seeing each other that night. So there."

"That's your take on it. When LJ was conceived, I was mad at you for holding back on the pussy and the tightness of it frustrated me. And, the night you came here, I was happy to see you, but I was angry that you'd married Collins and had my ass confined to the bed while soaking in my tears."

Nokea sadly looked down and was quiet. "Thinking about things, we have really caused a lot of hurt to each other, haven't we?" she said. "More so you disappointing me, but I've had my share of doing the wrong things to you too."

I kneeled in front of her, holding her hands together with mine. "I agree, but by far, our good times outweigh our bad times. Our love for each other continues to prevail and I can't stress to you enough that if you're pregnant, there's no way in hell you're not having my baby."

"Jaylin, I don't even know if I'm pregnant. You're getting ahead of yourself and I don't want you to be disappointed if I'm not."

"Of course you are. Why else would you be throwing up?"

"Because I've been sick. The stress I've been under can cause my body to react in such a way."

"Yeah, well, when are we going to find out? Call your doctor and set up an appointment. Better yet, let's go get a pregnancy test."

"I will do all of that, when the time is right. For now, I need for you to do some things for me."

"What?" I asked while still holding her hands.

Nokea was hesitant to talk, but she sternly looked into my eyes. "I don't trust you anymore, and the love we have for each other is not good enough for me. I now know that every time things don't go your way, you're going to run out of that door and do whatever it is that feels right to you. For your own satisfaction, you will risk losing your family and I never want to feel what I felt while you were away. Your children needed you and I had no answers for them. You did not take into consideration what I was going through here without you, and staying away for that many days made things worse. There have to be some changes in this marriage. Cooking me breakfast and telling me you're sorry is not enough for me to have another child. I don't . . ."

I stood up, pulled Nokea up to me and held my arms around her. "Whatever you want me to do, I will do it. I will do it because I love you and you know my children mean the world to me. If you're pregnant, don't deny me my child, Nokea. I can't explain what took over me, but I'm more than sorry for what happened. Ju . . . just tell me what it is that you want me to do."

Nokea touched my eyebrows and straightened them. She then placed her index finger on my lip. "Hear me out and don't say a word until I'm finished. As soon as possible, I want your name removed from this house and mine put on it. Every savings and checking account that you have separately and jointly with me, I want them put in my name solely. All of your stocks, bonds, mutual funds, real estate deals and any additional investments that you have, I want to be the overseer, and arrange it where any money made on those accounts belongs to me. As for your children, I want you to agree to, and legally put it in writing, that if we ever divorce for infidelity reasons on your behalf, I get sole custody. For any other reason, of course, we share joint custody. Lastly, the three-million-dollar deal you just made, if it hasn't been paid out yet, I want the check written out to me and deposited into my account. You can keep any credit cards that you have and the cars can remain in your name. I'm sorry that it has to be this way, but after all that's happened, I can't afford to let you walk out on me and our children and leave us with nothing. Right now, all I have belongs to you, and if you pull the rug from underneath me, I'm screwed. I trusted you before, but I can't trust you now. This is the only way I'll feel comfortable with this marriage and the only way I will ever consider having another child."

I looked at Nokea with a stoned face and didn't know what to say. I had already released my arms from around her. When I finally opened my mouth, all I could say was, "Are you out of your mind? The money issues can be negotiated, but I'm not about to give up custody of my kids. I can't believe you stepped to me like that. You know damn well I'm not going to agree to no bullshit like that."

Nokea sat back on the bed. "If you love me, and your intentions are to remain faithful to me, then the issue with our children should not be a problem for you at all. However, I can understand your frustrations, if you feel as if Scorpio should be able to walk back into our lives without any repercussions. Even though I understand her way of thinking, I'm not going to stand for her to come back again. Like I said, this should be easy for you and I'm a bit worried about your concerns."

"Fine, Nokea. I'll agree to the issue with our kids, but what about you? What if you commit adultery?"

"I'm not the one who can't be trusted, you are."

"Oh, I doubt that. You've got some skeletons too, but I just haven't found them out yet."

"If I did, I'm sure you would know about them by now. Besides, I have nothing to hide. You're the one who got caught with your pants down, not me."

I walked to the other side of the room and thought about Nokea possibly trying to set me up and leave me broke. "Are you trying to break me? Why would you want all of my money like that? If I agree to your request, don't you know what that leaves me with?"

"It makes you a very rich man, like you've always been. I'll never deny you any of your money, Jaylin, because you've worked hard to build on what you have. On the other hand, I can't say that you won't deny me. You reminding me that *you* pay the bills here and this is *your* house was a wake-up call for me. The risk I'll take, if I don't do this, is not a risk I'm willing to bear."

"So, still, it sounds like you want to leave me high and dry. I don't like that."

"Jaylin, what's mine is yours. You're still in control of your own destiny. If you love me, I don't understand why you're giving this much thought. It's simple. And, if the shoe was on the other foot, I'd hand everything over to you on a silver platter."

"Well, the shoe ain't on the other foot, damn it. You got me in a bind and I need some time to think about this."

"Take all the time you need. But, the sooner we can come to a resolution with this, the happier I will be and we can focus on repairing our marriage. You want that to happen, don't you?"

"You know I do, but I got a feeling that if I take too much time with this, that baby you're having will never see daylight. Nokea, I swear to you that if you have an abortion, I will never, ever forgive you."

"Don't base your decision on me being pregnant, because I told you that I didn't think I was. You're giving us false hope and I don't want to disappoint you again."

Thinking hard, I told Nokea I'd be right back. I couldn't help but walk down the hall and shake my head. I stand to lose a lot, but the big questions were . . . was Nokea worth it, did I trust her, and could I agree to never react as I did this time around? I went into my office and closed the door. I sat at my desk and picked up a picture of my kids. After gazing around at the many pictures of me and Nokea, I reached for the phone to call Frick.

His secretary answered.

"James Frick, please," I asked.

"He's on another call. Who shall I say is calling?"

"It's Jaylin Rogers and, uh, tell him to hurry and wrap up his call. This is important."

"Hold on, Mr. Rogers."

A few seconds later, Frick got on the phone. "If you're in jail, I can't help you," he said.

I laughed. "You'd better be able to help me, but this time, all I need is your advice, and possibly, a contract."

"I'm listening," Frick said.

I broke everything down to him. Once I finished, he was very quiet. He cleared his throat. "Are you even considering something like that? Jaylin, that's a bad move. You've worked too hard to get to where you are. I like Nokea a lot, but she shouldn't be requesting that of you. I guess it all boils down to trust. Can you trust her?"

"Yeah, I trust her. And, Nokea knows that I will seriously hurt her if she ever denied me my money. Our children, I'm not too worried about them because I won't have a problem being faithful to her."

"You just told me that, less than a month ago, you had sex with another woman. Are you sure this is something you want to do? I think you need to take as much time as possible to think about this. You are worth millions and I'd hate to see anybody walk away with it. I'm not comfortable with drawing up a contract of that nature, but it's your call. I will add every clause possible to protect you, but again, I don't like it."

"I'm not too thrilled about it either, but it's what my wife wants. I told her I'd do anything to make this work and I meant it. Start putting a contract together for me and call me once you have everything in writing."

"What about your will? Any changes need to be made to that?"

"Nope. Nokea is my sole beneficiary and Nanny B my contingent. I don't think any changes need to be made to it."

"Okay, then what if anything happens to Nokea? Everything you own could be tied up in probate because your name isn't on it. Now, I can make you the executor, but you still might have some issues. As for the accounts, you'd have to stay on as the secondary account holder. This will allow you to withdraw from the accounts, but Nokea can stop access to you at any time. By the way, does Nokea's will list you as the beneficiary too?"

"Yes. That's all taken care of. Just make sure all of those accounts are set up where I can still get to my money."

"No problem, but I will have to get you to sign off on numerous papers. How soon do you need to get this done?"

"As soon as possible. Once you have everything ready, can you bring the papers to me so we can sit down with Nokea and discuss everything? Possibly within the next two or three days?"

"Two or three days is going to cost you," he laughed. "That's a lot of work . . . ."

"Whatever it is, you know I'm good for it."

"Always," he said and laughed. "That's why I rush off the phone when you call."

"I'll bet," I laughed back and hung up on him. I sat for a few more minutes thinking, and couldn't help but call Shane.

"I take it breakfast must have failed," he said, sounding sleepy.

"Are you still in the bed? It's almost eleven. I can't believe you're still sleeping."

"When we spoke earlier, didn't I tell you that I didn't get to bed until after five? Shit, I'm tired."

"Well, I'm sorry to bother you, but I have to be very sure about something. While you and Nokea were sexually forced at the motel, did you release anything inside of her? I'm asking because she might be pregnant and you know I don't want no shit."

Shane was quiet, and then rushed his response. "Jay, I was too mad to release anything inside of her. My dick barely got hard and I am one hundred and ten percent positive that nothing came from me."

"Nothing?"

"Not a drop. If she's pregnant, how far along is she?"

"I don't know because she hasn't been to the doctor yet. I'm sure it's been a minute because she's been throwing up for a while now. In addition to that . . ." I filled Shane in on Nokea's requests.

"Hell motherfucking naw!" he laughed. "Are you serious?"

"As a heart attack. I just talked to Frick about the shit a li'l while ago."

"Talked to Frick about what? Are you considering it?"

"Yeah, it's in the making, as we speak. Basically, I had no choice and you know that this money means nothing to me, if I don't have Nokea and my kids."

"Jay, I have to say that you continue to shock me, but there is no way in hell I would have done anything like that. Nokea deserves a lot of what you have, but . . . I don't know about everything."

"Listen, if you think about it, it's really not a big deal. I still have access to my money and all I'm doing now is sharing everything with my wife. I should have been doing that all along, so what's the difference?"

"The difference is, she'll be in control of everything now. If you fuck up, she can cut your finances and the relationship with your kids completely off. Are you willing to take that risk?"

"Nokea would never deny me either. And if she did, I would make her life so miserable that she would regret ever fucking me over. I trust her with everything I own. If I wasn't out here tripping, maybe we wouldn't even be here."

Shane and I chatted for a little while longer. Like Frick, he continued to stress that I needed to rethink some things, mainly because they didn't trust me to be faithful. With all that was at stake, I knew I could be the best husband ever.

I left my office and made my way back into the bedroom. Nokea wasn't on the bed, but I looked in the bathroom and saw her in the bathtub. She was relaxed and her head was resting on a pillow. I cleared my throat and sat on the edge of the tub. She opened her eyes.

"I thought hard about what you said and I called Frick to make the arrangements. He'll be here in a couple of days to work out the details. Before then, is there anything else you'd like for me to do?"

Nokea puzzlingly looked at me and rolled her finger around her lips. "I want you to take off your clothes and get into the tub with me. Wash me like you always do, and I will do the same in return. Sex between us will happen in due time, but I just want to be as close to you right now as I possibly can."

I stepped out of my pajama pants and eased myself behind Nokea. She lay her back against me, holding my arms tightly around her waist.

"I love you," she whispered.

"And, I love you more."

Chapter 22

Nokea

I wished things didn't have to be this way, but I was not going to lose out again. For now, I didn't trust Jaylin as far as I could see him. If he went off on another one of his rendezvous, I was not going to leave me and my children without.

We got married so quickly that money issues were never discussed. I felt content with my bank account, but every account that I had, Jaylin's name always came before mine. Yes, all of the money was his, but I'd given up my life and career in St. Louis just to be with him. I did it because I loved him, so I didn't think it was selfish of me to ask him to do the same in return. Besides all of that, I had his children and took good care of my family. I wasn't looking to be rewarded through money. All I ever wanted was for Jaylin to do right by me and his kids. By being with Scorpio, he failed me. This was the only way I'd get what was due to me. If he ever turned to her again, he'd pay for it dearly.

Frick was supposed to come by today. Before our meeting with him, I finally made a doctor's appointment. Jaylin had been working my nerves and I had to know what was going on with me. On our way to the doctor, he was excited, but I had some doubts. I wasn't concerned with the baby being Shane's, because neither of us came that day at the motel. Anyway, my sickness started way before the real deal between us went down and Shane used a condom. If I was pregnant, it was definitely Jaylin's baby. My sickness didn't feel like it did when I was pregnant with LJ or Jaylene. I had more like an ill feeling inside and the feeling gave me regular headaches.

Either way, we were at the doctor's office to see what was up. When the nurse called my name, Jaylin stood up to go into the examination room with me.

"Baby, stay out here. As soon as I find out what's going on, I'll come share the news with you."

He hesitated, but took a seat. I followed behind the nurse as she led me to the examination room. She asked me to remove my clothes. When I put on a gown, I waited for my doctor to enter the room. When he came in, he smiled and looked at me on the examination table.

"How's my girl doing," he said, always very upbeat. He was a Black older doctor who had broken the news to Jaylin and me about my inability to conceive. I felt comfortable with him and that's why I stuck with him.

I explained my sickness to him and he quickly ordered some tests. The pregnancy test was first and then he did several more tests. He told me to relax and said he'd be right back.

Dr. James' right back status turned into him being gone for over an hour. Even Jaylin had come into the room with me and he paced the floor, until finally taking a seat on the stool.

"What is taking so long?" he griped.

"I don't know, baby, but you're really making me nervous. Will you relax, please?"

Jaylin seemed a bit more relaxed when Dr. James came back into the room. He shook hands with Jaylin and then pulled up a stool in front of us.

"I apologize for taking so long, but I had to look at all your tests. I know you guys are anxious to know about the pregnancy test, but I'm sorry, it came back negative." Dr. James paused, as Jaylin got up and left the room. "Again, I'm sorry," Dr. James said looking at me.

"You don't have to apologize. I had a feeling that I wasn't pregnant."

"I know how anxious you and your husband are to have children, but again, the possibilities are slim. That doesn't mean that it can't happen and I see miracles happen every day. You might want to stress that to him."

"I will. But in the meantime, what's going on with me?"

"Nothing that a little rest, maybe some medication, and taking a bit more care of yourself can't cure. You're in pretty good health, Nokea, but your blood pressure was slightly high. Not too much to worry about, but I think that might be why you're having those headaches. Your regurgitating episodes might have come from stress. If you've been under a lot of pressure, your body might be reacting. The flu has been going around too. I'll give you a flu shot before you go. Other than that, you're good. Again, I wouldn't give up on your attempts to conceive a baby because you just never, ever know."

I took a deep breath. I was glad to hear there was nothing seriously wrong. I was disappointed about not being pregnant. Even though I said I wasn't ready for another child, a huge part of me kind of hoped I was pregnant. I had a feeling Jaylin had set himself up for major disappointment. I hurried back into my clothes to go check on him.

Once the nurse gave me a few prescriptions, I left the room and headed out into the waiting area. Jaylin was sitting in a chair massaging his hands together while looking down at the floor. I stepped up to him and he lifted his head to look up at me.

"Are you all right?" he asked.

"I'm fine. I have slightly high blood pressure, minor stress or possibly the flu."

He stood up and took my hand. "Come on, let's go," he said.

When we got to our Hummer, he opened the door for me and I got inside. Before he started the truck, I placed my hand over his. "Dr. James said there is still a chance for us. He encouraged us to keep trying. Don't give up on me. I need for you to stop walking away from situations when you get angry. Can you do that for me?"

Jaylin didn't say a word. He started the truck and drove off. In less than thirty minutes, we were home. Frick was supposed to be there in an hour. I knew Jaylin wasn't up to our meeting. I told him to call Frick to see if he could come by later.

"Naw, let's get this over with," he said, tossing his jacket on the bed. He walked out of the room. I could tell how upset he was about me not being pregnant.

Almost an hour later, Frick showed up. Jaylin invited him in. Once he toured him around the house, they took a seat in the Great Room. Shortly after, the doorbell rang again and I answered. It was an attorney, Mr. Perry, whom I recently retained to help me with this matter. He walked in and I introduced him to Jaylin and Mr. Frick. They both stood up and shook his hand. Jaylin gave me a strange look, but there was no way for me to go through these contracts with Jaylin and Frick without representation. Frick always had Jaylin's back, and I knew for a fact that he wasn't happy about Jaylin's decision to do this.

"Please have a seat," I said to Mr. Perry. He was a sharp dresser and reminded me a lot of P Diddy. Jaylin and Frick looked him over from head to toe.

Remaining calm, I took a seat right next to Jaylin. I didn't want him to feel that I was against him because I wasn't. I just had to make sure some things . . . well, a lot of things changed.

Frick pulled out three stacks of papers. He kept a copy, handed one to Jaylin and gave the other to me. I gave my copy to my attorney and looked at Jaylin's copy with him. As Frick started to read it, within the first paragraph, we already had some issues. My attorney complained about the constant uses of the words, "reversal" and "termination of contract."

Perry looked at Jaylin. "Mr. Rogers, maybe your attorney isn't clear about what your wife is asking. All of this is unnecessary. The second paragraph states that, the seven bank accounts listed above shall be transferred in the name of Nokea Rogers and she shall remain the primary signee on such accounts so as long as, a) . . . b) . . . c) . . . d) . . . e) . . . f) . . ., etc. If any of these instances shall arise, then all of the above accounts shall revert back to the previous signee and owner of the accounts, Jaylin J. Rogers, and this entire agreement becomes null and void." Mr. Perry looked at Mr. Frick. "Give me a break. If Mrs. Rogers even sneezes, this contract terminates. You didn't expect for her to sign anything like this, did you?"

Frick looked at Jaylin. "I'm just trying to be reasonable and do what's best for you. If you want to make any changes, just let me know."

Jaylin sat back on the couch and rested his arms on top of it. "I know you got my back, but let's do this and do it right."

Frick cut his eyes and continued. Every single paragraph, Mr. Perry tore it apart. I couldn't believe the many stipulations Frick had put into the contract. I think even Jaylin got frustrated. Either way, we spent the next several hours, "working things out." What shocked me the most was when Frick revealed Jaylin's total "money on hand." I was in disbelief. After all this time, I never knew what it was. I didn't ask because his money didn't faze me. All I knew was, we didn't want for anything. Everything we wanted was well within our reach. I'd estimated more than ten but less than fifteen million, but the totals revealed in the contract averaged out to be approximately $41.9 million dollars. Those totals were only his "money on hand" and did not account for his net worth. Frick never specified what that was. The bank account statements showed earned interest on money he'd had in the bank for many years. His stocks and mutual funds had made him a fortune, and several real estate deals he'd gotten into since we moved to Florida had really paid off. I was amazed and the expression on my face showed it. As his wife, how could I not know about all of this? Jaylin had never mentioned any of this to me. If I had known he had this much, I never would have asked him for such a huge request.

Once all of the changes were worked over, Frick lay several authorization papers in front of Jaylin. One by one, Jaylin signed them. Before he signed the last one, he turned his head and looked at me.

"I told you I'd do anything for you, didn't I?" he said. He scribbled his signature, dropped the pen on the table, stood up and looked at Frick. "I got a headache so I'm going to get some rest. Thanks for everything. Once all of the amendments are made, make sure we receive copies."

He shook hands with Frick, then with Mr. Perry. As Jaylin walked off to our room, he told me to walk them out of *my* house. He smiled, giving me a wink.

I thanked Frick and Mr. Perry for their time and escorted them to the door. Once they left, I went to our bedroom. Jaylin was lying sideways on the bed. His eyes focused on the TV, but I knew he saw me come through the door. I went over to the bed and lay sideways in front of him.

"I hope you're not angry with me," I said. "I'm deeply sorry about the baby and had I known you had so much money, I never would have asked you to do that."

"You didn't stop me, did you? But, I'm not bitter about the money, Nokea. I have no problem sharing my wealth with you. My only concern right now is having another baby. I hate like hell what happened to you. I can't stop blaming myself for these mistakes I keep—"

I touched the side of his handsome face. "Don't be so hard on yourself. I'm the one who went ballistic and didn't see those steps. I promise you that some way or somehow I will give you another child. Right now, let's just enjoy the two that we have. If or when another pregnancy happens, it just happens."

Jaylin leaned in to kiss me and I kissed him back.

"Let's get out of here and go get something to eat. I'm in the mood for steak and shrimp," he said.

"That sounds delicious."

We left the house and drove to a quiet seafood restaurant we'd gone to on several occasions. The place was expensive, but they had the best seafood I'd eaten thus far. The waiter sat us at a cozy wide booth that had a hanging ceiling fan above it. The table was covered with a crisp white tablecloth and a lit scented candle was in the middle. The entire restaurant was dimly lit. As I looked around, all I saw were a bunch of couples who looked to be enjoying each other's company.

Once I scooted into the booth, Jaylin eased in beside me. There was plenty of room across the table, but I guess he wanted to be close to me. When the waiter asked what we wanted to drink, I suggested water and Jaylin asked for a bottle of wine. Before the waiter left, he lay the menus on the table and told us he'd be back with our drinks.

Jaylin picked up the menu and looked at it. "Since I don't have much money, I'm on a budget. You don't mind picking up the tab, do you?" he said.

"If you were on a budget, then you wouldn't have just ordered a bottle of wine that cost one hundred and fifty dollars. So, no, I'm not picking up the tab, you are. Besides, looking at the prices of this food, I can't afford it."

Jaylin smiled and stared at me. His eyes dropped to my lips and he gave me a peck. Afterward, his hand touched my thigh and he rubbed it. "Do you have buttons on your pants or a zipper?"

"What?" I said, thinking. "My pants have buttons. Why?"

"I was just wondering. I checked out how nice you looked in them, that's all."

"These are my favorite brown pants and short jacket combination. I like the way the pants lay on my waistline and hug my hips."

"Let me see," Jaylin said. "I don't know what you mean when you say lay on your waistline."

I sat back and slightly lifted my peach fitted shirt. I felt around my waistline and patted my hips so Jaylin could see.

"Yeah, I had noticed that too, but, uh, I like the way the pants display your tiny gap and raise that ass."

I lowered my shirt. "I knew you were leading to something ridiculous. I don't have a gap and my butt isn't anything spectacular."

"Have you lost your mind?" Jaylin laughed. "If your butt wasn't anything spectacular, I wouldn't have married you."

"So, you married me for my butt?"

He didn't respond and I gave him a shove. He turned slightly and placed his hand on my flat stomach. "Yes, Nokea, I married you for your butt. I married you for your pretty eyes, your gorgeous hair and your sexy lips. Most of all, I married you for loving me as you do and for being such a great mother to our children. How could I ask for more?"

Jaylin kissed me again, but this time, his hand lowered to the top button on my pants. The button came loose. When he unbuttoned the second button, I placed my hand over his.

"What do you think you're doing?" I asked.

"I'm about to have some fun. This place is boring and it needs a little excitement in here."

"We're in a restaurant. How exciting do you want it to be?"

He went for the last two buttons on my pants and unbuttoned them. Using the tablecloth to hide his activity, he touched my silk panties, and then moved them to the side. His finger rotated around my clit, and then separated my slit. I squeezed my legs tightly together and whispered.

"Now isn't the time to do this. I can't believe you're doing this here." I saw the waiter coming our way and leaned slightly forward. He put my water in front of me and poured out Jaylin's and my wine. Trying not to be obvious, I sat still.

"Are you ready to order?" he asked.

Jaylin kept his hand in place, dipping his finger in and out of me. He looked at the waiter. "I am in the mood to *eat* something really, really good. You know, something that makes my mouth water. Something tasty . . . but sweet. What would you recommend?"

As the waiter talked, Jaylin continued to work his finger. I was soaking wet, and the tighter I squeezed, the more force he used.

I sighed, placing my hand over his underneath the tablecloth. I tried to move his hand, but he was too strong.

"That all sounds good," Jaylin said, once the waiter finished speaking. "But, I won't be satisfied with just any ole steak. Are you sure the steak you have will whet my appetite? I am very hungry and I like my meat thick and juicy. What kind of white creamy sauces do you have?"

The waiter told Jaylin about the sauces. As the waiter spoke, Jaylin turned his fingers inside of me, teasing my clit with his thumb. I put my elbows on the table, dropping my forehead in my hands. I interrupted the waiter.

"Sir, could . . . Would you do me a huge favor? I like lemon with my water and I'm really thirsty. Would you mi—" I paused and slowly sucked in some air. "Mind getting me a few cut up lemons?"

"Sure," the waiter said, and then walked away.

I looked at Jaylin. "You've got to sto . . . stop it, now," I whispered.

"But you are so, so close," he said. "I feel it."

I was very close to coming. As I felt myself getting ready to, I tightened my legs and crossed my arms on the table. I lowered my head into my arms to hide my expression. My muffled lips didn't allow me to say what I wanted to. I was so glad when it was all over. When the waiter came back over to us, Jaylin removed his hand and rubbed my back with his other hand.

"Baby, are you feeling okay?" he asked. "I think my wife is feeling a bit ill. She might want to get out of here."

I sat up and looked at the waiter. He had already put my lemons on the table. "No, I'm fine. I am really hungry. Once I get back from the restroom, I'll be ready to order. Give us about ten more minutes, please?"

The waiter smiled and walked away again. I scooted Jaylin over with my hips. "Move," I said. "I need to go to the restroom. You know better than to do something like that."

Jaylin rubbed his finger around his lips and then sucked it. "I told you I was hungry. I don't know why you keep depriving me, but that's what you get. Now, is it on tonight or what?"

"Maybe, but we'll talk about this more after dinner. Now, move."

As he moved over, I quickly buttoned my pants and picked up my hand held purse. I scooted out of the booth and stood up. Jaylin leaned over, whispering in my ear. "I don't care what you say, that pussy been missing me. You gon' be in the bathroom for a minute, so when the waiter comes back, I'll go ahead and order for you."

I rolled my eyes at him and walked off.

Dinner was spectacular. Jaylin and I were full as can be and I was slightly tipsy from helping Jaylin drink two bottles of wine. The night was full of laughs. This was one of the best nights we'd had in a long time.

When we got back to the house it was late. I took off my clothes, changed into my nightgown and plopped down in bed. Doing the norm, Jaylin cuddled with me and held me in his arms.

"You're not going to stay up with me?" he asked.

"Baby, I am tired. I will see you in the morning."

Jaylin kissed my cheek and I was out.

What seemed like hours later, I woke up and turned in bed. When I reached over for Jaylin, he wasn't there. I looked at the alarm clock. It showed three forty-five in the morning. Anxious to know where he was, I pulled the covers back and got out of bed. After searching around the house, he was nowhere in sight. I looked in the garage but all of the cars were there, including his Hummer that he normally drove. I returned to our bedroom, and stepped outside on the balcony to look down on the beach. I could see Jaylin sitting on the sand near the water. He had on a pair of shorts, but his chest was bare. I wanted to join him, so I went into the closet to look for something to put on. I thought about a swimming suit, but I decided against it. Instead, I looked through my lingerie to see what I could put on. I knew what he was in the mood for and I had sexy attire for whatever mood I thought he'd be in. I left the silk long pieces on the hangers, and found a pair of pink panties

Jaylin had bought me, with a strapless half top that matched. Once I dolled myself up in the bathroom, I rubbed my body with some smell good lotion and tied the panties low on my hips. I looked at my hard nipples poking through the skimpy fitted top and turned to look at the panties that barely covered my butt. Pleased with what I had on, I left the bathroom to go keep my man company.

Since it was in the wee hours of the morning, I didn't expect anyone to be on the beach. Barefoot, I made my way outside. When I got close to Jaylin, I quietly crept up, making my way in front of him. While sitting on a towel with his knees bent, he looked up at me. His eyes searched my body. Without saying a word, he reached for my hand and pulled me to him. He got on his knees, laying the side of his head against my stomach.

"You looked as if you needed some company. Don't you want to go inside?" I asked.

"No," he said. He turned his face, placing tender kisses on my midsection. He then turned me around and untied both sides of my panties. They fell to the sand. After Jaylin kissed my butt cheeks, he turned me back around.

"Why you out here naked?" he asked. "If our neighbors look outside, you know they can see you."

Jaylin pecked my coochie, but before he could go any further, I backed into the water. It was warm and I stepped back until the water met up with my hips. I removed my top and let it float in the water. "Can they see me now?" I asked.

Jaylin looked behind him, turned back around and then smiled. "When a shark bites that fat-ass, I ain't gon' see you either."

"Well, I thought it was your job to protect me. I can count on you to protect me, can't I?"

Jaylin stood up, stepped out of his shorts and came into the water with me. He held me, as I wrapped my legs around his waist. I moved my wet flat bangs away from my eyes so I could see all of him. I could tell he wanted to say some-thing, but the look in his eyes implied that he didn't know how to say it.

"Words . . . no words can express how sorry—"

I placed my fingers on his lips. "I'd really like to go inside so we can sample the rooms like we always do. But if we stay out here," I said, "you'd better make it good."

Jaylin held my face in his hands, while search-ing deep into my eyes. "I need your forgiveness, Nokea. I can't stop thinking about what I've done to you. This time, I went too far. No matter what, though, I hope you know that I love no one but you. You do know that, don't you?"

I nodded and closed my eyes as I thought about my time with Shane. I wanted to tell Jaylin how sorry I was for what I'd done, but this was our time to heal from the mistakes that had been made in the past.

"I forgive you," I said. "What's done is done. We've got to get beyond this."

With Jaylin's hardness pressing against me, it made me anxious for him. He carried me out of the shallow water, laying me back on the towel that covered the sand. As he sucked my breasts, I raked his hair with my fingers, while looking up at the beautiful star lit sky. My eyes welled with tears, as I thought about how much I love him. My mind wouldn't let me think about what we'd been through, only where we were headed. I knew that only good things awaited us, and for that, I felt grateful.

The sudsy water occasionally rolled in, splashing on our naked bodies. Jaylin had already entered me, causing a deep arch to form in my back. My legs were wide open, and I accepted the pleasurable beating that his big dick was giving to me. As his wife, I mastered how to hang with him. We had perfected our love making skills. I knew what he wanted, and he also knew what my body needed. He got gentler with his strokes, stirring up my juices and waiting for them to flow. Within a few minutes, I had reached the level only he was capable of getting me to. My body gave off vibrations, from the tips of my toes, to my hands that I had squeezed tightly. Jaylin dipped low to catch my raining cum, and from the way he cleaned me with his mouth, I suspected not one single drop went to waste. He licked his lips from one side to the other, teasing me about tasting my clit that he often referred to as his "juicy raisin in the sun." He made it clear that he was in no way finished with me and I welcomed more. As we changed positions, the heated sex session went on. I kissed Jaylin over and over again, rubbing my face against his.

"How could you ever want more than this?" I whispered in his ear. "I love you and no one will ever love you as much as I do."

Jaylin's strokes and kisses came to a halt. He looked down at me with red eyes. "I know. I will do everything in my power to make you trust me again."

We continued to express our love for each other. That day, along with so many others, was one of the best days of my life. There was no way in hell I would ever allow another woman to take this feeling away from me. Scorpio was a darn . . . damn fool if she ever thought Jaylin would walk away from something as secure and good as this.

Chapter 23

Shane

It was Saturday and I took a break from all the hard work I'd been doing. Since I had not been in a committed relationship with anyone, I'd become a workaholic. Work kept my mind off things. I didn't have much time to think about how Scorpio had played me, or my feelings for Nokea. It wasn't as if I couldn't get over my feelings for her, but she did leave quite an impression on me. I guess my connection to her made me realize that maybe I didn't love Scorpio as much as I thought I did. For both of us to be able to move on so quickly, that pretty much said a lot about our relationship.

For the time being, an old friend Amber and I were kicking down heavy conversations over the phone. I hadn't gone to see her yet, and I hadn't invited her to my place either. For a very long time, she'd been my late night booty call woman and I'd cut her off during my relationship with Scorpio. I didn't feel right running to Amber again because I knew her feelings were strong for me. Thing is, I just wasn't feeling her as much. She was very good company, was dynamite in bed, but still, there was something about her that I couldn't connect with.

Around 10:00 A.M., I started lifting weights in my office. The place was crammed, but it was so easy for me to handle my business and work out in the same room. Working out relaxed me. Once I finished, I took off my sweaty wife beater and lay it on the bench. To contain my sweat, I tied a red, white and blue scarf around my head. Then I changed into a pair of painter's pants I had previously lay on my desk. My plans were to paint the day away, so I gathered my materials and started to work on a painting I hadn't touched in months. I was so indulged, that when the phone rang, I ignored it. It rang again, so I tapped the speaker button to answer.

"Yes," I griped.

"Good morning," Amber said. "I was on my way to a home décor show at the convention center. I'm calling to see if you'd like to go with me."

I kept painting. "Naw, no thanks. I'll catch you next time."

"Come on, Shane. All you do is work, work, and work. You need to have a little fun, don't you?"

"Right now, I'm having a lot of fun. Trust me."

"Do you have company?"

"No, I'm painting. Let me finish up and give you a call later."

"Sure, but, uh, I was wondering if I could stop by. I made some delicious blueberry muffins this morning and I couldn't help but think of you."

That's what I didn't like about Amber. She had a hard time accepting the word no. I knew if I told her I wasn't in the mood for muffins, her feelings would be hurt.

"Amber, feel free to bring the muffins by. I can't entertain for long because I'm busy, okay?"

"Sure," she said. "I'm on my way."

I hung up and straddled the stool in front of my picture to get back to it.

Almost thirty minutes later, the doorbell rang. I was surprised to see Scorpio outside. At first, I wasn't going to invite her in. Instead, I did.

"What brings you by?" I asked.

"Since you haven't returned my three measly phone calls, I figured you were still upset with me. You've avoided me for long enough. I wanted to stop by to say hello, that's all."

"I'm a little busy this morning," I said, walking back to my office. She followed, and by the way she was dressed in her fitted soft blue skirt and low cut blouse, I knew she was there to get my attention. I straddled the stool again and continued with my picture.

"Talk," I said, as she stood close by me.

"Where do I start?" In her high heels, she switched over to the chair behind my desk and took a seat. "Shane, I—"

The phone interrupted her, and instead of picking it up, I hit the speaker button again. "Yes!" I yelled.

"Shane," Jaylin said.

"What?"

"I'm about to tell you something that I never, ever thought I'd say before."

I looked at Scorpio who was tuned in. "And, what may that be?"

"My dick is out of order! This muthafucka is tired and it can no longer function. Nokea . . ."

I jumped up and quickly put the phone to my ear. I also looked at Scorpio, but she turned her head.

"Jay, what did you say? I couldn't hear you?"

"I said . . . I am tired. Man, I must be getting old because, believe it or not, after two or three consecutive days of sex, I need a day to rest. Nokea is over here like the energizer bunny."

I laughed and so did Jaylin. "Well, maybe you are getting old. Going at it for two or three consecutive days doesn't seem like a problem."

"I mean, all day, and every day. For me not to handle Nokea, it says I'm slacking."

I looked at Scorpio again and decided to end my call. "Hey, Jay, let me get at you a li'l later. I got company right now."

"Is it Scorpio?" he asked.

"Yes."

"Did you find that out for me?"

"I'm getting ready to. Like I said, I'll hit you up later."

"Cool," Jaylin said and hung up.

I put the phone down and headed back to my stool. "Sorry about that," I said. "I didn't expect for him to say that, but Jaylin is full of surprises."

"You got that right," she said, clearing her throat. "So, I guess him and Nokea worked things out? I don't understand how, but Jaylin has a way with her, me, and everybody else."

"You know better than anybody, don't you? But, I'm sure that Jaylin turning all of his finances over to Nokea might have helped speed along the forgiveness process."

"He did what?" Scorpio yelled. "Are you kidding me?"

"No, I'm serious. He gave her everything, including the house. She requested that everything be in her name, and because he loves her, he did as she asked."

"Bullshit, Shane. If Jaylin turned everything over to Nokea, it was because of guilt. I doubt that he gave her everything. That doesn't sound like the Jaylin I know."

"Well, I'm not going to argue with you about it. I'm just telling you what he told me. Besides, a man doesn't turn over forty plus million dollars to a woman he doesn't truly love, especially without a court order. Maybe you need to face the facts about them and realize that nothing you can do will separate them."

Scorpio tooted her lips, still in denial.

"I don't care what you say. Jaylin would never share forty million dollars with anyone. Now, he might have given Nokea a little security to keep her mouth shut, but I can't see anything more than that. If he loves her so much, then he wouldn't have shared his bed with me."

"I would share with you my theory about that, but I don't want to hurt your feelings. I will, however, say one word to you, and I hope you figure out the rest—convenience. The bottom line is, they experienced a very difficult time in their marriage. Because of the love and history they share, they prevailed. You, I or nobody will ever come between them and that's a fact. Now, I suggest that you wake up from this imaginary dream you're having, and have had for a very long time. You'll never have Jaylin, Scorpio. You finalized our relationship for what you thought could have been, and you fucked up. I'm damn mad about it. You allowed Jaylin to step into this and break us apart. Now, he's living happily ever after, and look at us. Our so called love damn sure didn't hold up. I could kick myself for loving you. Thank you for opening my eyes."

She folded her arms and tried to defend what she'd done. "I'm upset too, Shane, but I never would have turned to Jaylin had you not lied to me."

"That's bullshit and you know it. At least woman up and fess up to your mess. I have serious problems with a woman who doesn't admit when she's wrong. If I can admit to being wrong for lying, so can you."

She sat with a frustrated look on her face and didn't say a word. The doorbell rang. I dropped my paint brush on the easel.

"Stay right here," I said. "I'll be back."

Amber was at the door. She came inside with the muffins covered in a basket. I hadn't seen her in a while and her long hair made her look different. It was parted through the middle and flowed down the sides of her face. Her trench coat was opened and showed her frame that looked as if it had thickened up a bit. She removed her glasses and stood tall in the foyer with me.

"My, don't you look sexy," she said, observing my cut six pack. "Were you working out?" she asked.

"I was earlier, but I'm finished."

She handed the basket to me and moved in close. She placed her hand on my chest, rubbing my solid abs. "If you'd like to *catch up*, the home décor show can wait. I can give you one of those amazing back rubs I always give you and—"

"And, he's busy right now," Scorpio interrupted. "Can you and your basket of whatever that is come back once we're finished?"

I turned my attention to Scorpio. "Hold up," I said. "Please don't come out here giving my guest any orders. I got this, all right?"

Amber took a quick glance at Scorpio and quickly addressed me. "I thought you said you didn't have company. Had I known, Shane, I never would have come here."

"I didn't know she was coming over here. She'll be leaving shortly. Still, is it necessary for me to explain?"

Amber shrugged her shoulders. "I . . . I guess not. Surely by now, I should know the rules, right?"

"I couldn't agree with you more. But, uh, listen . . . I appreciate you bringing the muffins by. I'm sure I'll like them. Have fun at the décor show and call me when you get home. We'll talk then."

Amber looked over my shoulder at Scorpio, put her glasses back on and pecked my lips.

"Be good," she said, and opened the door. She winked at me and closed the door behind her.

"Just like your friend, neither one of you waste much time on going after the next best thing. How long has this been going on?" Scorpio asked.

I ignored Scorpio and walked by her. She grabbed my arm and squeezed it.

"So that's how it is, huh?" she asked. "You and I break up and you immediately run to another woman? I can't believe you, Shane. Even though I've made some mistakes, you've made plenty of them too. I forgave you on numerous occasions. Have you even thought about forgiving me?"

"Forgive you? Oh, I forgive you, but if you think that you and I are going to patch things up, you are out of your mind. I care deeply for you, Scorpio, but I will not be your fool. You made your choice. Unfortunately, your choice didn't work out for you. Don't think you can run back to me and I'm supposed to rescue you again from your let down from Jaylin. I did it once and it backfired. There's no way in hell I'm doing it again."

I pulled away from her and went back into my office. Getting back to my picture, I picked up my brush, and did my best to ignore Scorpio. She stood beside me and touched the side of my face.

"I'm not going to say I'm sorry because I know how you feel about those words. What can I say, other than I lost out on a good thing. You knew how I felt about Jaylin and so did I. I should have never gone back to him, but a part of me felt the need. You know that I never meant to disappoint you, don't you?"

I moved her hand away from my face. "I never meant to disappoint you either, but I want out of this Scorpio. This thing between all of us is driving me fucking crazy. I need closure, and you and Nokea need to stop using me to get at Jaylin. It's ridiculous and I'm tired of it."

"What does Nokea have to do with this? How do you feel as if she's used you?" I ignored Scorpio and continued to paint. "Shane, be honest. Did you and Nokea . . ."

"No," I said, sternly. "Now, if you don't mind, I'd like to finish my picture. I didn't make plans for this conversation today, and I'm really not feeling up to it."

Scorpio stared at me. From the corner of my eye, I could see her suspicions growing. "Every time I mention Nokea, you get real defensive. You can ignore me, but I can tell that something is up with you. Jaylin and I weren't the only two who had sex. You and Nokea did too, didn't you?"

I ignored Scorpio and when she continued to press for answers, I asked her to leave.

"I'm not going to discuss anything with you," I said. "Like I said, it never happened and you can believe whatever you'd like to."

"You are not good at lying and you need to stop it. You can protect her all you want, but I plan to make sure Jaylin knows about his precious wife. The both of you put Nokea up so high on a pedestal, and she's no damn better than me. She manipulates the both of you. If she convinced you to have sex with her, and not tell Jaylin, then you are a fool. A big fool."

"Scorpio, again, I'm going to ask you to leave. I don't have time for this, baby. Whatever has happened, I'm done with it. I'm out of this, and I don't know what else you want from me."

She continued to press and would not leave. "Just so I can sleep at night for what I've done,

I want nothing but the truth from you. I need to hear you tell me that you and Nokea were intimate without being forced."

"I'm not telling you shit. You go ahead and take that mess to Jaylin. I assure you he's going to laugh behind your back. You need to face it, no matter what you say or try to do, it's over Scorpio. Find a fresh new start elsewhere. You blew it with me, but maybe you'll have success with someone else."

Scorpio leaned down and whispered in my ear. "We'll just see about all of this. When the truth comes out, you'll have to look me in my face and admit that you fucked up, too. I'll be waiting, Shane. Maybe, once you face reality, you and I can begin to work this out. You let me know, okay?"

Scorpio walked out. When I heard the door slam, I got back to painting. I forgot to ask about her period, so I hurried to call her. She answered her phone in a sharp voice.

"What?" she said.

"I didn't want us to end our conversation on a bitter note. I hope we can still be friends. I think maybe your anger stirred from you having a bad day, or you're just suffering from PMS or something."

"My day was going along just fine, until I came over there. I already had my period this month, so you can't go blaming PMS for something you brought on yourself. We'll always be good friends, but at this time, distant friends work better for me."

She hung up and I took a deep breath. I wasn't sure if I should call Jaylin to confirm Scorpio's period, or if I should call Nokea to warn her.

"Damn!" I yelled. I wanted out of this mess so badly, but shit just kept on happening.

Chapter 24

Scorpio

I didn't expect for anyone to feel sorry for me because I brought this situation on myself. My love for Jaylin was something I couldn't control. If I had to do it all over again, I'd go see him again. Hell, if I can't be with the man I want, then so be it. Maybe I wasn't cut out for the marriage thing. I guess it's time I started to accept that.

After I left Shane's place, I quickly had a change of heart. I wasn't telling Jaylin anything. If Nokea had screwed Shane, then more power to her. The way Jaylin had played me was downright uncalled for, and for him to call Shane and brag about all the sex he and Nokea had been having, that was gut wrenching. Thing is, Shane was wrong by saying I hadn't faced reality. I had a feeling that Jaylin and Nokea would stay together, but why cry about it when I know that

Jaylin will never be happy with just one woman. No doubt, he will come back to me again, and how can a man like him forget what I'm capable of putting on him? Like he said, we have a sexual connection, and that connection will drive him back to me each and every time Nokea can't get her shit together. I've prepared myself to cope with the situation. Until I meet a man who can shake me from feeling any differently, my attitude will stay the same. Unfortunately, because Shane was so close to Jaylin, he stayed in my thoughts. Under the circumstances, there was no way for me to get over him. I had fooled myself, and just like Shane, I felt like fuck it!

As for his trick, Amber, I was mad that Shane seemed to have moved on. Amber had nothing on me and he knew it. No curves, no nothing. She was a plain Jane and I knew she couldn't give Shane what he really wanted. Eventually, he'd come running back to me too. Whether I decided to ever deal with him again depended on my status. Yes, I intended to take a break from men. I'd had enough. Relationships brought about too many headaches and heartbreaks. Being with Shane taught me a lot, but nobody taught me more than Jaylin. He was unbelievable, and talk about game . . . the brotha had it! He had a lot more to add with his game, and the total package he continues to deliver will forever be my weakness. It was kind of funny, though, that he couldn't find it in his heart to give up his precious wife. For me, I promised myself there would be no more tears. There would be no more losing my mind. There would be no more Jaylin or Shane, until I say so, especially if Jaylin had put Nokea in charge of his money. I still didn't believe it. I didn't know he even had that much money. If Nokea had been smart enough to get that much money into her possession, then I had to give credit where credit was due. Definitely, she had his ass exactly where she wanted him, but it wasn't as if she ever didn't.

Chapter 25

Shane

Whichever one of them answered the phone, that's who I was going to speak to. I dialed the Rogers' place, and after four rings Nokea answered.

"What's up?" I said, always happy to hear her voice.

"Hi, Shane. Long time no hear from. I know you've been talking to Jaylin, but I don't get a chance to talk to you anymore."

"That might be for the best," I laughed. "But, uh, is Jaylin around? If not, I need to talk to you about something."

"I think he's outside somewhere with the kids. What's up? Is everything okay?"

"So-so. Today, I spoke to Scorpio and some things I said led her to believe that you and I had sex. I didn't confirm anything, but she is determined to call Jaylin and make him aware of her suspicions. I just wanted to warn you, and make it clear to you that I will not tell anyone what happened between us, unless you ask me to. I might not say anything if you ask me to because there's a lot of damage that can occur. You know what I mean, don't you?"

"Yes, I do. I appreciate you calling me. Jaylin and I are managing to work things out. I'd hate for something like this to surface and put us back where we started. A part of me wants to tell him the truth. I know if Scorpio speaks to him, he's going to question me about it again. Honestly, I don't know what I'm going to say. I love my husband, but I do not regret giving myself to you before court that day. It was a beautiful time, but I know we're past that now. These last several weeks have been wonderful for Jaylin and me. My wish is that you someday find true love as I have. You really deserve it."

"I know. When the time is right, my time will come. I'm in no rush, you know?"

Nokea laughed. Before we ended our call, I told her to tell Jaylin to call me.

Chapter 26

Jaylin

I was shocked as hell, as I held the phone in my hand and listened to the entire conversation. I knew Nokea had given herself to him, damn, I knew it! Never in my life had I felt like such a fool. For the both of them to lie to me about the shit was unforgivable.

Why didn't I just listen to my gut? What made me trust Nokea and Shane more than I trusted myself? I couldn't believe that she made me out to be the villain, when all along, she had fucked my friend. And, Shane, his words were so convincing. "I wouldn't do that to you, Jay. I've had my way with Scorpio, but I know Nokea is off limits."

Bullshit! Was all I could say. No word in the English dictionary explained how I felt.

I put the phone down, took several deep breaths to calm myself and made my way into the bedroom where Nokea was. I couldn't even think straight. There was so much anger inside of me. Before somebody got hurt, I needed to get out of the house—fast!

I entered our bedroom. Nokea was sitting in the chair, while paging through an *Ebony* magazine. She looked up at me. By the look on my face, she knew something was wrong.

"Who was that on the phone?" I asked.

"Nobody, the caller had the wrong number. Where . . . where are the kids?" she asked.

"They're outside with Nanny B." I sat on the bed, roughly massaging my hands together. "I need to go, uh, take care of something for a couple of days."

She closed the magazine, giving me her attention. "What . . . Where and what for?"

"Frick said there were some issues with the paperwork. He's not coming here, so I have to go there."

"Would you like for me to go with you?"

"No, I need . . . I'm going alone. The kids need you and I don't want to leave them with Nanny B."

Not saying another word, I got up and went into my closet. I put a few things in my suitcase and removed my keys from the nightstand.

Nokea stopped me. "Why are you rushing out of here Jaylin? Tell me, is something wrong?"

I shook my head and stepped up to her. I touched the side of her face and kissed her cheek. "I'm cool. This is so important to me. I gotta go now so I can take care of this. I'll call you as soon as I get there."

Nokea nodded and I left the room. Hurrying, I said good-bye to Nanny B and the kids, then left.

Going to see Frick in St. Louis was not on my agenda. I got a room at a nearby hotel and checked in. I was so numb. I didn't know where to begin. I wanted to fuck Shane up, and Nokea too, I hated the thoughts of what I wanted to do to her. Before I did anything, I needed time to think. My mind was saying . . . kick her ass to the curb, but my heart was trying to understand.

Yes, I'd cheated on Nokea, but she was supposed to be better than me. That's what I loved so much about her. If I wanted a woman like me, then I would have married Scorpio. I knew Nokea could tell something was up, but I was drained from arguing with her. Looking at her made me want to snap, but something was holding me back.

Until I figured out what I wanted to do, I planned to stay at the hotel in Florida and chill. It seemed like the logical thing to do, so once I checked into the room, I put my suitcase on the floor, stripped down to my jockey shorts and got in the bed. For a while, I just lay there. Then, I thought about it. My name is Jaylin Jerome Rogers. This was my world and so many women lived in it! I searched through my wallet and pulled out Mia's business card that I'd found in Nokea's drawer. I fumbled through several other phone numbers I'd picked up from time to time, totaling sixteen different phone numbers. I visualized these ladies in my mind and thought about my next move. Definitely, the numbers had come in handy, but the big question was . . . what was I going to do with them?

Chapter 27

Nokea

Something with Jaylin wasn't right and I knew it. I didn't think Scorpio had called him that fast, but maybe she did. If she had, I was 100 percent sure he would have said something to me. Just to be sure nothing was up, I called Frick and he confirmed Jaylin's appointment. Still feeling uneasy, I called Shane and he told me to calm down.

"If Scorpio had called Jaylin, he would have called me or said something to you," he said.

"But Shane, you should have seen the look on his face. He looked worried. I'd never seen him get out of this house so fast. I . . . I need to talk to Scorpio. Would you please contact her and ask her to call me? That's the only way I'll feel at ease with this."

"If it upsets you that much, then tell him the truth. He'll forgive you, but you know him and me might have some challenges. I'm game, though, and whatever happens, it just happens."

"No, I don't want your and Jaylin's friendship to end. You mean a lot to him, and for those months you all didn't speak, I could tell it bothered him. We have to keep this a secret. As long as we continue to deny it, everything will be fine."

"However you want to handle this, I'm with you. Now, I will contact Scorpio and ask her to call you, but I don't know if she'll do it."

"Just see for me, okay? I want to find out if she's spoken to Jaylin."

Shane hung up. Almost fifteen minutes later, Scorpio called. When I answered the phone, she responded, "What do you want?"

"Scorpio, I talked to Shane. He mentioned to me that you intended to contact Jaylin about some serious accusations. I truly wish you wouldn't do that. Haven't we all been through enough? Can you find it in your heart to move on and leave my husband and me in peace? You shouldn't live your life this way. I can't believe you have wasted so much time on a man who clearly doesn't want you."

"Oh, I doubt that, but to hell with you and Jaylin. I haven't spoken to him, nor do I intend to reveal your sneaky ways. I truly believe that you had sex with Shane, because history always repeats itself. Just like you used Stephon, you also used Shane. Someday, Jaylin will see you for what you really are. Where in the hell does anybody get off by thinking you're so much better than me? If and when Jaylin learns of your infidelities, it won't come from me. If I had the facts, surely, I'd present them to him. Since I don't have much to go on, for now, you're good. Just for the record, if he ever needs me, I will always be there for him. You hear me . . . Always, Nokea so, enjoy your fame and fortune while it lasts."

Scorpio hung up and I held the phone in my hand. I realized there was no way Jaylin knew anything so I waited to hear from him.

Finally, that night, Jaylin called around midnight. I was worried about him, but glad that he called.

"I had a delay at the airport," he said. "Because of the weather, there are a lot of power outages in St. Louis. If you need me, call me on my cell phone, okay?"

"Okay, but how much longer will you be?"

"Hopefully, Frick and I will be able to wrap up things in a day or two. I will let you know, soon."

"Okay. Hurry home. I love you."

He hesitated. "Me too."

Jaylin hung up and I felt relieved. Not only that, but I felt sick. I covered my mouth and rushed to the bathroom.

Chapter 28

Jaylin

After two nights at the hotel, I was ready to go home. I had been in touch with Frick and was waiting for the paperwork to be delivered to me at the hotel. As soon as FedEx delivered the papers, I read over everything, nodded my head with acceptance, and without any hesitation, I signed.

My decision had been made. Knowing what kind of man I was, there was no way I could deal with Nokea having sex with Shane. Realistically speaking, I'd make her pay for it through my own infidelities. If I did step out on the marriage, I'd lose everything. I wasn't prepared to do that. A couple of things that saved me in those contracts were clauses that stated, if I filed for a divorce from Nokea, and no infidelities had been committed on my behalf, then the contracts were void. Her name would be removed from everything. In addition to that, if Nokea had ever been unfaithful to me, she was subject to whatever financial offer I made to her. By signing her name on the dotted line, she agreed to it, and assured me that no infidelities had been committed on her part. How could she keep lying to me? The thoughts of what she'd done made me furious. It was time to get this show on the road.

Feeling as if I didn't have much of a choice, I was satisfied with everything. I left the hotel to present her with our divorce papers. I knew this wasn't going to be easy, but this was about nobody but me. I felt hurt, betrayed, and numb at the same time. I didn't intend to leave Nokea with nothing. By all means, she deserved part of what I had. The house was hers and I was prepared to offer her one fourth of my money. At this point, all that really mattered were the kids. I wanted custody of them, but I knew she'd want it too. Joint custody would give me limited time with my kids. The thought of it devastated me.

As I drove back to our house, I couldn't stop visualizing Shane making love to my wife. I was full of emotions. As I waited at the light, I rubbed my eyes with my fingertips. Soon, my cell phone rang. When I looked to see who it was, it was Nokea.

"Yes," I answered.

"I know I've been bugging you, but the kids and I miss you. Will you be home soon?"

"I'm on my way. I'll be there shortly."

"Okay. You sound tired, are you?"

"Very. I'm feeling a bit sick too."

"I'll have Nanny B whip up some chicken noodle soup for you. You know I can't make it like she does." Nokea laughed.

"Yeah, that might help. I'll see you in a minute."

I hung up. Driving home seemed like the longest drive of my life.

When I got there, I pulled into the driveway and turned off the lights. It was dark outside, but I stayed in my truck for fifteen more minutes. I gazed over the divorce papers again and folded them in my hand. I was sure about what I needed to do, but paced back and forth before going to the door. Once inside, nothing could have prepared me for this moment. I already knew how I felt, and I didn't expect Nokea to take the news well.

The entire house was dark. I didn't hear Nanny B or the kids, but I saw flickering lights coming from the kitchen. When I got there, Nokea was sitting at the kitchen table with her legs crossed. She wore a gray silk negligee and candles were all over the room. The table was set for two, with crystal glasses and a bottle of wine on display. Our expensive china was covered with a top and Nokea lifted it to show me the food.

"Welcome home. I thought you'd be hungry so I cooked you a steak, some potatoes and string beans. The chicken noodle soup didn't turn out too well, but I have dessert too. If you're not too sick, you can have your dessert later," she smiled.

I moseyed over to my chair to take a seat and Nokea stopped me. "Can I at least have a kiss? I know you didn't walk up in here without giving me a kiss."

I walked over to Nokea and bent down. My eyes looked into hers. I knew she saw my pain. She touched the side of my face and rubbed it. "Baby, are you okay? You're kind of warm. Do you think you might be running a fever? I hope I didn't give you the flu."

I shook my head implying no, and then leaned in to kiss her. We kissed for a very long time, before I made my way back to my chair. With the folded papers still in my hand, I lay them next to me on the table. I gazed at Nokea through the flickering candles on the table and spoke up.

"Baby, this is real nice and everything, but, uh, we need to have a serious talk."

"Jaylin, if it's about that contract you and Frick have been working on, I've had enough of that, okay? Let's just eat our dinner and talk about that later. Please?"

My head was banging. Since I hadn't eaten anything in a couple of days, I was hungry. I lifted the top, removing the crisp napkin that covered my food. I stared down at the food, but no food was there. Instead, there were several pictures of a beautiful little girl lying on the plates. Of course, I recognized the girl in the pictures as being my oldest child and long lost daughter, Jasmine. Her mother, Simone, had jetted with Jasmine when she was three. I hadn't seen her since. Over the years, I'd hired several private detectives to find her, but had no luck. I thought this day would never, ever come. All I could do was sit speechless while holding the pictures of my now ten year old daughter in my hands.

"In case you don't recognize her, that's Jasmine," Nokea said. "Since the possibilities of me giving you another child are slim, I've been working hard with another private detective to find your daughter. I know how much your children make you happy. That's all I ever want is for you to be happy. Of course, that makes me happy too. The private detective told me where she was, and yesterday, I met with her and Simone at their home in Tampa Florida. We all had a wonderful time together and I took those pictures. She is just as beautiful as she was when you last saw her, and baby, she's excited about meeting you. After so many years, you'll be able to be with your daughter again."

Not saying a word, I dropped my forehead into my hand and rubbed my temple. I continued to look through the pictures. The previous harsh feelings inside of me quickly went away. I smiled and looked up at Nokea. "She lives right here in Tampa?"

"Yes. You once said that they'd moved to Florida, but you didn't know where. Well, baby, they're right here. Once they get back from their family reunion in Dallas, she's coming here to see you."

I was overwhelmed with joy I was almost speechless. "This . . . That's very good news. Did Simone give you a number where I can call them?"

"Yes, and earlier, Jasmine already called to see if you made it back from St. Louis. She's anxious to talk to you."

"Does she even remember me? When Simone moved away, you know that Jasmine was just three. I doubt that she remembers me."

"She said that she didn't, but when I showed her your pictures, she smiled and talked about how handsome you are. She said that she couldn't wait to meet her handsome daddy and for him to meet her friends. She's a bright girl, Jaylin, and she can play the hell out of a piano. I can tell that Simone raised her well."

"How long have you been at this? I mean, I've dished out so much money trying to find her. Every private detective I hired came up empty. I guess I gave up too soon, huh?"

"Maybe, but I'd been at it since I had my accident on the stairs. I noticed this sadness about you. Even though we're going to keep on trying, I knew that finding Jasmine would give you peace. As for the private detectives you've hired, all it took was the right one to find her. He's been at it for quite a while too. When he called, I couldn't believe it."

Nokea walked over to me and kneeled down. "I know you're stunned, but say something, would you?"

I set the pictures on the plate and held Nokea's hands together with mine. "Yes, I'm happy, Nokea. I'll be even happier when you give me the biggest kiss and hug you've ever given me."

Nokea leaned in and gave me a kiss. I held her waist, stood up and lifted her in my arms.

"You know what?" I said. "I was really feeling ill, but I'm feeling so much better now. What would I do without you in my life, huh?"

"I don't know—you tell me. What would you do without me in your life?"

"Lose my motherfucking mind."

Nokea smiled, and once we kissed again, I lowered her to the ground. She reached for her plate and forked up some potatoes.

"I'm sorry, baby, but I have starved myself all day. I had to taste the potatoes," she laughed.

I helped her tear into the food as well. "I'm hungry too. Come on, though, let's take that plate to the bedroom. I got a phone call to make then we got to get down to some serious and enjoyable business."

Nokea laughed and picked up the plate. Before we left the kitchen, she stopped by the table and reached for the papers.

"Here, baby, you left these on the table."

She was getting ready to unfold the papers, but I took them from her hands. I tucked the papers underneath my arm. "We'll talk about that mess some other time."

Nokea walked in front of me.

"A boy or girl?" I asked. "Which one?"

"What are you talking about?"

"I'm preparing myself for the festivities, after I make my phone call. Are we going to make another girl or shoot for a boy?"

"Well, since you have three girls . . . Jaylene, Jasmine and Mackenzie, I'd say we shoot for another boy. LJ needs a little brother."

"To make a boy, it takes hours and hours of work. Are you up for it?"

"Maybe tomorrow. Tonight, I just want to celebrate finding Jasmine, okay?"

"Okay, but since we're on the subject, what do you suggest that I do about Mackenzie? I know I don't talk much about her, but that's because I know how you feel about Scorpio. If you want me to forget about Mackenzie, I can't make you any promises that . . ."

Nokea poked at my chest. "Not right now, okay? First, let's deal with what's in front of us. Allow me some time to deal with the situation with Mackenzie, and I will take into consideration how much she means to you."

"That's all I can ask for," I said, reaching for the phone to call Simone's cell phone to speak to Jasmine.

Chapter 29

Jaylin

I was in a deep sleep. When I woke up, sweat dripped from my forehead. I wiped it and slowly widened my eyes, only to see a blurred vision of Nokea coming toward me. She had an aspirin bottle in one hand and a glass of water in the other hand. I didn't know what the hell was going on, so I quickly sat up to gather myself.

"Wha . . . Where are we?" I asked while looking around.

"Promise me you'll never drink like that again," she said, sitting next to me. She gave me the glass, along with two aspirin. "Here, take these. You have been out for almost twenty-four hours. I thought I'd lost you. Your snoring told me you were alive, but you gave me quite a scare. This is one anniversary you'll have to work hard at making up to me."

I puzzlingly looked around at my surroundings. We were still on our yacht. I popped the aspirin in my mouth and guzzled down the glass of water. Nokea wiped the sweat from my forehead with a cold towel.

"Wha . . . what day is it?" I asked.

"It's Saturday. Late Saturday. Like I said, you've been out since yesterday afternoon."

In disbelief, I lowered my head and rubbed my temples. "Baby, I am so, so sorry. I did not think drinking that much Remy would have this kind of an effect on me. I . . . I had the most awkward-ass dream. It seemed so damn real. Please pinch me, slap me or do something to let me know I'm awake and that dream did not happen."

"How about I just give you a hug," Nokea said. She reached over to squeeze me in her arms. She gave me a kiss too and her lips were very real. I touched the sides of her pretty face, rubbing it with the back of my hand.

"Damn, I'm glad that was just a dream. Baby, it . . . the dream was so—"

"Just relax. Why don't you go take a shower, calm yourself down and meet me upstairs in the stateroom, okay?"

Nokea gathered some towels for me. Since I still seemed to be so out of it, she washed me up in the shower. Once finished, we lay snuggled up in the comfortable queen-sized bed with the lights down low.

"Okay, now, tell me about this dream that seems to have you so shaken up."

"It started with you going to St. Louis, which by the way, when you leave next weekend, I'm going with you."

"That's fine. I'm glad you changed your mind. Anyway, continue."

I told Nokea about everything, except for my encounters with Scorpio and the exact amount of millions I'd turned over to her. She couldn't believe that I'd dreamed about her and Shane hooking up.

"Now, that was ridiculous. I couldn't even see myself getting down with Shane like that, and if you would have divorced me for something that seemed to be beyond my control, I would've killed you."

"Baby, I was so fucking hurt. I wanted to just die. All I can remember is Shane touching you and . . . and you liked it. The only thing I wish was real was finding my daughter. That's where the dream ended."

Nokea chuckled and rubbed my chest. "No, I wouldn't enjoy Shane touching me. And, pertaining to your daughter, some things are meant to be, and some things aren't. I wish you'd find her too, but it's been so long. For the sake of your happiness, maybe you should just . . ."

"Never. She gotta be out there somewhere. First thing Monday, I'm going to hire one of the best detectives out there to find her. I think the other detective gave up on me."

"Whatever you want to do is fine with me. You know I hope you find her."

Nokea and I continued to discuss my dream. Once we started to make love, I was so glad that my dream was over! I would've never been able to forgive myself for causing her so much drama. I doubt that I would've forgiven her so easily for sleeping with Shane.

Chapter 30

Jaylin

We had a change of plans because of my dream. There was no way in hell Nokea was going to St. Louis alone. Our plane had touched down in St. Louis about an hour ago. Once Nokea and I had gotten a room and rental cars, we headed to her parents' house first. They were upset about us not staying with them, and even more upset that we hadn't brought the kids. Nokea promised she'd bring the kids for Thanksgiving and Christmas. That somewhat put her parents at ease.

After sitting and talking with them for hours, I told Nokea I was heading to Shane's place to see him. She was leaving shortly to go see Pat. Before I departed, I gave her a kiss and told her parents I'd see them soon.

On my drive to Shane's place, I felt real uneasy. I'd been feeling that way all day starting at the airport. Nokea and I didn't get down in the bathroom stall, but it sure would have been nice to. I could tell that many of the women's stares made her uncomfortable. She kept looking at me for a reaction. I showed no interest in the women, and that confirmed how important my marriage was to me.

As for Shane, we hadn't talked much at all, but my dream encouraged me to work on our friendship. I didn't know if I was doing the right thing or not by going to see him, but maybe my bitterness toward him caused my dream to surface.

I pulled in his driveway, and saw his new pearly white Lexus truck he'd told me he'd gotten. Another car was parked beside it, but I wasn't sure whose car it was. I'd thought about calling to make sure the coast was clear, but since I was already there, what the hell?

Dressed in a white and black striped Kenneth Cole woven shirt and black jeans, I knocked on the door. A chick, Amber, that Shane had been seeing on and off again for years, opened the door.

"Hi, Jaylin," she said with a surprised look on her face. "Come in."

With my hands in my pockets, I stepped inside and looked at Amber's slim and tall figure covered in one of Shane's long white T-shirts. "Is Shane here?"

"Yes, he's in his office. You can go on back. I'm sure he'll be pleased to see you."

"Thanks," I said, as Amber checked me out from head to toe.

"Those are some nice black leather shoes, Jaylin. And that watch on your wrist about to blind me. Can I see it?"

I lifted my wrist, which displayed a new diamond faced Rolex with a white gold band I'd just purchased. Amber observed the watch and smiled. "Everybody ain't able. That's nice—really nice. I would like to get Shane something nice like that for his birthday, but that might be way out of my budget."

"If you know Shane like I do, a watch like this wouldn't even excite him. Get him some jockey shorts, cologne and some good pus . . . good loving and the brotha will be just fine."

Amber smiled and agreed. I made my way back to Shane's office and got a whiff of the seasoned fried chicken that lit up the kitchen. When I got to his office, his back was turned and his face was aimed at the flat screen monitor in front of him. He was shirtless and had on some white and yellow basketball shorts. I lightly knocked on the door, but he didn't turn around.

"I'm busy right, now, baby. In a minute, okay?"

"What if I don't have a minute?" I said. He quickly turned, cracking a tiny smile.

"What's up, Jay?" Shane stood up and adjusted his shorts. I walked up to him and slammed my hand against his.

"Nothing, fool. What's been up with you?"

"Doing what I do best . . . working," he laughed. "Have a seat."

I took a seat in a chair that was next to his weight bench.

"Man, I didn't know you were coming to St. Louis. What made you want to stop by and visit li'l ole me?"

"Nokea's friend Pat is having a baby and she came for the shower. I came too, just to get away and see what you've been up to."

Shane leaned back in his chair, placing his hands behind his head. He looked down, and then looked up at me. "Well, as you can see, me and ole girl ain't together anymore."

"Yes, Amber answering your door kind of validated that for me. What happened between you and Scorpio?"

"Nothing," Shane chuckled. "After she lost the baby, things went downhill. I did tell you she lost the baby, didn't I?"

"Yes, but we didn't talk much after that."

"Yeah, well, she lost the baby. She got mad at me when I confronted her about my suspicions. Honestly, I don't think there ever was a baby. I think Scorpio lied to me so I wouldn't move to Florida. I got tired of the games, and just like Felicia, she's been playing games too. She sent me a picture of her baby, but she did admit to it being Stephon's, not mine. The baby looks just like him. I hate he got killed. Maybe him having a baby could have saved his life and gotten him off crack."

I thought about the good times Stephon, Shane and I had, doing my best not to comment on the fucked up times while he was on crack. Before then, he was my right hand man, but things quickly took a turn for the worse. "You knew Felicia's baby wasn't yours," I said. "We all had a piece of that, and ain't no telling who the father is."

Shane opened his desk drawer and pulled out a picture. He tossed it over to me so I could look at it. Felicia's baby looked just like Stephon, when he was a baby. "Damn," I reminisced. "Stephon spit this baby out," I paused and continued to look at the picture. "Before I leave, make sure you give me Felicia's contact information. This li'l dude and LJ need to know each other. Besides, Felicia don't need no damn baby. I'm sure she's still whack and that bitch owes me some favors. As for Scorpio, I'd bet every dime in my bank accounts that she lied, but that's just how *some* women are."

"Yeah, but to lie to me about something like that was crazy. We kept arguing, and honestly, our relationship was starting to revolve around nothing but sex. Now, I ain't complaining, but it was hard to focus on other things when all I could think about was making love to her."

"I definitely understand what you're talking about. She's got that snapdragon pussy and once it snatches you up, it's hard to let go."

"Right," Shane nodded and laughed. "Anyway, like I said, we couldn't get along and the next thing I knew, Mackenzie's father, Bruce, was back on the scene. I didn't trip 'cause I'd started seeing Amber again."

"Bruce? So, she's seeing that fool again, huh?"

"From what I hear, yes. And a little birdie told me that wedding bells are in the plans."

"Is that right," I said, rubbing my goatee. I was surprised. "So, uh, is this thing serious with you and Amber?"

"Not at all," he whispered. "I'm not feeling another relationship right now, Jay. Ending my relationship with Scorpio kind of left a bad taste in my mouth. I've been working hard at building my book of business and seeing where it takes me. That's all I can do for now."

"Well, what if I make you the same offer I made you a while back? Would you still move to Florida and consider going into business with me?"

Shane took a deep breath and clinched his hands together in front of him. "I . . . I would like that more than anything in the world. I wanted to call and talk to you about doing something together, but I knew you were upset with me about Scorpio. At the time, I saw nothing wrong with me loving her. My feelings were beyond my control. Now, I see things differently. I apologize for the damage I cost our friendship. My being with her should have never happened or been a priority over my career."

"No comment from me. You already knew how I felt. I'm pleased that you're accepting my offer. How soon can you make this transition?"

"A month, maybe two. I'll need to clear up things here and work on a place to stay in Florida."

"You work on clearing up things a.s.a.p., and as for a place to stay, you can stay with us until you find a place of your own. Until you do," I said smiling. "if you even look at my wife like you wanna get with her, I'll kill you."

"What?" he laughed. "Why would you say . . ."

"Man, I had this crazy-ass dream that you were fucking Nokea behind my back."

Shane laughed, but I didn't understand his humor.

"What in the hell is so funny?" I asked.

"Nothing. I can't believe you'd dream something like that, but I guess you might have some trust issues with me, huh? Because of my relationship with Scorpio, I understand, but I assure you that Nokea and I will never be secret lovers."

I lightly rubbed my goatee. "Shane, all jokes aside. If I'm making a big mistake inviting you into my home, then you need to stay right here. If you have any feelings, whatsoever for Nokea, I don't think this is a good idea. After all, you did kiss her . . . ."

"Jay, relax. I don't know the details of your dream, but it ain't that serious. Kiss or no kiss, Nokea loves you and only you. I know it might be hard for you to believe, but I respect our friendship more than you will ever know. It ain't going down like that, trust me."

"Yeah, that's the same mess you said in my dream. But, Negro, you were all up on my shit."

"Straight?" he smirked and folded his arms. "Okay, so tell me about this dream. Maybe I can analyze some things for you."

I told Shane about my dream and he seriously thought the shit was funny. I didn't leave out one detail, as I'd left out a few things when I told Nokea.

"Now, as soon as that muthafucka put a gun to my head, you should've woken up from that dream. Ain't no way in hell it would've gone down like that, and you and Scorpio added big flames to a burning fire, didn't you?"

"Yeah, buddy. That shit was wild and I was insane! No offense, but I couldn't stop fucking her ass, man, and enjoyed every damn bit of it too. Then my money . . . I gave away all of my money to Nokea and she was still screwing you."

"Yeah, the money thing was messed up too. That was another time you should've snapped out of it. You know damn well you wouldn't turn over your life savings like that."

"Never," I laughed. "I love my wife and she can have anything she wants, but the bulk of my money stays with me."

"I hear you. If I had nearly as much money as you do, I would feel the same way."

For the next few hours, I ate dinner with Shane and Amber and we chatted about his move to Florida. Amber seemed disturbed by the conversation. The news about Shane leaving in a few months made her upset. She left immedi-

ately after dinner and told Shane she'd call him
later. I asked him if Amber would be okay without him. He assured me that he wasn't going to
allow another woman to interfere with his plans
for the future. According to him, he was moving
and that's all there was to it. This time, I believed
him. As I got ready to leave, he walked outside
with me.

"So, are you headed back to the hotel?" he
asked.

"Yeah, it's almost eight P.M. so I'm gon' call it
a night. Why don't you hook up with Nokea and
me for breakfast, and maybe, we can go shoot
some hoops tomorrow afternoon."

"Sounds like a plan to me. Thanks for stopping by, Jay. I'll see you tomorrow."

Shane patted the roof of my car and I drove
off. Wanting to know how Nokea's day was going, I reached for my cell phone to call her. She
answered the phone laughing.

"So, I see you're having a good time," I said.

"Baby, Pat is so crazy. I wouldn't dare tell you
what she just said."

"Keep your little secrets, all right? I wanted to
let you know that I'm headed back to the hotel.
I just left Shane's place and we had a good talk.
He's going to move to Florida in a few months."

"I'm so glad to hear that the two of you reconciled your differences. I probably won't get to the hotel until two or three o'clock in the morning so don't wait up for me."

"Be careful and I hope you haven't been drinking. You sound like you have."

"I've only had one . . . two glasses of wine. Besides, drinking affects you, not me."

"You're so right about that. I don't want to see another drink for the rest of the week."

Nokea laughed. Allowing her to get back to her friend, I told her I loved her and said good-bye.

For whatever reason, instead of going back to the hotel, I took a detour. It led me to Scorpio's place. Before going to the door, I sat in the car thinking hard about the past. Why was I even there? My dream was heavy on my mind. When Shane mentioned Bruce being back in the picture, I had a queasy feeling in my stomach. I had to see what was up. That's what prompted me to go to the door. I rang the doorbell. When no one answered, I rang it again. Soon, I heard Scorpio's voice, as she asked who I was.

I cleared my throat. "Jaylin."

"Who?" she repeated.

"I said Jaylin."

She slowly pulled open the door and stood in her soft yellow sheer nightgown. Her long thick hair was full of wavy curls. She looked to be in a trance. My eyes couldn't help but wander to her visible almost bare breasts and her yellow panties that covered her goods down below.

"What a surprise," she said. "I was expecting someone else."

"I don't mean to intrude, but is it okay for me to come in?"

"Sure," she said, widening the door. "If you're looking for Mackenzie, she's at my sister's house. My fiancé, Bruce, will be here soon."

I looked around at the cozy dim living room and the several lit candles around it. Ironically, "Like You'll Never See Me Again" by Alicia Keys was playing and the aroma of soul food was in the air. Scorpio invited me to have a seat, so I did. She sat on one end of the couch, and I sat far away on the other end. I looked at my watch. "I came here to talk to you," I said. "How long do I have before your man gets here? I'm not up to fighting . . . ."

"How much time do you need? I have no problem calling and telling him to push our plans back for a few hours."

"That's fine. Just give me about an hour."

Scorpio stood up and walked into the other room. I couldn't help but feel guilty about the way her sexiness still turned me on. To see her go all out for another man kind of made me jealous. I looked around the room, thinking about the many times we'd had sex in this type of atmosphere. My dream was still fresh in my memory and damn did she look good. She came back into the room and returned to her position on the couch.

"Done deal," she said. "He won't be here until later. I'm glad you're here. I'd been meaning to contact you about a big problem that we seem to have. Mackenzie's father, Bruce, and I are getting married. He's anxious to get back custody of his daughter. Since you've moved on without her, I think it's only fair that we do the right thing."

I surely hated that Scorpio had already struck a nerve. "For the record, I have not moved on without her. I think about her every single day. When she turns eighteen, because of me, she will be a millionaire. Now, I'm happy for you and Bruce, but giving custody back to a man who walked out of his child's life years ago, and signed away his parental rights, is not going to jive with me."

"That was a long time ago. He's a different person now. We've all made mistakes. Mackenzie is his child and—"

"Look, we can sit here and debate about this all damn night. Like I said, I wish you and Bruce all the best, but things will have to be left as they are. I've been talking to Nokea about my situation with Mackenzie and she's coming around. Mackenzie will know her brother and sisters. She's old enough to understand that things just didn't work out between you and me."

Scorpio's mouth hung open. "So, let me get this straight. When Nokea decides that it's okay for Mackenzie to visit you all, then she can? It's been years, Jaylin; I'm the one who's had to explain why she can't see you. Mackenzie doesn't give a damn about your money—all she wanted was to be with you. You left, and I watched my child hurt and behave badly because you wouldn't come for her. Now, she's over that stage and I will not allow her to go through that again. So, how dare you come in here and tell me what's not going to happen. You need to get with your lawyer and do what's best for Mackenzie."

"I don't need to do shit!" I yelled then lowered my voice. "Sorry, but my mind is made up. I will tear Bruce's past up in court and you know it. You get so caught up in these fucking relationships. By next year, that sucker will be history. *My* daughter needs a stable father figure in her life and she will have one. I mean that shit, Scorpio. That's just how it's going to be."

Scorpio shook her head in disgust. "After all this time, you still haven't changed one bit. It's gotta be your way or no way and there's nothing I can do. I've told you about all of the setbacks we'd endured since you left, but you won't listen. You expected for me to accept things for what they were and go live happily ever after. Well, that didn't happen for me, up until recently. Bruce and I—"

"I don't give a damn about you and Bruce, Scorpio. You said the same mess about you and Shane and look at how that turned out. You're starting to sound like a broken record. Your reputation is getting awfully ugly."

"Fine," she said, standing up. "If you don't want to listen to me, then why are you here? I don't understand the purpose of your visit."

"Let's just say that I had a feeling something wasn't right."

She folded her arms. "Something like what? Like I have an opportunity to be happy and you're here to steal my joy? You do it to me every time, Jaylin. From Shane to Bruce, or anyone else I might date, you'll continue to cause problems for me. After playing me how you did, I hoped you'd want me to find happiness. For years, I've struggled with being without you. Even while with Shane, I could never get you out of my system." Scorpio swallowed and plopped down on the couch. She dropped her face into her hands and rubbed her hair back. "I never told you this, but I wanted to die. After you went off and married Nokea, I wanted to roll over and die because of your decision. Since then, yes, I've made many mistakes with men. I wanted all of them to be like you. Who could blame me? Even with Shane, I felt as if being with him would keep me close to you. Once the two of you stopped speaking, it was as if I had no need for him." She turned to me and displayed true honesty in her eyes. "God help me for loving you so much. I . . . I just want to move on with my child and be with a man who truly loves me."

I hated to see Scorpio so broken. I knew what our failed relationship had done to her. The repercussions showed as she fought her emotions. I stood up and went to her end of the couch. I pulled her up and put my arms around her waist. She resisted a bit and turned her head to the side. I placed my finger on the side of her face, turning it to face mine.

"Tell me something. Did you lie to Shane about being pregnant?"

Scorpio hesitated. Her eyelids fluttered and she slowly nodded. "I couldn't lose him too. That meant losing my connection with you. I was so confused. I hated to lie to Shane, but even he knew how much I still loved you. Please don't tell him the truth about the baby. I never meant to hurt him as much as I did."

I shook my head in disgust. "Damn, Scorpio, but you did. He gave up so much for you and you—"

"I know. But, you haven't walked in my shoes and you don't know how difficult all of this has been for me. I've made so many horrible mistakes, all because I didn't know how to deal with being without you. The relationships I've had, none of them made me feel as I do now with Bruce. I know he's the one for me, and . . ."

I knew Scorpio too well and I didn't believe her. "You said that Bruce loves you. Not once have you said that you love him. Please, don't marry a man just to escape your hurt. You'll make a big mistake and I'm not saying this because I'm jealous. I'm telling you this for your own good."

Scorpio wrapped her arms around me, lightly scratching her nails up and down my back. Without a blink, she gazed into my eyes and I could feel what she'd been going through. Her look was so powerful that it caused me to blink and look away. This time, she turned my face to hers.

"I do love Bruce, Jaylin," she confirmed. "But, I will never, ever love a man as much as I love you. So, if that's what you came here to hear, then I have no shame in saying it. Yes, I still love you, but there isn't a darn thing I can do about it. Who in the hell could blame me, after what you did for me and Mackenzie? You changed my entire life around. At the time we met, my life was headed for destruction. We endured a lot in our relationship, but overall, you were a blessing to me. Therefore, losing you was tough. I . . . I can't forget what we shared and I will never forget. Call me stupid or whatever you want, but my love for you can never be replaced."

I was speechless and continued to stare at Scorpio. She was so damn sexy and her watery brown eyes, along with the thoughts of my dream, and Alicia Keys' song replaying had me so caught up. As I felt a rise down below, I slightly backed up and cleared my throat.

"Listen, I gotta jet. I hope everything works out for you and Bruce and, uh, I appreciate you sharing with me how you feel." I loosened our embrace and made my way to the door. When I reached for the doorknob, Scorpio's hand covered mine.

"I'm getting married soon. This might be our last chance," she said. "Please stay with me for a while."

I turned to face her. "Our last chance for what?"

She got on the tips of her toes and whispered in my ear, "Last chance for us to be naughty. I will never interfere with your marriage to Nokea again. I wish you and her nothing but future happiness. I hope you feel the same way about me and Bruce, but please allow us to have this one last time together."

I stood for a moment, seriously debating with myself. I was so weak when it came to Scorpio, and the thing is, she knew it. She stepped forward and when her lips touched mine, I held her face in my hands, sucking her lips in like kissing was going out of style. "Call Bruce," I ordered. "Tell him to come much later. I . . . I gotta tell you about a dream I had, but you gotta promise me that you and I will be *Naughty No More*."

Scorpio reached for my belt buckle. "After tonight, you go your way and I'll go mine. I promise you there will be no phone calls, no questions and no attachments. Let's just get this over with and do something that we both have been dying to do."

I didn't say another word. I followed Scorpio to her bedroom. When she removed all of her clothes, there was no turning back for me.

***

I reached the hotel at 1:15 in the morning. I wasn't sure if Nokea had made it in yet, but I hurried to slide the card in the door. When I didn't see Nokea, I rushed out of my clothes to take a shower. All I could think about was where in the hell I'd just come from. I kept telling myself that Nokea didn't deserve this. Feeling frustrated with my decision, I threw my cell phone across the room and broke it. I hurried in the shower. While my hands were pressed against the shower's wall, I let the soothing cold water drench me to calm down my dick. I closed my eyes and visions of Scorpio played in my mind. *Damn*, I thought. *Why couldn't she have just let me leave!* The betrayal I felt from being inside of her made me ill. My stomach turned in knots. I had the nerve to hold my dick and look at it, as if it was the one who made the decision. "Fuck," I said loudly and rubbed up and down my dripping wet face. *Why? Why did I go there?* Never, ever would I do this shit again. I didn't like how being with another woman made me feel. Yes, Scorpio's performance was good . . . damn good, but I had no idea I'd feel like this.

The cold water dripped from my face. As I was reminiscing about what had just happened, the shower curtain slid over and startled me. Nokea stood outside the shower and stared at me with a blank expression on her face.

"What?" I hurried to say. "Is . . . is everything okay?"

She gave me a puzzled look and the knot in my stomach felt like it was being pulled tighter. "Everything is fine, Jaylin. I saw your broken phone and called your name several times. You didn't answer, so I thought something had happened."

To release my tension, I took a deep breath and turned off the water. "I got mad at the damn thing because I couldn't get a signal. I tried to call you, but it wouldn't dial out."

Nokea reached for a towel and slowly wiped my body. When she got to my back, she stopped. "Where did this red mark—long scratch on your back, come from?"

I turned my back toward the mirror to see what she was referring to. There was a long scratch on my back and I had to think fast. "Shit, I don't know, probably from Jaylene climbing on my back yesterday. Remember, when I was on the floor and she . . . ."

"Yes, I remember," Nokea smiled and yawned. "I'm so tired. Pat's baby shower is tomorrow, and can you believe I'm already missing home? I can't wait to get back to my babies."

"I can't wait to get home either. I wish we could leave now, but I know how important it is for you to be there for your friend."

"Very important," she said. "Pat would die if I left this soon."

As Nokea got undressed, I got in the bed. The feeling I had inside was unlike anything I'd ever experienced before. From the disturbing look on my face, it was so easy for Nokea to tell that something was wrong.

"Out with it Jaylin Rogers, what's on your mind?" she teased while climbing underneath the sheets with me. We cuddled, and as I held her, she lay the back of her head against my chest.

"I just had a long day, that's all. I'm glad that Shane and I worked things out. I'm looking forward to him moving to Florida. My mind's been preoccupied with our new business venture."

"I knew it was something. I've been here for almost thirty minutes and you haven't even kissed me."

Nokea looked up at me and that same powerful feeling I felt with Scorpio came across me. There was no denying that I was in love with Nokea, but now, it was easy for me to admit that I had *some* love for Scorpio too. For me to have gone as far as I did, it was obvious. I continuously interfered with Scorpio's relationships. Being as jealous as I was of them, the proof was in the pudding. No matter what, though, the love I had for Scorpio could never amount to the love I had for Nokea. Deep down, I knew it and Scorpio knew it as well.

As I kissed Nokea, it was hard for me not to think about where my lips had been only a few hours ago. I paused and pecked Nokea's forehead. The step I'd taken tonight required me to close my eyes and ask for forgiveness. Already, I could see my mother shaking her head and Nanny B looking at me with disgust. Even Stephon was yelling that I was a dog-ass nigga who didn't deserve Nokea. I could hear Shane telling me how wrong I was for making such a move. I was human. Even though I hated to admit it, I wasn't perfect. My flesh was weak, and this was first-hand experience as to just how weak it was.

With my eyes still closed and head laid back on the pillow, Nokea interrupted my thoughts.

"Hey, baby, can I ask you something personal?" she said.

"Of course."

"You mentioned that in your dream, you had millions and millions of dollars. I don't keep up with your financial status, but isn't it fair to me that you be a bit more specific about those kinds of things?"

"Yes, and if you ever want to know, all you have to do is ask. Anything you want or need, you can have it. What's mine is yours. It's not that I've been keeping our finances a secret, it's just that you rarely ask about our financial status."

"I do look at our bank statements, but you have accounts that belong solely to you. For the sake of our children, I don't know if that's a good idea."

"I agree. It's not."

"All I want to know is, is there more than fifteen million in your combined accounts?"

"Yes."

"Twenty-five?"

"Yes."

"Thirty-five?"

"You're on to something."

"Fifty?" she looked shocked.

"You're very close. I promise you that when we get home, I'll reveal everything to you."

Nokea laid her head back on my chest and rubbed it. I thought it was ironic that she had brought up this subject at this particular time. A woman's intuition, I guessed. "Can I ask why, all of a sudden, you're inquiring about our finances?"

"Because I'd been thinking about the yacht you'd purchased. That thing cost some serious dollars. I felt so foolish for not knowing that we could afford something like that. I don't like being kept in the dark, and I do want to know about all of our assets. A husband and wife should know those kinds of things. It's only fair to me."

I was real uneasy. I didn't know if it was just my guilt eating away at me or if Nokea knew something she wasn't telling. I love her more than anything in the world, but nobody could be trusted with the amount of money I'd given away in my dream. After my *interesting* night with Scorpio, this was a touchy subject for me. Surely, though, if Nokea knew I had been intimate with Scorpio, I wouldn't live to see tomorrow, nor would we be lying in bed having a civil discussion.

"Like I said, baby, it's whatever you want. Next week, I will make arrangements for us to meet with my financial advisor and Frick."

"Thanks," Nokea said, as she lifted her head to give me a tiny peck on the lips.

Afterward, she reached in her purse and pulled out a silver picture book. When she lay back on my chest, she opened the book and it displayed many digital pictures of us.

"This was your anniversary gift," she said. "I was too embarrassed to give it to you."

"Why?" I said, admiring the cute and memorable pictures of us. "Woman, this book is priceless. We make an adorable couple, don't we?"

"Yes, and look at this one," she said. "This was taken when you were nineteen and I was eighteen, remember? You were so handsome and bad to the bone."

I smiled at the picture. I couldn't believe Nokea was embarrassed to give this to me. The yacht didn't compare to our memories together. As we lay in bed laughing at the pictures, I told her just that.

Chapter 31

Scorpio

Nearly a year and a half ago was the last time I'd seen Jaylin. I was now a happily married woman and Bruce and I were doing well. At first, I'd talked myself out of getting married because that interesting night with Jaylin couldn't be forgotten. He admitted to being in love with me, but made it clear that he'd never, ever leave Nokea. The moment he strutted in my house with confidence, casually dressed, tanned as ever and smelling good, I knew it would be a life changing moment for me. There was no way in hell I was going to let him leave without giving me something to remember. I'd waited a long time to feel the satisfaction only he could give me, and it started with a juicy long kiss. It was like magic, and when all of the touching, feeling and stroking was over, he left.

Yes, I hated to see him go. To put me at ease, he called and talked to me until he reached the hotel. During our conversation, he made me smile. We talked about how we'd missed making love to each other. We discussed his dream, and I was glad we made part of it a reality. According to Jaylin, I'd gotten my feelings hurt in his dream, but to me, being with him, that kind of hurt came with the territory. He continued to pressure me about marrying a man I didn't love. When I asked if he ever thought he'd be available, he responded again, *"Unfortunately, that day will never come."*

With that being said, my wedding day went off without a hitch. Surely, because Jaylin had revealed his love for me that night, I kept hoping he would show up and I'd be able to drop my bouquet on the floor and run away with him. I even thought I'd seen him peeking around corners, but I knew it was just my imagination playing tricks on me. Then, several months later, out of the blue, I received documentation from Jaylin's attorney. Jaylin gave up custody of Mackenzie. I knew that closed the final chapter of our lives. He had his own family and was with someone who was destined to be his. So was I.

A few months after I was married, Bruce and I purchased a new home and we shared it with our two children. Almost nine months after the honeymoon was over, Bruce Jr. was born. As he sat on my lap at the park, I held his hands with mine. I then turned him to face me. Every time I looked into his eyes, it took me back to that unforgettable night with Jaylin. Bruce Jr. had many of Jaylin's features. Even Bruce had commented on how his son looked more like me, not him. When it came to making babies, my credibility had been shot. I refused to go through the headache of finding out the truth. My desires for Jaylin were gone. I had no intentions whatsoever to ever disrupt or disturb his happy home. We both agreed not to share the detailed events of that night with anyone. In order for peace to prevail, my secret would go to my grave with me.